The Betrayal

Henry Kreisel

The Betrayal

Introduction: S. Warhaft
General Editor: Malcolm Ross

New Canadian Library No. 77

McClelland and Stewart

PR
9199.3
K-697
B4
1971

To Esther

The Canadian Publishers
McClelland and Stewart Limited
25 Hollinger Road, Toronto

0-7710-9177-X

Manufactured in Canada by Webcom Limited

Introduction

How can we distinguish victim from betrayer in a world gone mad? Where do the responsibilities of man toward man begin or end? In an irrational, brutal existence, who is destroyer and who healer? Who hero, who coward? These are the kinds of questions that Henry Kreisel in *The Betrayal* has Mark Lerner, Ph.D., Assistant Professor of History, confront in 1952, when one of the numberless tragedies produced by the Nazi madness invades his Edmonton peace. From being simply academically interested in history, Lerner is drawn into history; as the recent European past moves into his bland territory, the scholar is forced to become a true learner, not from books but from life itself. But the lesson, if any, is hard, and, twelve years later, as he comes to tell the Stappler-Held drama, he is still turning his experience over, still wondering where blame lies, who is to judge, "what it is to live like a human being in a rational society," what can be done about betrayal and the desire for revenge it engenders.

On the surface, it is a simple story: one Theodore Stappler arrives in Edmonton seeking revenge on one Joseph Held for having given him and his mother up to the Gestapo some thirteen years before. Yet the issues are by no means clear-cut, and complications set in very quickly. Held, it appears, was also betrayed, a helpless victim bitterly made to seem responsible for his own fate and misery. Nor is Stappler quite without blemish, for not only has he deserted his mother, as he believes, by not trying to save her or at least by failing to have undertaken to share her trials with her, but he has also been faithless to himself, to his own vision of himself as hero. Also, something like love for Held's daughter shortly intervenes to take the edge off his quest and to confuse his desire for revenge. What is more, despite his absolute insistence on the existential quality of Held's guilt ("A man's action must be his own"), the heroic dimensions of his longing for vengeance, nurtured through so many years, are suddenly much deflated when he at last comes face to face with its object: a "tired, pot-bellied, middle-aged man." Then, too, his treatment of Katherine, however fervent his protests that he does not want to hurt her, must be seen as tainted by perfidy. And to what extent is Lerner to be blamed? In his refusal to come to grips with the terrible problem that has sought him out, in his evasion of responsibility in the whole affair, is he not being untrue at least to his own liberal convictions? Is it enough in our day simply to be a witness? These questions will be looked at later, but the point at issue here seems obvious: there are many betrayals in *The Betrayal* – of man by man, by love, by principle, by life itself – none of them easily definable or categorically evil, none of them to be casually judged or censured.

This tale of moral ambiguity, if not moral uncertainty, is told with considerable craft. To begin with, it is developed to quite an extent through a subtle complex of evocative parallels, contrasts, allusions, and motifs. Right at the start, for example, there is the Jean Paul Marat-Charlotte Corday lesson, which not only brings history to Western Canada, but also sets the theme of guilt and revenge. Related to this is the motif of the moral desert, closely connected to that of the distortion of reality, both of which are communicated through the recounting of dreams (mostly nightmares), through references to detective stories and to labyrinths, and through sudden apocalyptic announcements (including ironic play on the image of the dragon). Existential drabness, part of the moral desert, is evoked by a number of vignettes (which also bring the past into the present), by descriptions, which tend to become symbolic, of various dingy streets and places, by the Cafe Sturm (storm, turmoil) and the ironically named hotel, Victoria, where Stappler stays. The question which the latter frequently has put to him, "And what brought you to Edmonton?" though on the surface an inanity, takes on by dint of repetition in significant contexts such an ominous metaphysical force as to threaten to disturb the universe. Canada, too, with its great spaces, its snow and rivers, its innocence, crudeness, and unthinking assurance of endless security and invulnerability, plays an important role in the unfolding of the story. Finally, there is a host of Conradian touches which evoke a great battery of associations, many of them ironic, with works like *Lord Jim*, *Victory*, and *The Heart of Darkness*. The doppelganger theme (Stappler is identified with Held as well as with Lerner); immense romantic longing for absolutes and for heroism (which is made bitter by apparent cowardice); the indeterminacy of victory; the corruption, emptiness, and vanity of European civilization (as exemplified by Dr. Stappler, for instance); the indispensibility of potentially dangerous illusions; the indirect approach to the narrative; "the horror, the horror" – all of these aspects of Conrad's novels are smoothly and tellingly integrated into *The Betrayal*. Thus the whole is woven together by a myriad of suggestive parts, giving it body and cohesion and a rich unity which the necessarily careful and scholarly spareness of Lerner's style demands.

As far as the characters are concerned, the work seems to have been conceived more along the lines of a morality play than a modern novel. For the characters are developed rather as "flat" than as "round" figures, more as representatives or embodiments of ideas or moral qualities than as three-dimensional people. It is true that their ambiguousness seems to add some depth to them (particularly in that it tends to give them some of that capacity to surprise which belongs to the rounded character), but that is more an illusion than fact, because the ambiguousness is deliberately built into them, deliberately made a part of their morality delineation. Thus, there is the narrator, Lerner, the teacher and pupil – "A man of conscience. Of conviction. Of principles" – the Jewish middle-class academic whose habitual posture of dispassionate irony prevents him from helping those who have appealed to him. Then there is Joseph Held, who, as his name indicates, is the "hero" (in both senses) – shabby and tired toward the end but still a hero of sorts, revered to his death by his clear-seeing daughter, Katherine (whose name means "pure" or "innocent"). Finally, there is Theodore Stappler, a rather more complex figure but still portrayed through a few simple traits. In some respects he is Everyman, everybody and nobody, seeking to find out who and what he is in the world. His first name means "gift of God" or "beloved of God" – and those whom the gods prefer die young. His family name means "stalker" or "strider," but it also means (if derived from *Hochstappler*, as Kreisel once said it was in a private letter) "fashionable or elegant swindler." He is both the romantic Lord Jim who has failed his test of heroism and the defiant Axel Heyst snatching victory out of defeat. Now he is a dandified Satan, now a Christ on his way to the last supper; now Hamlet bemused before the riddle of humanity, now Lohengrin in search of the holy Grail, declining to say who he is (which is no wonder, for how is anyone to arrive at self-knowledge or at other than a deceptive definition of self in an arena of vicious absurdity?).

The matter of the choice of narrator deserves further attention, for Lerner is at least as important a character in the story as any other, and perhaps, in the final analysis, more important than any. Although the point of view that Kreisel decides to tell his story from is similar to that which Conrad often adopted, Lerner is no Marlow. In fact, there are many signs that he is designedly made different from Marlow. Of course, the obliquity of the structure is much the same – both narrators tell the stories of others so that the author can explore the meaning of the reality before him at leisure – but, unlike Marlow, Lerner does not brood over the events he recounts. He turns aside the repeated invitations to be a secret sharer, to acknowledge close kinship with Stappler. And he does not take us into the heart of darkness. Again and again, just as he is on the verge of penetrating the horror, his ironic detachment forces him to draw back and to say "Nothing" to the awful question. In many ways he resembles rather the speaker in Thomas Mann's *Doctor Faustus*, Serenus Zeitblom, Ph.D., who is also confronted with the torment of uttering the unspeakable. Yet here too there is a difference. Thoroughly alive to the nuances and pressures of the tale he must unfold, Zeitblom himself is transformed, changed from a rather complacent, over-scrupulous scholar to a sensitive, enlightened and committed human being. Such a transformation seems to have been beyond Lerner. He is sensitive enough, to be sure, but he appears to end up much the same kind of person he was at the beginning – aloof, unromantic, dispassionate – a somewhat sadder man, yes, but not much wiser.

Some readers will undoubtedly find such a distant character rather distasteful. As Kreisel has him admit at one point, his is not the kind of life that would suit everybody, and many would readily agree, because for many, in Francis Bacon's words, "in this theatre of man's life it is reserved only for God and angels to be lookers-on." Certainly it is hard to warm up to his Olympian detachment. One wonders if it is true after all that he is a man of conscience. Does not his delicate, even fastidious rendering of the monstrous perversion that ruined the lives of so many people fail to convey the horror that it was? Does he share any of Stappler's "ruthless honesty"? Though he understands that both Stappler and Held are victims, could he not have done more to bring them together? Is it enough to decide just to set their story down – unresolved, without catharsis – "so that the fact of writing would in itself be a kind of relief"? Is his not the final betrayal? And yet, even as the questions rush to mind, the suspicion nags that they are perhaps not entirely to the point, that Lerner is kept by design from descending into the darkness and hell of Stappler or Held.

If this is so – and there is plenty of evidence to substantiate it – then Lerner suddenly becomes, as Marlow never does, the main character in the novel. What has happened to the others is important enough in all conscience, but, seen in this way, the story comes to focus on the man who tells it: it comes to be about how *he* sees and reacts to the people and events he describes, how *his* values assert themselves in collision with insistently different ones from outside. And thus understood, though hardly less an ambiguous figure than before, Lerner surely becomes more sympathetic. After all, Stappler, for one, found him sufficiently to his liking, and if it took the latter's death to establish the fact that he was his next of kin, that too was something. It is one of the ways that the Canadian identity is being formed. For Lerner is primarily a Canadian, relatively innocent and untried, not too sophisticated, not too sure of ethical or other absolutes, reasonably confident in reason, fairly happy about the future, and resentful of any attempts to drag him into European miseries. What is more, he is a university man in Canada, not only a person trained as an objective observer, but also one committed to establishing a meaningful civilization in a new country. From this point of view, collecting Canadian paintings, pursuing bookish research, writing studies of the French Revolution, and teaching his reluctant students about Europe's past – this life of his (which would clearly *not* suit everybody) becomes highly significant if the land of his birth is to have any past of its own worth building on. It is not a romantic life nor a heroic life, and its moral outlines remain rather uncertain, but it is a respectable one. It is a life marked by a certain obtuseness, a certain corporation-man's lack of insight into the more refined ecstasies and torments of man's predicament. His is a failure of the imagination to grasp the mystery of romantic yearning or at least the importance of such yearnings to others. It may be that this is a form of betrayal, but if so, how many in Canada can cast the first stone?

Though it would appear that Lerner will probably never learn in the marrow the Swiftian lesson that man is not a reasonable creature but one only capable of reason, there is no doubt that, while we are still trying to digest the Nazi experience, he affirms for his author not just a commitment to Canada but also a fundamental belief in life. In one sense this book could have been called *The Sun Also Rises* (by way of

Thomas Mann, perhaps), for although generations pass away in it, the earth abides. The snow falls, "merciful and forgetful," on all alike. The river continues to roll through Edmonton, and the narrator begins to think he could not live without it. The city itself develops into "a great circle of light" coming out of an immense darkness. Art and Mary's party turns out to be a celebration of life, for, drab though their existence may be, it is free of barren illusion, since, as Stappler puts it, "Life has no time for nightmares in its endless quest to reproduce itself." Katherine marries and has three lovely children. Stappler undergoes a kind of rebirth, changing from destroyer to healer, discovering at last, in the Arctic wilderness, "a kind of peace, and a sense of unity with elemental forces." And Lerner, moved but still ambiguous, still puzzling over the dark immensity of romantic desires, finds it strange that now that Stappler is dead, he seems to him most alive. The past, which was before just history, he comes to understand, has touched sensitive Canadian nerves and has evoked powerful Canadian responses. Perhaps in this understanding is the birth of that imagination which must accompany, if it is to save, the development of Canadian civilization.

S. WARHAFT
University of Manitoba

❦ I

NOW, WHEN I LOOK BACK, IT SEEMS STRANGE THAT I SHOULD HAVE got involved with Theodore Stappler at all. The affair began, as such affairs have a habit of doing, in the most casual way, simply because I noticed that one of my students, an alert and intelligent girl – good-looking, too, I might say, not perhaps beautiful but certainly striking – was not doing as well as she had been doing in the first term. There was, after the Christmas vacation, a noticeable falling-off in her work.

I noticed, to begin with, that she seemed at times to be preoccupied, her eyes wandering away from her notes, so that I was sure, seeing her looking out of the window, that she was not paying a great deal of attention to the finer points of the various conflicts between the factions that were fighting for control of the destiny of France during the Revolution. Even the high dramatic moments seemed to stir her only momentarily, and then she would turn her head away from the window and look at me with her large, striking, grey-green eyes, and I would feel my ego rising and a flush of satisfaction mounting into my cheeks.

I am, I think, a fairly effective lecturer. There is something in me, I think, of the actor. At any rate, when I was a student at the University of Toronto, I used to do some acting with various undergraduate drama societies. If nothing else, that experience made me aware that there is such a thing as an audience, and that this audience needs to be captured and held. Perhaps that is why, given the choice between Political Science and History, I chose History, because it is less exclusively concerned with the theory of government; perhaps also because, when I returned from the war, invalided after the invasion of Sicily, I was more than ever interested in the large sweep of events and in the causes of wars and revolutions, all the more so since I had lived a relatively sheltered life in a country removed from the great battlefields and the centres of revolutionary upheavals in the modern world.

It is hard, for instance, to walk the streets of this growing, unself-conscious western city, where I have now been living for two years, teaching the turbulent history of Europe to young Western Canadians, and to realize that elsewhere the past is not merely history but something that touches sensitive nerves, evokes powerful responses.

Take Sicily, for example, where nothing is forgotten, and betrayals are remembered that took place generations ago. But this is too easy a generalization. For here, too, in this western city, so peaceful, stodgy even, in spite of all its activity, its growth, its feeling that the world has only just begun and history is a tomb, a collection of dry bones, here too the old ghosts stir, walk beside many a man or woman on the crowded, peaceful pavements or stand beside them as they look down into the river valley and see the great Saskatchewan River flowing dark-grey in the summer or lying stiff and white and frozen in the long winter. But history has a way of exciting even those students who have grown up here, in the West, who are conscious of little turbulence, and are no longer much aware even of the war so recently past. It seems strange that soon, for many of them, the names of Hitler and Mussolini, Stalin and Roosevelt, Churchill even, will be names only dimly attached to living men, who gave commands, inspired and terrorized, and in one way or another affected all our lives.

One of my colleagues, a dark-haired, ascetic-looking scholar with thin, rimless spectacles, said to me when I first arrived that our students were the best students he had ever taught, and he had taught all over the United States and Canada. Not, he said, because they are sophisticated. Precisely the opposite. They knew little, were aware of the fact that the mainsprings of history were elsewhere, and therefore wanted to know, were avid for knowledge, he said; they wanted to drink knowledge like a thirsty man who, wandering in the desert, suddenly sees water.

My colleague was perhaps somewhat too rhapsodic. I found that most of my students could keep their enthusiasm under strict control. Some, of course, were enthusiastic, but others made up for them by their total indifference. Some would come alive briefly, like a feeble candle, at certain moments. Perhaps the drama inherent in a certain situation roused them, perhaps my actor's instinct, breaking to the surface and illuminating, more sharply, more memorably than is usual, some man, some event.

For instance, Jean Paul Marat. Is it possible, I asked my class once, to arrive at some final estimation of him? How do we judge him, this little, slender, broad-nostrilled man, afflicted by some awful disease of the skin, who was the "friend of the people," who thundered against the villainous attempts of princes to ruin the liberty of the people and brought into the light of day some of the dreadful acts of depotism, but who later preached the physical extermination of all who supported the old régime. "I believe," he cried, "in the cutting off of heads." Though himself too sensitive to attend a post mortem, he was nonetheless a moving spirit in the Prison Massacres, in which supporters of the old régime, and some others too – debtors, thieves, some prostitutes – eleven hundred souls in all, were executed, without benefit of tribunal, by the "just vengeance of the people."

Revulsion against the event Marat dismisses, speaking from the tribune in a hollow voice, a handkerchief round his head, shirt open at the neck. Though shunned by most members of the Assembly, he commands the loyalty and veneration of many outside and, through that loyalty, gains power. Once, as a court physician, he had lived in a silk-curtained drawing-room, upholstered in blue and white damask, with a brilliant chandelier hanging from the ceiling and superb porcelain vases filled with rare and delicate flowers on the tables. Later, a hunted, persecuted man, he hid in cellars and sewers and contracted the disease whose pain can now be eased only when he sits, his face yellow, his skin shrunken, submerged in a warm bath.

Here, in the austerely furnished room he inhabits as a Revolutionary leader, Charlotte Corday finds him. She brings him news from Caen, where the escaped Girondin leaders, betrayers of the Revolution, are trying to raise Normandy. He asks their names, sitting in his bath.

"They shall soon be guillotined," he says, and Charlotte Corday, that beautiful young girl, draws out a knife and stabs him to death.

Thus the hunter becomes the hunted and at last the victim. Dead, he becomes a martyr and a saint. His body is carried in triumph to the Pantheon, only to be disinterred again four months later.

This account galvanized my students, caught their interest as it had mine, because here all the ironies, all the paradoxes of history are so classically present.

How, I repeated, do we judge Marat? How do we judge that beautiful girl who assassinated him? How, in general, do we come to terms with violence, especially the violence generated by revolutionary fervour? I attempted to draw a distinction between the violence unleashed by the French Revolution, which, however destructive, also released positive forces, and the violence of the Hitlerite movement in Germany, which was essentially negative and nihilistic. Marat, I said, like Robespierre, like Danton, was an idealist. But his idealism, turning into a kind of fanaticism, consumed him. He lacked self-knowledge. Perhaps all fanatics lack it. They do not understand the action of time, nor all those other things that make human life so wonderful, so absurd, so grotesque, so infinitely complex. Fanatics lack that quality which we call judgement, a quality which, needless to say, I felt myself to possess in great abundance. And, lacking so vital a quality, they are in a real sense mad. But this madness enables them to drive toward a goal in a blind fury, eliminating obstacles because they stand in the way of the goal. If the goal seems eventually acceptable to men, then men forgive the madman, even call him divinely inspired. If the goal itself is ultimately judged to have been evil, men call him satanic. But sometimes the divine and the satanic are so finely balanced that no ultimate judgement is possible, and the figure remains forever paradoxical.

I stopped to let my students absorb what I had said, to let them think it over, pleased that I had stirred them up so that their turning brains seemed almost palpable in the suddenly very quiet room. I looked out of the window onto the quiet campus. It was a cold day toward the middle of December. Icicles hung from the drainpipes of the building across the way, and the walks were white, for it had been snowing during the night.

A student raised his hand. It was John Cairns. He frequently spoke, and frequently off the topic. So I felt myself bristle as I nodded my head in his direction.

"How far," he asked, "was Marat motivated, not by a striving toward some ideal, but by pure hatred, by . . . by," he hesitated, groping for words, "by personal malice, motivated by a subconscious drive for revenge which had nothing to do with social justice, but expressed his own subconscious needs?"

"You have been reading Freud," I said.

"Well, what if I have?"

There was a little titter from two or three rather prim girls who sat together in the middle of the room, as if something indecent had been said, and I was at once sorry that I had dragged Freud into it, since the question was perfectly serious, and legitimate too, but sometimes the psychological clichés which come glibly from the tongues of undergraduates are annoying. Silly tittering is, however, even more annoying. So I silenced the titter with what I conceived to be a stern look, a look which a friend once told me makes me appear merely pompous. At any rate, the titter stopped.

"You haven't answered my question, though," said Cairns.

I felt the exciting atmosphere which my tale of Marat and my speculation about the divine and satanic balance had built up dissipating, and I said rather testily, "I can't give you an easy answer, and if you expect me to solve the problem for you once and for all, I can't do it. It can't be done."

It was then that she raised her hand and that I noticed her really for the first time. I had of course seen her, but only as one in a group of some forty or fifty students, not in any way distinguished. She had never made any comment during a lecture or contributed anything to the discussion.

"Of course," she said now, leaning forward slightly in her chair, "of course he was motivated by purely personal feelings at times. That seems only logical and obvious. We all are. You said once," she addressed me now directly, "that history is a play of forces, and that may be so. It probably is so. But human beings play the roles."

"All right, then," said John Cairns. "So everything ultimately must be traceable to subconscious drives. The man thinks he's serving justice and all that, but really he's working off some awful grudge which he got because once, when he was a child, he was rejected."

"Are you suggesting, Mr. Cairns," I said in the most acid voice I could muster, "that all we need is to stretch everybody, particularly politicians and statesmen, out on couches and have them psychoanalysed?"

There was laughter, and I felt for a moment like a very superior sort of animal, though I knew also that I would soon feel embarrassed, for nothing is easier for a professor than to score a cheap victory over an inexperienced undergraduate. I found myself also, surreptitiously and perhaps even subconsciously, looking at the girl and trying to remember what her name was. Her eyes were firmly fixed on me, as if she were trying to draw me to her. She had, I now saw, dusky-gold hair and a rather pale face with a long, aquiline nose.

"The suggestion," said Cairns, and so drew my eyes, reluctantly, back to him, "has been made. And perhaps it wouldn't be such a bad idea at that. Considering the mess the world's in. It might be worth a try."

"Well, then," I said, "let us start. The trouble will be persuading men of power to lie down on that couch. Or to get them to allow for immediate world release any suggestion that what they are doing is motivated by deep subconscious drives and not by high devotion to some eternal principle. Everybody does things on principle only, you know. At least for public consumption. Everybody wants peace and everybody is merciful. It is always the other man who is cruel and vindictive. That is the world's tragedy."

The bell rang, and so I was able to terminate the lecture on this rather high and sombre note, and I had the satisfaction of seeing little groups of students beginning to discuss some of the issues that had been raised.

"What," I heard one say, "do you make of the girl – what's her name? – who stabbed him in the bathtub? Why'd she do it? I didn't get that. She only got her head chopped off for it."

"Well, she did it because she thought she was saving France."

"Sure. That's what she said she thought. I wonder – was she ever in love with the guy? Maybe he threw her over for somebody else."

The Cairns influence, I thought, was strong and plain.

They were moving over towards my desk, where I still sat, gathering up my notes, listening to what was being said, and feeling in general very satisfied. After a good lecture I always feel as I do after a good meal – sated, self-satisfied, a little smug.

"The death of Marat." I said to one of them, rising, "has all the aspects of a cheap melodrama. In fact, a writer wouldn't dare to invent it. It would seem too absurd, too corny."

John Cairns and the girl with the dusky-gold hair, for so I designated her for the time being, joined our little knot, and Cairns must have heard what I said about cheap melodrama, for he said in his I-have-solved-this-problem-once-and-for-all voice that I found most of the time rather hard to take, "Objectively speaking, a person out for revenge always looks corny, because the objective bystander doesn't understand his powerful subconscious drives. All he sees is exaggerated emotion. But once he understands the inter-personal conflicts and the inner-directed subsconscious drives. . . ." He lapsed now into textbook jargon which he had only very imperfectly understood, and I stopped listening to him, although, out of courtesy, I nodded and, when he finished, I made a non-committal comment, and walked out.

Then, as I walked along the corridor towards the stairway leading up to my office on the second floor, she was suddenly at my side.

"Do you think, Dr. Lerner, that an act of revenge could be quite impersonal? That Charlotte Corday, say, could have been motivated by entirely unselfish motives?"

"Doesn't that," I asked in turn, "contradict what you said before in class?"

"No," she said. "I don't think so, not really. I said that Marat was motivated by purely personal feelings at times." She stressed the last two words. "But at other times he may not have been. What starts out as a personal thing can become totally impersonal, totally pure, in fact."

"That's a strange use of the word 'pure,' " I said.

"I like to think that Charlotte Corday, when she stabbed him, was pure."

"Why do you like to think that?" I asked her.

My question seemed to fluster her. "I – I really don't know. Now that you ask. I don't know why I said that. Except that I don't want to think she did it as a matter of just vengeance or revenge. I think vengeance is a sordid thing."

"Yet very human," I said.

"Yes."

"And don't you think," I asked her, "that at times it may be a very proper emotion – to want to take vengeance?"

"I – I suppose," she said. "But I wish it wasn't."

I looked closely at her as we walked side by side slowly up the stairs. She had on a light-green velveteen dress, and – I must confess this – I let my eyes travel downwards – professors are not immune to this sort of thing – and observed with pleasure the soft rise and fall of her full, young breasts.

She recalled me. "What I really wanted to ask," she said, "was – you see, I'd begun to work on one of the topics you assigned. But now, if that's all right, I'd sort of like to do an essay about Marat and Charlotte Corday. Is that – do you think that it would be all right for me to do it?"

"Yes," I said. "It would certainly be all right." I found myself idly wondering how old the girl was. She seemed a little older than most undergraduates – in her early twenties perhaps. "What precise topic do you have in mind?"

"Well," she said, "I don't yet know. I really only got interested when you talked about Marat. Could I have a day or two to think about it?"

"Certainly," I said. "Oh – you must forgive me, but it is difficult to remember names when there are forty or fifty students in a class. What is your name?"

"Held," she said. "Katherine Held."

"You can drop into my office and discuss the topic with me, Miss Held. When you have thought a bit about it."

"Thank you," she said and turned and walked away.

I looked after her and noticed particularly her long, slender, and rather elegant legs. She walked with a gentle swaying motion, and she presented a picture that was aesthetically pleasing. That is a way, I realize, of rationalizing, of distancing, of wrapping in words, a perfectly simple, fleshly response. Still, it is the dignified way out. Outwardly I keep a stern, impersonal demeanour, befitting a man solely concerned with academic questions and wholly involved in his own little corner of his subject.

I am a bachelor, still in my twenties – well, that is putting things optimistically, since in a few months time, on the 26th of September, 1952, to be exact, I am going to be thirty. But why hurry time? Why not hang on to the last possible moment to the comforting thought that I, though only a fairly junior assistant professor of History, am not yet too much older than at least some of my students? Am still, like some of them, like Katherine Held, I felt sure, in my twenties.

I live in a nice (though the sound-proofing could be somewhat improved) two-bedroom apartment which I have furnished with some rather elegant modern Scandinavian furniture. I have also three distinguished (at least I think so) oils, the prize being a rich British Columbia forest scene by Emily Carr, which is now quite valuable. I rather fancy myself a patron of the arts, a hobby

I'll probably have to give up, if the experience of my married colleagues is at all typical, once I myself enter the blessed state of matrimony. Most marriages have a way of being fruitful, and then dentist's bills and children's shoes (my colleagues seem to be forever taking their children to dentists and buying them shoes) and oil paintings and the salary of an assistant professor don't somehow mix.

About once a month my mother, who lives in Toronto, inquires, with ever so much tact, whether I have at last met the right girl. Once she came right out with it.

"I don't want to hurry you," she wrote, "but it really is time. Your father and I would really like to see you settled. Miriam's children are lovely."

Miriam is my lovely sister. She is a standard model of the young bourgeois wife and mother. Her husband is a lawyer climbing the lovely ladder of success. Lovely job, lovely man, lovely surburban house. Three children, all lovely.

Dear mother! How she worries about me. My father told me, tears in his eyes, that she nearly went out of her mind when word came that I had been severely wounded in Sicily. For three weeks, he said, until at last I could write to say I was out of danger and doing reasonably well, she hardly ate anything at all.

I think that she has also never reconciled herself to the fact that I became a Ph.D. instead of an M.D. History! Who ever heard of such a thing? Who can possibly make a living telling somebody else what happened in the past?

"This," my father told me once, "this is the country of the future. Here no one cares about the past. They come here to forget the past."

And indeed, both my father and mother, though they were born in Toronto, were the children of immigrants. And the first generation notoriously looks to the future and tends to play down the past, tries indeed perhaps to forget it altogether. It would be difficult to look at my mother, a fairly tallish, grey-haired Jewish matron, a bit stout, but still, especially when she is properly corseted, a very fine figure of a woman, and to remember that her father had come to Canada as a nearly penniless youth, with a thick, unkempt black beard, straight out of the crowded slums of the Warsaw ghetto – the same that during the war was to be so completely, so tragically annihilated. There, but for the grace of God, might I have been.

Ironically, it was my grandfather who instilled in me a love, I might almost say a passion, for history. He was not a learned man. He read the Yiddish papers that were published in New York, and when I was about ten, one of these papers ran a potted serial version, very sensational, of the French Revolution. Whenever I saw my grandfather, which was about twice a week, he gave me the latest news about the French Revolution. Together we waited anxiously for developments. Would Robespierre himself be guillotined in the end? Would Danton? We debated these questions seriously. And it was he who was really proud when I became a student of history.

By now of course my parents have accepted the *fait accompli*. Apart from her campaign to get me married, my mother would like me to come back to Toronto. In a way, these two goals are one, since she thinks there would be a greater choice of eligible girls there. In vain I tell her that I live in a fairly big city. She doesn't, I think, quite believe it. For her, little exists west of Toronto. She knows there are mountains somewhere, and she knew, before I went to the prairies, that on the Pacific coast there is Vancouver. She knows New York fairly well, and she knows Florida, for my father and she have been going there the last two or three winters for two weeks or so. Right after the war she forced my father to take her to Italy, because she wanted to see the place where her dear son was wounded and so nearly lost a leg. If I don't return to Toronto for good, she wrote, she would come and visit me here next year to see how I live.

I keep telling her that I do not intend to return to Toronto. I like it here. I like the University, I like my colleagues and, to be frank about it, I prefer to live at a distance from my close relatives. I love my parents, I love my sister, but at a distance of two thousand miles familial love has a greater chance of flourishing. Reunions are then such lovely occasions.

I like to be able to come and go pretty much as I like. I am now working on a book about the intellectual currents generated by the French Revolution, and I have been going down to the United States during the past two summers to use the great libraries there. When I get tired and weary, I drive to Jasper or Banff for a weekend, to ski in the winter and walk in the spring and autumn. In the mountains one feels free. So I am content and reasonably happy. As happy as any man can be, thinking about the carnage of the recent war and the general murderousness of our time.

And so, after I had watched Katherine Held walk down the long sweep of stairs, I went into my office. On and off during that day my thoughts kept straying to her, and I saw always the rather long, palish face framed by the dusky-gold hair.

She presented herself at my office during the afternoon of the next day and asked if I could see her. She had done a little preliminary reading, she said, and she wanted to write an essay about Charlotte Corday, the girl who had assassinated Marat.

"I thought you wanted to write about Marat," I said.

"Well, I'd be writing about Marat, of course," she said, "but I want to concentrate on Charlotte Corday. I came across a contemporary account by. . . ." She stopped and rummaged among her notes. "Here it is. By Louvet. He says Charlotte was 'a mixture of sweetness and pride that proclaimed her celestial soul.' "

"Louvet was very emotional when he wrote that," I said.

"But I was right, too," she said. "She acted quite unselfishly. She didn't even know Marat. She only wanted to make a great gesture."

"Well, she certainly did," I said. "You could hardly do more than hunt someone down and kill him. In the bathtub yet. That is a gesture all right."

We both laughed.

"Of course," I went on, "all assassinations are gestures. That is what the Nihilists were doing at the end of the nineteenth century and the beginning of the twentieth. They assassinated ruling personalities to assert a principle and make a gesture. But such gestures are also political acts. Charlotte Corday's murder of Marat was a political act. We must not forget that. She was of course a very romantic girl. She had read Plutarch. She saw herself as a great heroine. She knew she was going to sacrifice herself." I was playing with a pencil and I suddenly found myself pointing it at Katherine Held and asking her in a rather inquisitorial tone, "Do you admire what she did? Are you by any chance identifying yourself with Charlotte Corday?"

The question startled her, as it was meant to do. "No," she said firmly. "No, I don't think so. In a way I admire her, I suppose."

"Why?"

"It's hard to say. Perhaps because she dared to act out of conviction. She had courage."

"But courage by itself isn't enough, is it? And is conviction? Some of the most evil men in the history of mankind have had plenty of both. Conviction and courage are not good in themselves. I think we have to ask what they're used for."

"Of course," she said. "I agree. But when one looks at all the little people just jogging along, then one longs for some great events, some sort of great declaration."

"You are romantic," I said.

She cocked her head to one side and gave me what I took to be a flirtatious smile. "Is that bad?" she asked.

"Not necessarily," I said drily. "So long as you don't get all maudlin and sentimental. Write about Charlotte Corday, but don't get all soft. And don't psychoanalyse her. Analyse the political situation which made a Marat and a Corday possible. This is not so dramatic, but it leads to understanding."

"All right," she said. "I'll do that."

"I meant to ask you what your major field of study is," I said.

"Psychology."

"Everybody is studying psychology these days."

"Is that bad?"

"No. Except that many students expect to get a shortcut to human understanding. And there are no such shortcuts."

"I want to understand," she said, "but I don't expect shortcuts."

"I'm glad to hear it. Is this your last year?"

She smiled. "I hope so. If I pass all my courses."

"Why shouldn't you?"

"Oh," she said, shrugging her shoulders, "you can never tell."

"And what will you do after you get your degree?"

"I don't know quite yet," she said. "I've been thinking about social work. But I'm not sure."

She looked at me uncertainly, as if she expected another question, but when I didn't say anything she rose to go.

I wanted her to stay. She seemed interesting and I wanted to find out a little more about her.

So I said quickly, "Before you go, Miss Held, let me ask you an admittedly hypothetical question."

She sat down again.

"If you found yourself in Charlotte Corday's position – you know – full of passionate conviction, full of a sense of desperate mission, could you select your victim as she did, could you hunt him down, and could you then, do you think, kill him?"

"That's a strange question," she said.

"Let me put it another way. Would you be capable of killing someone?"

I leaned forward and looked straight at her and saw that her eyes were very beautiful, the colour of a mountain lake.

"You told me," she answered, and an ironic glint came into her eyes, "not to psychoanalyse historic figures. And now you want me to psychoanalyse myself."

"Well," I said, slightly on the defensive, "this is a parlour game we all play from time to time."

"But isn't this just an academic exercise?" she said. "If I say 'yes' would this mean anything?"

"It might mean something. Even as an academic exercise."

"Well, then, I don't think I could kill anybody." She then artfully turned the tables. "Could you kill someone?"

"I was a soldier," I said. "A soldier's job is to kill. And I was almost killed myself."

"But there is a difference between a soldier's job and the kind of act Charlotte Corday did."

"Yes," I said. "And in many ways her act was more human. A modern soldier is an inhuman instrument. He drops bombs or fires a heavy gun, and half the time he doesn't see the consequences of his acts. It is all very impersonal. That is what is so horrifying. Nobody is ultimately responsible. Or at least each one of us can persuade himself that he really isn't. And the end result is a dehumanization. People become dehumanized." I had not intended to swim into these waters. I had only meant to keep her talking for a few more minutes.

"Well," she said. "I refuse to become dehumanized. I don't want to kill anybody. I want to help people. That's why I was thinking of social work. I want to be useful."

"You are idealistic."

"You like to put tags on me," she said and managed to make me feel uncomfortable. "First you called me romantic. And now you call me idealistic. And you use these terms as if they were somehow bad."

"Forgive me," I said. "I didn't mean that. Not really. But you surprise me. You are unusual. So many students I talk to want only to go out and get good jobs. Very few speak of service and usefulness. Then also," I added, rather irrelevantly, "you are a very striking-looking girl and you will probably get married before long."

A flush came into her cheeks. "And if I do," she said. "What has it to do with anything?" She was quite belligerent, so that I felt like looking for cover. "Some men talk as if everything is finished for a girl once she marries. I don't accept that."

"I didn't say that, and I certainly didn't mean to imply it."

"Oh, yes, you did."

"I'm sorry then."

I admired her. She had spirit. She could stand up for herself. That was a good thing.

"If I'd been a bit older when the war finished, and had some training," she said, "I would have tried to get over to Europe to work in some of the refugee camps."

"Oh," I said, very surprised. "Why that?"

"Because," she said very quietly, "I would have liked to do something to help. Something, anything. These people came out of concentration camps all over Europe. I remember when I first saw photographs in the newspapers. It was terrible. I cried. And I wanted desperately to do something. You will probably call me romantic and idealistic again."

"No, no," I said quickly. "I must apologize. I don't think I took you seriously enough."

"Because, you see," she went on, pursuing her own thoughts without bothering to answer me one way or the other, "I could have been there myself. More likely I would have been one of the dead."

Her words gave me a jolt. Was she talking about a purely hypothetical situation? Was she merely given to dramatizing herself, or was her assertion based on some fact?

"How possible was this?" I asked.

"Very possible," she said. "We fled to England in 1939. From Austria. And came to Canada just weeks before the war started. I was only a child of course at the time."

"You were refugees then?"

"Yes," she said, "we were."

That astonished me. She looked so like most of the students who were born here and had lived here all their lives. Her English, too, was not very different from that of other students.

"I wouldn't have known," I said. "I thought you were a Canadian girl."

"I am now," she said. "At least I hope so. We came to this country from England. Then we lived in the East first, in Toronto, until three years ago when my father suddenly decided to come out here. He is like that. Impulsive. He's been very restless for a long time now. And that's not surprising. It hasn't been easy for him. He never really found a place for himself after we left home. He was a lawyer in Austria, and a good one too, I think, but he hasn't been able to practise his profession since. The law is so different. In different countries. And he has never had the patience to study again. So it's been a pretty hard life for him. Then my mother died almost as soon as we arrived here. Now I feel I have to make something out of myself."

"Of course."

"I feel that somehow I have to repay some debt. That may sound odd. I don't know if you understand. It's only a vague feeling I have. Something I can't really explain. At least not in so many words. But I sometimes ask myself, Why were we saved? Why could we escape? The margin was so narrow. We left London exactly three weeks before the war broke out. I sometimes wake up in the middle of the night in a kind of terror and say to myself that I might have been dead. One of those millions of corpses."

Her words sent a shudder through me. Because what might have been was more than a mere abstraction. I felt suddenly as if a sombre reality, the spectre of Auschwitz, had invaded my office. I felt all the more uneasy because I was taken by surprise. I don't usually wish to avoid facing unpleasant realities, but nothing had prepared me for the turn our conversation had taken. The murder of Marat was far enough in the past so that the blood had had a chance to dry. But the bones that had been here evoked had not yet crumbled.

There was nothing I could say, but I thought, looking at her sitting there across the desk from me, her hands folded in her lap, how little we really know about anyone, and yet how ready we are to make easy assumptions. I had categorized her, put her into a pigeon-hole labelled "Romantic student. Dreamily idealistic. A bit naïve. But bears watching. Streaks of independence." And it was all wrong.

"Well," I said at last, "unfortunately you may yet have your chance to help. I say 'unfortunately,' because I could wish the suffering were all over. But that's not so. The aftermath will be with us for a long time. There will always be much to do."

"Yes," she said. "I know."

"The refugee is the everyman of our time. As soon as some are salvaged, more are created elsewhere. So it's no wonder that the world grows callous."

"Yes," she said again.

We sat silently for a while, each brooding vaguely about man's fate, I suppose. Then she picked up her books and rose to go. I went to the door and opened it for her and then I held out my hand to her, an unusual way for me to terminate an interview with a student. But then it had been an unusual interview.

After that I took naturally a very lively interest in Katherine Held. I was very pleased when she got a first-class mark on her Christmas examination paper, and I was looking forward to her term paper on Marat and Charlotte Corday.

But when the second term began, I noticed a distinct flagging of interest on her part. Her mind seemed to be, not in the lecture room, but elsewhere. She did not hand in her essay when it was due. Then she began to attend lectures fitfully. Two or three lectures would go by and she would not be there. So at last I sent her a note, asking her to come and see me in my office.

She came, hesitantly, toward the end of January. In the course of our conversation she hinted about some involvement with a man. She did not yet mention his name. But it was in fact Theodore Stappler. And that is how I became involved with him.

❦ II

SHE WAS CLEARLY ILL AT EASE, EMBARRASSED EVEN, WHEN, after a light knock and my "come in," she opened the door of my office. She wore a long, beige winter coat and fur-lined overshoes. She also had on a hat, which she took off immediately, and then quickly smoothed out her long hair with rapid, irregular strokes of her fingers. She must have just come into the building, for her cheeks were glowing from the cold.

"Please sit down," I said. "Perhaps you'd better take off your coat, too."

"Thanks," she said. She took off her coat and draped it around the back of the chair, and then sat down.

"I'm sorry I didn't get my essay done," she said. "I suppose that's why you asked me to come."

"Well, partly," I said. "I don't usually prod senior students. They should know what they're doing. But you did seem very interested in the subject. After all, you proposed it yourself. And you did seem capable of coming up with something interesting. That's why I took a special interest in you. But now I have noted that your interest seems to have evaporated."

"Oh, no, it hasn't," she said quickly. "Only I. . . I suppose it must seem like that to you." She broke off and shrugged her shoulders. "I can't explain, really. I do like your course. And I like your lectures very much. And you mustn't think that because I've been staying away. . ." Her voice trailed off and she didn't finish her sentence.

"Well, I don't really much care about that," I said, trying to make it sound as casual as possible. Because I really do care. I always feel responsible when students stay away from lectures for a prolonged period of time, or come irregularly. "I was, however, looking forward to your paper more than I usually do. Especially after the conversation we had here before Christmas."

"I hope you don't expect too much. So you won't be too disappointed when I finally do hand it in. If you will accept the essay, although it's already very late."

"Have you got it done?"

"No," she said. "No, I haven't. I've read a lot, but I haven't written much."

"But you do intend to write it?"

"Yes," she said. "If you will still accept it."

"I will," I said, "if you get it in within a week."

"I'll try," she said. "But I can't promise."

I was getting annoyed, because I felt she was trying to bargain with me and, worse even, that she was trying to take advantage of me. Something of this irritation must have been manifest in look or manner, for she said quickly, and rather piteously, I thought, obviously trying to prevent some kind of explosion on my part, "It's not just your course, Professor Lerner. I'm behind in all my work, and I feel terrible about it."

"You're a fool, then," I said. "Are you going to throw the year away? The finals are less than three months away."

"I know," she said. "I constantly think about that, and I feel sick when I do."

"Why don't you get to work, then?" I asked. "That will soon take the feeling of sickness away."

"Because I can't," she almost whispered, "because I can't concentrate on my work."

"Why not?" I asked. "Has something happened to you?"

She shook her head lightly. Then she closed her eyes and passed her left hand slowly down her left cheek. The reddish glow had gone from her cheeks and, with her eyes closed and her head slightly inclined towards one side, she looked a little like some suffering madonna and called forth all my sentimental instincts.

"Everybody hits some rough patches in the road," I said, speaking in my most paternal accents. I really hate myself for turning on that particular faucet, though I don't do it quite consciously and by the time I'm aware of what I'm doing it's too late to turn off the flow of paternal honey dew, and so I go on. Besides, I tell myself that it's sometimes quite effective. "The best thing to do in order to get over a particularly rough patch,"

I found myself saying, "is to grit your teeth and get down to work."

She suddenly looked at me and smiled in such a quizzical, ironic manner that I stopped talking, and then stammered, in a flustered kind of way, "I – I don't want to preach at you or give you a pep talk."

"I don't mind, really," she said, "except that it's not going to be of very much use to me. I know what I should do, but I just can't do it. My mind won't stay on the subject."

"On any subject?"

"On academic subjects."

"That can only mean," I said, exchanging the paternal for the ironic tone of voice, "that there is a man involved here somewhere."

She sat up with a start, as if I had just touched a particularly sensitive, exposed nerve. "How did you know?"

"That's not so difficult to guess at. It's a quite normal condition, I suppose. But the first flush of excitement wears off, and then you'll be able to work again. Let's just hope it doesn't last too long."

"I wish it were as simple as that."

"It always seems complicated. More complicated than it is."

"But sometimes things really are complicated. . . . But I don't really want to bother you with personal problems of that kind. That wouldn't be fair. And you have so many other things to do. I just wanted you to know that my sudden neglect of my work had nothing to do with a loss of interest. . . ."

"But with the acquisition of a new and different kind of interest," I completed her sentence and she smiled. "How hard have you fallen?" I asked her, and the smile vanished.

"What do you mean?"

"I mean that I presume you have fallen in love."

"I don't think you can presume that," she said. "If things were as straightforward as that, there wouldn't be any difficulties. But I'm not sure of my own feelings. That's what makes things difficult."

"I sympathize with you. Unfortunately I have no advice to offer you. On that subject I speak without any kind of professorial authority."

For a moment the distance that separates professor from student seemed to have narrowed, indeed to have disappeared altogether. And after all, I thought suddenly, I was not so very much older than she. I might indeed be courting someone very like her myself. The thought startled me.

"It would be easy if one could be sure one way or the other," she said, though she left the exact nature of that assurance undefined.

"Things must have happened very suddenly," I said. "These matters were not agitating you the last time we talked together."

"It all did happen rather suddenly," she said. "Just about a month ago, when the Christmas holidays started. That's when he suddenly appeared."

"A mystery man."

"Just about," she said. "He suddenly turned up and said he'd known my father many years ago. I thought at first they had been friends. But it turned out they hadn't. Yet he and I – the man, I mean – have become friends."

"Romeo and Juliet," I said.

"Hardly," she said. "But my father certainly disapproves of the whole affair. Violently."

"I thought fathers no longer had much to say about these matters," I said. "I thought the modern girl was quite independent."

"I suppose I could do what I wanted," she said. "But that isn't really it. Even if I knew exactly what I wanted to do. Besides, I am very fond of my father. I don't want to hurt him. We've been very close, especially after my mother died. He's very restless and nervous. . . . Oh, I don't know what's going to happen."

I wanted to ask her exactly why her father disapproved of this man, but at that moment my colleague Bill Sommers stuck his head in my door and said, "Oh, I'm sorry. Didn't know you were busy. I'm going over to have a cup of coffee. Thought you might be interested."

Katherine Held got up quickly and looked at her watch. "I don't want to keep you, Professor Lerner," she said.

"Not at all. Sit down. I'm not in a hurry."

"I really have to go anyway. I'm late as it is. I have to meet someone. It was very nice of you to listen to me."

"Not at all," I said. "I'm only sorry I couldn't be of much help to you. Things will work out."

"I hope so." She reached for her coat.

I got up and walked around my desk to help her on with it.

And then again, just as I had done the first time we spoke together, I held out my hand. Her hand was warm, and I held on to it rather longer than was strictly necessary.

"Don't worry too much about things," I said.

"Thank you very much for your time and for taking all this trouble."

"That's all right. And, Miss Held," I said, in a curious mixture of my paternal and ironic styles, "don't throw away the year. It wouldn't be worth it."

She just smiled, Mona Lisa-like, a cross between the enigmatic and the haughtily superior, and walked away.

Bill Sommers had been waiting for me just outside my office. He is a boyish-looking man, and his boyishness is accentuated by a crewcut, although his hair is beginning to turn grey at the temples and bears witness to the fact that the first flush of his youth is gone. He stood leaning against the wall and watched Katherine Held walk down the long corridor and turn to go down the stairs. Then he looked at me and said in his capital letters voice, "Playing Father Confessor To Troubled Girls, Professor Lerner?"

"Nonsense," I said.

"Didn't hand in her paper on time, eh?"

"No," I said. "How did you know?"

"I've been in this business for damned near ten years," said Bill. "I know all the situations that arise. Or are likely to. You have a trusting soul, old boy. Once word gets around, they'll all be sitting in your office, telling you sob stories. You watch out." He looked down the corridor, as if he could still see her.

"She is a striking-looking girl, though," he said.

Uncomplicated fellow, Bill Sommers. Very good sort, though. I'm very fond of him. He's now working on a book about the *voyageurs*. Uncomplicated fellows and adventurers. He's exactly the man to write about them. No constitutional wrangles. No complex problems of conscience. Just the drive to open up untrodden wilderness. Make money. Uncomplicated relationships. Simple trading. When that's not possible, simple if violent solutions. If passion is aroused and a likely Indian girl is ready, then that passion can be satisfied. Tents pitched under the vast, star-studded sky. And then the sudden shudder of the loins. I am simplifying matters, of course. Bill Sommers will write a fine book about it all.

"I'm interested in the problems of my students," I said.

"Ho, ho," said Bill. "Come off it, old boy. You sit there listening to heart-throbbing tales and you feel sentimental and protective all over. I know you, Mark Lerner. Now listen to wise and experienced William Sommers. Harden your heart. Stiffen your sentiments. What's the matter with her, anyway?"

"A love affair of some sort, I think. That may be overstating the case. She's involved in some way with somebody who just showed up."

"And therefore can't write essays," he said." "A likely story."

"I think she told me the truth," I said, somewhat on the defensive.

"Of course she did. They always tell the truth. They all have trouble with their immortal souls and their unformed emotions. Especially if they have such beautiful big eyes."

"You notice everything," I said.

We had now come to the stairs, and Brian Maxwell and Don Brent of the English department joined us there.

"How are our symbolic friends today?" Bill Sommers called out to them.

Maxwell and Brent were hot in pursuit of symbols. The world to them in fact was a vast forest of symbols that needed to be deciphered and interpreted.

"Better than ever," said Maxwell.

Tall and lanky, austere in appearance, he looked quizzically at us. He is a specialist in the poetry of Yeats and Eliot. Brent was all taken up with Jung at the time. He was playing about with the theory that *The Tempest*, symbolically speaking, really takes place under water.

"Lerner here is turning himself into the wailing wall of Jerusalem," said Sommers. "And the lovelorn are beating a path to his wall."

"To wail?" said Maxwell.

"He has a sympathetic face," said Brent.

Maxwell, who evidently hadn't been listening very closely, said innocently, "So Lerner has fallen in love. I thought it was about time. The example of all the married men about him. . . ."

"You have it wrong," said Sommers. "Although, symbolically speaking, perhaps that's just what has happened to our friend."

"Oh, shut up," I said.

We stepped out of the building, and the cold hit us suddenly, and we all pulled our coats tighter about us and humped our shoulders. It was about ten below zero, and there was a light wind which made it seem much colder than it was. We walked quickly, without speaking. It was about a hundred yards to the cafeteria, and then warm air welcomed us, and we got our coffee and sat down.

Brent began to stir his coffee in his own characteristically ruminative manner, and I knew that a portentous statement was about to issue from his lips. He did not disappoint me.

"Will they ever agree about the prisoners?" he said. "There was an item in the paper yesterday saying the two truce teams had wrangled for three and a half hours without getting anywhere. They were just accusing each other of dishonesty and treachery."

"That's not unusual," said Sommers drily. "Imagine yourself as one of the negotiators. Day after day you meet the other side. You don't budge. They don't budge. You know what they're going to say. They know what you're going to say. So it goes day after day. So you have to liven things up a bit. That dishonesty and treachery song is just the thing. What a dreary prospect."

"But in the meantime real men are really dying," I said.

The Korean war, which was then dragging on, aimlessly it seemed, was like a running sore. It gnawed at our consciences.

Brian Maxwell said suddenly, very quietly, as if he were talking to himself, "After what you have told me, I cannot but conclude the bulk of your natives to be the most pernicious race of little odious vermin that nature ever suffered to crawl upon the surface of the earth."

Bill Sommers looked at him, startled, and said, "What is this in aid of?"

"The king of Brobdingnag speaking to Gulliver and delivering judgement. Old Jonathan Swift had our number."

"The gloomy old Dean," said Sommers.

"Not gloomy all the time," said Maxwell. "Sometimes he is funnier than any other writer I know. He had searing insights without any illusions." He continued mockingly, peering at Sommers and me over his coffee cup, "You're historians. Tell us how it will all end."

"How will what end?" I asked. "The war in Korea?"

"No, no, not just that. The world. Will it end with a bang or a whimper?"

"It will not end at all," I said. "It will go on."

"A touching faith," he said.

"Well, you've got to have that," I said. "No conflict ever would be worth blowing the human race to smithereens forever. As long as they keep the monster bombs out of it, it will somehow end."

"And do we have a guarantee of that?" asked Maxwell.

"No," I said, "no guarantee. Only hope."

"Hopeful Lerner," he said.

"I have to believe in the essential rationality of men," I said, "or I couldn't go on living."

"That's a noble declaration," said Maxwell, "even if a little melodramatic."

"Speaking of melodrama," said Sommers suddenly. "Look who's just coming in. Lerner's love-sick child."

And there, indeed, she was.

"And who," continued Sommers, "is that with her? Certainly no love-sick callow youth, at least by the look of it."

"Who," asked Brent, "are you talking about?"

"The couple who just walked in," I said.

"You don't have to stare so rudely," said Sommers to Maxwell and Brent, who had turned round in their chairs. "Whatever it is," he went on. "This is not a student romance. An elegant fish, eh?"

"It's not difficult to be elegant among students and professors," said Maxwell.

The man who had come into the cafeteria with Katherine Held was tall. He wore a dark-blue homburg and a well-cut, grey overcoat. He was assuredly not a student. His homburg was set at an angle that gave a slight suggestion of rakishness, but at the same time he managed to look reserved and rather distinguished, largely because he carried himself with an air of easy assurance.

"A good twelve years older than she, I'd say," said Brent.

"Father objects," I informed them. "Perhaps that's why."

Sommers said, "Look, Jean is eight and a half years younger than I am. Her father didn't object when I married her. In fact he was damned glad. Thought it was a splendid match."

"Watch it, Bill," said Brent. "You're wide open to all sorts of cracks. But I will show Christian forbearance."

"Funny," said Maxwell.

"What's funny?" asked Sommers.

"I was only thinking. You see our students all about us." He stopped dramatically, looking at each of us in turn.

"Yes," I said. "What's the revelation?"

"Only this. Here they sit, our students, looking at us, thinking, what marvellous conversation is going on over there, round that table! What philosophic gems, what intellectual sparks must be flying! And here we sit, like a bunch of old women gossiping out on the verandah on a hot summer evening. When I was courting Mary, I had to walk past a gauntlet of old crones who chattered away like so many sewing-machines, and looked at me with X-ray eyes, especially at my baggy trousers. I'm sure they predicted disaster for poor Mary. It got so I was so self-conscious that I went out of my way, about three blocks, to avoid them. And here we sit, the intellectual élite of the country, gossiping about trivial matters and trying to guess the age of some poor guy we don't even know, and what's more, have no business yakking about."

Bill Sommers applauded. "Bravo!" he cried. "That was a great speech. Brian Maxwell for Prime Minister!"

"Enough of this nonsense," said Maxwell. "I've got to get back. My freshmen have battled and murdered poor Swift. I must survey the carnage."

"Are you coming?" Sommers asked me.

"You three go ahead," I said. "I want to find out more, in a casual way, about my love-lorn child."

"Mark Lerner, Private Eye," said Bill. "Be diplomatic, my boy. I doubt whether they really want your company."

They sat, heads leaning towards each other, Katherine Held and the tall, elegant man, talking earnestly in low voices. I sat for a while alone after my colleagues had left, watching the two out of the corner of my eye. After a few minutes of what seemed intense conversation, the man leaned back and took out a package of cigarettes, offered a cigarette to the girl and took one himself. She smiled and said something and they both laughed.

I judged the moment to be right. I would saunter by their table, casually say "Hello," stop and say a few words to her, and then, if this seemed appropriate, begin a conversation with the man.

But these elaborately casual preparations proved unnecessary, for as soon as I got up Katherine Held – whether by accident or also by elaborately casual prearrangement I don't know – saw me and got up, and when I was about two yards away, she said, "Oh, Dr. Lerner, I – I. . . ." She didn't quite seem to know how to proceed and turned to her companion and said, "Theo, this is Dr. Lerner. And this," she turned to me, "is Theodore Stappler."

"Mark Lerner," I said to him, holding out my hand.

Theodore Stappler got up and made what I thought was a very formal bow, shook my hand, and said, "I am extremely pleased to meet you. Katherine has talked about you a lot."

"I hope she hasn't been running me down," I said.

"Oh, no," he said. "She speaks about you with the greatest enthusiasm and respect." His voice was crisp, yet not unmelodious. Its modulation and inflection led me to surmise that he had spoken English first in England, but that his native language was another – German perhaps, perhaps French – it was difficult to tell.

We were all standing, and I said, "Please sit down. I don't want to disturb you."

"Not at all," said Theodore Stappler. "Would you join us for another cup of coffee?"

That seemed a fine opportunity to play Private Eye Lerner, and so I nodded assent, and he said, "Good. I'll go and get you a cup."

I sat down facing Katherine Held, who now seemed somewhat flustered. Her fingers played nervously around the rim of her cup. "I – I'm sorry," she said, "I – I didn't want to take any more of your time, but. . ."

"Not at all," I said. "Mr. Stappler, I take it, is not a student."

"No," she said. "Of course not. He hasn't been here long," she added by way of explanation. "In the city, I mean. Or for that matter in the country. He originally comes from Austria, as we do. That's where he knew my father. I think I mentioned that to you before."

I was about to ask her what he was doing here when he returned with the coffee and sat down beside her. I wished now that I had not accepted the invitation to join them, for I began to feel rather out of place. Private Eye Lerner was not really a role I was cut out for. It was after all a very ordinary thing. A good-looking young girl of twenty-one or two meets and perhaps falls in love with a rather handsome man, older than she but not so very much older either, and neglects her work. That was all there was to it. It was foolish of me to sit there. What could I possibly hope to accomplish?

"Katherine," said Theodore Stappler, "hasn't been studying very hard of late. You must hold me in part responsible."

"That's all very well," I said, making light of the whole matter, "but I cannot fail *you*. You are not taking my course."

He smiled broadly. He had a sharply-beaked Roman nose, rather wide about the nostrils, and full, almost voluptuous lips. I noticed now that his hands were long and surprisingly delicate. His left hand drew attention to itself by a broad, brightly gleaming gold signet ring.

"Miss Held just told me that you haven't been in Canada very long."

"No," he said, "not very long. Only about three years. I've been living in Montreal and Toronto."

"Oh," I said. "And what brought you here to Edmonton? And to the West?"

He looked at me with a quick, wry glance, then lit a cigarette. "How extraordinary," he said, "that you should ask this question."

"Why extraordinary?"

"Because everybody asks me this. Why should a man not come here?"

"Well," I muttered, somewhat taken aback. "It's a long way to come. But you are right. People come here. They settle. They work. I had nothing in mind, really. Except that here we are, in the middle of the winter. It's a rather bleak time of the year."

"Indeed," he said. Then he went on, speaking slowly, reflectively, "One can't always choose the moment exactly. One gets – " he hesitated, "pushed or pulled. It's easier for me than for other people. I don't feel I belong anywhere. I am, you might say, a restless man. I've come to feel that restlessness is in my bones, in my flesh. The faraway city always seems to lead me to the end of my journey. Perhaps now I have really reached the end."

He turned his face slightly towards the girl, who sat beside him, her fingers still playing nervously with her cup. I thought he looked tenderly at her, but this might have been a subjective impression.

He turned to me again. "Do you know the story of the Flying Dutchman?" he asked.

"Yes," I said, puzzled.

"Love redeems the restless and uprooted wanderer there."

It seemed a strange remark. I didn't know what to make of it.

"Only," he went on sadly, "there the hero and the heroine both perish and the dream is over. What is gained?"

He fascinated me, though I didn't know what he was driving at.

"Theodore always thinks of the worst," said Katherine Held.

"But you are not a Dutchman," I said lightly. "Miss Held tells me you come from Austria."

"Oh, that," he said, very offhand. "That's such a long time ago. Some things in the past seem so long ago that they're no longer real. Others, mind you, that happened long, long ago are very real. They dominate the present. The past is a curious phenomenon. I have lived in Austria and in Italy and in France and in England and in Canada. When a man moves about constantly, as I've done, time and places begin to play tricks. Already it seems as if I'd left Toronto months ago. I was born in Vienna, but that – my youth that is – seems lost in a prehistoric fog. It's not real to me any more. . . . Well, that isn't true. Some things are very real. It must seem confusing to you."

He spoke so fluently, seemed so obviously highly educated, that I wondered all the more what he had come for and what he was doing.

"Are you by any chance representing a Toronto firm here?" I asked.

He reached into his side pocket, brought out a wallet and extracted a card, which he reached over to me.

THEODORE STAPPLER
WORLD-WIDE ENCYCLOPEDIA, INC.

"You are selling encyclopedias," I said.

I did not mean to make this sound patronizing, but evidently that is how he took it, for he said rather sharply, "Is there anything wrong with that?"

"Nothing," I assured him, "nothing at all."

"It is a fairly honourable way of making a living," he said. "I am trying to find out what the market is like here in the West, on the prairies, and then on the coast. Since I have been in this country I have represented Mr. Fuller and his brushes, and then the Encyclopedia Britannica, and now World-Wide Encyclopedia. Brushes for the body, my dear Professor Lerner, and brushes for the mind."

I smiled at that, and wished only he would not call me "Professor." It made me seem old and wizened, and yet he was older than I, though clearly not much older.

"I can always make a living by selling things," he said. "I found that out. It would have been a great surprise for my father.

He would have thought it represented a great drop in status. He was a very famous surgeon in his day."

I wondered how true that statement was, but he gave me no time to follow it up, for he said dramatically, "On the Rialto once, I sold an American a Venetian bridge."

I wasn't sure whether he was joking or not, but the sentence and the way he spoke it struck me as being very funny, and I laughed out loud.

"You find that amusing," he said. His face, which had been very set and very earnest, suddenly grew animated. "Katherine here obviously doesn't believe me."

"I haven't said anything," she said.

"Listen, then," he said. He spread his fingers wide and planted his hands on the table and fixed me with his eyes. Then, as if a map of Europe were spread out on the table, he drew a finger over this imaginary map, and said, "I fled from Austria to Italy. That was in the summer of 1939, two or three months before the war started, though Italy didn't get into it for another year or so. I fled after a particularly terrible experience with which I won't trouble you now." He opened the package of cigarettes that lay on the table, but it was empty, and he fumbled about in his pocket, found a fresh package and lit a cigarette.

"The Italians, in any case," he said, inhaling deeply, "had not gone raving mad about the Aryan superman nonsense. It was possible for a non-Aryan to breathe there, although I detested Mussolini's state. I was very idealistic. I was about twenty-two then. Not quite twenty-two, but close enough."

He was now, then, I calculated, about thirty-four or five, four or five years older than I.

"I couldn't take much money with me, and I tried to make the little bit I had stretch as far as it would go. I went to Venice first. Because I love the city. Because it is closest to the Austrian border. I met a young fellow there. His name was Ernst, and on a very hot August day we were standing on the Rialto hoping for something to turn up. Well, two Americans turned up. They were about thirty, and they came up to us and told us they had lost their way and could we help them. They didn't know where they were staying, where their hotel was. I knew English quite well. I had studied it in the gymnasium for five years. One of the Americans said if they could only remember the goddamned *calle* where they lived, they would be all right. But they didn't know. They didn't know the name of the *calle*, they didn't know the name of their hotel. And they were also not quite sober. They held on to the railing of the bridge, and they swayed.

"One of them said, 'This is a damn fine bridge,' and the other said, 'The place is crawling with bridges.' "

Theodore Stappler suddenly revealed great powers of mimicry, and, as he talked, it seemed as if the two Americans were really there, sitting with us at the table.

"I said casually, on the spur of the moment, not thinking about anything, 'You could buy a bridge. The government is selling them. They need the money,' and one of the Americans said, 'What do you know?'

"But the other said, 'The hell with it. Let's go and have a drink,' and he turned to us, to my friend Ernst and me, and said, 'You too. You come along too. We'll buy you a drink and afterwards you can help us find that damned *calle* we're supposed to live in.' Generous people, the Americans. So naturally we accepted. We went to a little café and sat around a little table drinking pernod, and the two Americans were getting drunker all the time, and then all at once one of them, with his eyes shining, said how wonderful it would be if he could get back to the States and say he was the owner of a bridge in Venice.

"My friend Ernst said suddenly, 'It so occurs I am owner of a bridge.' I can still recall the exact words, because they sounded quaint to me even then. After that Ernst spoke to me in German and I translated. My English, you see, was better. He said he would gladly part with the bridge because as of last year it was no longer possible to collect toll charges. 'You mean,' said one of the Americans, 'every time you crossed one of those bridges you had to pay?' We nodded, and he said, 'Well, what do you know!' and whistled softly through his teeth.

"After a while, and after several more drinks, he asked how much Ernst would take for the bridge, and Ernst said without hesitation he would take four hundred lire. The American said, 'Done!' He took his wallet out of his pocket and put four hundred lire down on the table. He demanded that we show him the bridge. He didn't care, he said, that it no longer brought any income. Four hundred lire was a lot of money to us and we took it."

Theodore Stappler went on to tell us how they had gone in search of the bridge. They all stumbled away together, Ernst

leading the way and Stappler following with the other American
morosely hanging onto his arm. At last in a back street, dimly lit,
the outlines of the shabby houses only barely visible and a stench
rising from the narrow, sluggish canal below them, his friend
Ernst stopped on a little bridge, and spreading his arms wide as if
to embrace it, cried, "Here's your bridge!"

"Better mark it, George," said the one who had been completely
silent most of the time. "Or else you'll never find her again." And
then he relapsed again into silence and said nothing more.

"You're damned right," said the other, and turning to Theodore Stappler, he asked, "You got a piece of chalk?"

He settled finally for a pencil, said Theodore Stappler, and
with it he slowly wrote his name in blockletters on the pavement
of the bridge, and then they all turned and walked back again
towards the Rialto.

"And after that we tried to help them find their hotel, but we
never did," Theodore Stappler said. "My last sight was of the
two standing on a bridge and looking down into a canal. For all
I know they are still there."

"That was dishonest," said Katherine, a bit primly, I thought,
"your taking that money."

He shrugged his shoulders. "There are degrees of dishonesty,"
he said. "What do you think, Professor Lerner?"

"Oh," I said, "I can find it in my heart to forgive you."

"Well, that is good of you," he said with a dry irony. "That
winter," he went on, "I spent in Rome because it was absolutely
impossible to earn any money in Venice. No one else wanted to
buy a bridge. It was a dreadful winter. The worst, I think, I've
ever lived through. I'm not sure any more how I really kept alive.
I peddled things. Dodged the police. I had no work permit, you
see. Was always afraid of being deported. But somehow, you see,
I survived, to find my way here to this city, in the bleak winter, as
you said before."

He was undoubtedly an interesting man. Yet, I found myself
thinking, looking at Katherine Held and wondering how far involved she was with him and whether anything would come of
their affair, that if she were my daughter I might well worry about
her, too.

It was nearly five o'clock, and I found myself saying suddenly,
"Why don't you and Miss Held come over to my apartment? I

have some eggs. I could concoct an omelette and we could have some drinks."

"Oh, no," she said quickly.

"We couldn't really put you to this trouble," Theodore Stappler said. "What would your wife say if we suddenly blew in?"

"She will say nothing, because I have no wife."

"I really have to get some work done," said Katherine. "You told me to get my essay done."

"I extend the deadline by two days," I said.

We all laughed. Then we moved off and went to my car and drove to my apartment.

❦ III

I COULD NOT KNOW THEN, AS WE DROVE THROUGH THE SNOWY streets of the cold city, pleasantly talking, how strangely, how dramatically, the evening was destined to end. I shall try to set down as clearly as I can and as precisely as I can what happened. Indeed, it is in order that I might clarify for myself the events of that evening that I sat down to write the record in the first place.

Things started quietly enough. I mixed some drinks. Then Theodore Stappler noticed my paintings. He thought they were good. This pleased me. He was particularly taken with my Emily Carr. I was surprised when he told me that he had never heard of her or seen any of her work. I began to speak about Emily Carr. He was particularly impressed when I told him how she had triumphed over indifference and hostility, and had gone on with her work quietly, but tenaciously. Tenacity, said Theodore Stappler, was what he admired. That and independence of spirit. The capacity to pursue a goal to the end and not give in until the task was finished and the goal reached. That was why, he said somewhat enigmatically, he had travelled across the world. But when I asked him what his goal was, he fell silent, as if he had not heard me, and when I repeated the question, he simply shrugged his shoulders but did not reply.

He turned his attention to the painting again. He went close up to it and looked broodingly at it. "The painting speaks to me," he said. "It expresses tangled emotions."

"Oh," I said. "That is interesting. It has never struck me like that." I'm not, I suppose, much given to psychologizing.

"I am of course subjective," he said. "I tell you what I feel. What the painting makes me feel."

The painting, mostly done in rich and subtle blues and greens, was of big, towering trees, and below the massive trunks of the trees there were bunches of leaves and creeping vegetation.

"Everything seems quiet," Theodore Stappler said. "But that is only on the surface. Below, everything is in motion. The landscape is static, but the colours are dynamic. So everything is still, and yet everything moves."

That was, I thought, a very acute analysis.

"You know something about painting," I said.

"A little," he answered. "At least I have looked at a lot of paintings. Galleries are warm. And that winter in Rome I spent mostly in galleries, partly to keep warm. But once I was there, I looked. Of course, I have always liked paintings, ever since I can remember."

I went out into the kitchen and concocted a giant omelette. Katherine came after me and asked if she could help, and I said she could set the table. Theodore Stappler didn't seem to notice what was going on around him. He sat, leaning forward in his chair, absorbed by the painting, or at any rate by whatever emotions it called up for him.

When everything was ready, Katherine went up to him and touched him gently on the shoulder, and said, "Theodore."

He tore himself away. "An extraordinary piece of work," he said as he took his place at the table. "Especially for this country."

I felt my nationalistic hackles rise. "Why for *this* country?" I said. "If a work of art is good, it is good. It doesn't make any difference where it was done."

"That's not what I meant," he said. "I merely meant that Europeans think always that this is an unsophisticated country, incapable of producing subtle works. A country of mountains and vast spaces and Indians and the mounted police. I thought so too, at one time."

"And you don't think so any more?"

He began to eat slowly, thoughtfully. "Of course not. But. . . ." He hesitated for a little while. "In a way, yes," he said then. "It is an innocent country."

"How do you mean?"

"I mean," he said, "that history – you must forgive me, you are a professor of history and I am an ignorant amateur – but history has been very kind to this country. At least so it seems to someone like me. So the country hasn't had to – to corrupt itself. To betray. To murder. Unlike a good many other countries one could mention."

"You idealize our country," I said. "There are black spots on the record. The treatment of native populations, for example. The treatment of the Japanese population on the west coast during the last war."

"Of course. I'm sure there are black spots. But these – these are not of such huge magnitude."

"Magnitude," Katherine Held said. "What has magnitude to do with anything? Evil doesn't depend on size or numbers."

"I certainly agree," he said. "Evil doesn't depend on size or numbers."

He busied himself with the food on his plate, but then, with his fork poised in mid air, he continued, "There are situations when a whole nation becomes corrupted. When corruption is so to speak in the air, when to be just decent, just ordinarily decent, is an act of heroism. I think this country has been spared that kind of hell."

We ate for a while in silence, and then I asked, "Do you think that any country is immune from corruption?"

"Of course not."

"Isn't it very dangerous to generalize about a whole nation?" I asked.

"I agree," he said. "It is dangerous. Still, everybody does it. Take me, for instance. I am a great Anglophile. And I generalize about the English people largely on the basis of my own experience with them. That's a very subjective basis. I admit that."

"Speaking of the English people," I said, "I've been wondering how you got to England ever since you said that when the war started you were in Rome."

"Believe it or not," Katherine Held broke in, "Theodore was part of the British Expeditionary Force that was evacuated from Dunkirk."

"An alien part of it," he said.

"You're travelling too fast," I said. "What were you doing in Dunkirk when the B.E.F. was taken out?"

"I had no business there," he said, "but I was there. You see, we left Rome, my friend Ernst and I, early in February because our situation had become desperate. We couldn't survive. There was no hope. Ernst had been very active in the socialist party and he had his connections. The party was outlawed, of course, so everything we did was illegal. But he had connections, and we decided that we should try to get to France. There was a kind of underground railway operating. There were rumours that France would form some kind of anti-Fascist international legion. That turned out to be false. But we made our way north, to Genoa, and then along the coast to San Remo. There we picked up our guides. There were five of us. The other three had arrived separately. The two men who took us acoss the border did this without pay, out of purely altruistic motives. They thought they were aiding a good cause. They took us along the coast in a small fishing-boat, during a cold, dark night, and landed us near Cannes. And there we were, on the Riviera, in Paradise! But we didn't stay. We intended to make our way to Paris, but we only got as far as Lyon, and there we were arrested. What saved us in a way was the fact that there were a lot of refugees in France at the time. Many of them had come across the borders illegally, and the French didn't deport them. They just interned them. So they shipped us north and we were interned near Paris. And there we sat, aspiring heroes, and waited. This was my first experience with internment camps. I got used to waiting. When you wait without knowing what you are waiting for, time is endless. I even wished I had stayed in Rome."

Katherine and I had finished eating, but he still had half his omelette on his plate, and he broke off and ate somewhat hurriedly. I said that all I had to offer for dessert was some canned fruit, and they said that was perfectly all right, and Katherine went out into the kitchen with me and helped me. She served the fruit and took the plates to the table, and I in the meantime put some water on to heat.

"We waited for two months for something to happen," said Theodore Stapler, "but all during April the tension rose, and all kinds of rumours floated around, and there was all kinds of wishful thinking. Then the terrible things began to happen. At first we heard that the Germans had broken into Belgium, and that the British and French troops had moved north to meet them. People were in despair. We were wondering what would happen to us, but nobody knew. Then suddenly everything changed. New troops arrived in our camp. Colonial troops. Mercenaries, commanded by French officers. There were rumours that France had been invaded, but nobody seemed to know for certain, and certainly nobody told us. But suddenly one evening we were told to be ready the next morning. For what we weren't told. On that morning we started to march. There were old men with us, and young boys, and the soldiers shouted at us all day. '*Allez hop!*' they kept shouting, '*Allez hop!*' When we asked where we were going, they just shrugged their shoulders, and you could see nerves getting rawer and rawer. After four days of marching, many of us couldn't carry on. Our shoes were torn. Our feet were blistered. The roads were full of people. All of France seemed to be moving, and nobody seemed to know where. After a while, I became indifferent. I no longer cared about anything. From time to time we stopped and the officers sat apart from us, talking together. Once or twice we sent a little delegation to them and told them that we wanted to fight with them, that we were on their side, that we believed in their cause, but they just laughed and shrugged their shoulders and said they were very sorry. On the fifth day our column couldn't march fast enough any more, and there were times when a man would just sit down and refuse to march on. Then we all had to stop and the soldiers tried to make him go on. Once one of the officers got angry and shouted that anybody who couldn't march on would be shot."

"You never told me about that march," said Katherine.

"There are a good many things I haven't told you," he said lightly.

"Were you frightened?" she asked him.

"No," he said. "As the days went on, I became more and more indifferent. I didn't really care, and I know my friend Ernst felt the same way. There was a moment when I thought I would have died sooner than walk on. But Ernst saved me. He dragged me along, he forced me to walk. There are times when death is more welcome than life. But more and more of the men, particularly the old men, found it impossible to keep the pace, and some of us heard the soldiers say that it would be better to shoot these useless and exhausted wrecks. At that moment one of us stepped forward and began to talk slowly and carefully to one of the officers. He was a little man and he talked to him in a disinterested way. I think he could do it because life and death were no longer really momentous, since we were already in a sort of life in death. Our spokesman must have been a lawyer once. I don't know his name. I never knew it, but I'll always remember him, particularly his hands. They were long and slow-moving and very expressive. They looked like spiders' legs. He never raised his voice. '*Mon capitaine,*' he kept saying, with just a touch of deference in the way he pronounced it. Even when the officer once lost his temper, our man never raised his voice. His French was very elegant, perhaps a little affected. But he did manage to talk them into slowing down the pace. Many of us on that march owe their lives to him. Many of course were killed later, in one way or another. So perhaps little was gained."

"You shouldn't say that," said Katherine. "Some were saved. So something was gained."

"The march ended," Theodore Stappler went on without replying to her, "in a field. In an open field. I had no idea where we were. Somebody said that we were close to the sea. Suddenly planes roared over us. Bombers. The field was green, and red poppies grew in it. Then I heard one of the soldiers say that we were near Dunkirk. That meant nothing to me. I only knew then that we were really near the sea. You know what I thought of at that moment. Something completely irrelevant. Xenophon. The march of the Greeks to the sea. And I remembered suddenly how the Greeks had reached the sea after marching – how long was it? How many miles was it? – a thousand, ten thousand? I'd forgotten all my Greek, but one word kept coming back to me, 'Thannata! Thannata!' And I thought of my old Greek professor, whose hands always trembled because he had Parkinson's disease. After a while I didn't think of anything any more, I just lay in that field, and if someone had come to me and had said, 'Here you, I'll kill you now,' I wouldn't have said anything, I would only have nodded my head. A long way away, or so it seemed, I could hear them dropping their bombs, way out there where the harbour was. It wasn't as far away as I thought. We seemed to be alone in the field. The officers and the soldiers were somewhere, but I didn't know where. They no longer cared about us, obviously. There was chaos all about me. There were troops on all sides, and people running about, and the bombers kept coming in and roaring out again. Once, only once, one of the bombers dipped down and strafed the field with machine-gun fire, and I realized that this was happening, but I didn't even lift my head after he had gone. I had abstracted myself from the world, and the part of me that was here was immaterial to me."

"Then how did you get to the ship?" I asked him, "How did you leave that field?"

"Because one of the bombers dropped a bomb short of his target," he said, "and fairly close to us. And what happened afterwards I don't know. I've often tried to think of it, but there is a block. I must have been half unconscious from the blast and the shock. I must have run and run. The only thing I remember is a soldier whose front teeth were missing, and he was shouting at me, 'Hurry up! Hurry up!' There was a mass of barges and ships and motorboats, but I barely remember. It is all confused. I can hear whistles still and foghorns blowing, and I can hear the bombers roaring in and roaring out. But exactly how I got on that ship I don't know. Eight others who were on the march got onto the same boat. I suppose in all that confusion we somehow were marched in. I was too shocked to know what was happening. I remember only one thing distinctly. I kept wondering if the Greeks had shouted *'Thannata! Thannata!'* or *Thallata! Thallata!'* Because I had forgotten the Greek word for the sea."

After a short pause he continued, "Once we were in Dover, they sorted us out, of course. The nine of us were immediately interned. They sent us first to an internment camp in the North, in a place called Pontefract. And then to the Isle of Man. And from there to Canada, on a Polish boat by the name *Sobiski.*"

He must have seen my look of astonishment, for he said, "That surprises you. I am a living example of how to get around the world with a minimum of documents and at government expense! Modern governments are masters at shipping people about. At any rate, I was in internment camps in Quebec and in New Brunswick, and then in 1943 I was sent back to England because I had agreed to join what they called the Pioneer Corps. This was not a combat unit. They wouldn't let me join a combat unit, for I was, after all, technically at least, an enemy alien.

"After the war I came back to Canada, this time on my own. And there you have at least part of the story of my life."

"Astonishing," I said.

"Not so astonishing, really. A typical odyssey of our time."

What was remarkable was the impersonal way in which he spoke. It was almost as if he himself were not involved and it was an impersonal fate about which he was speaking.

"In school," he went on, "we used to be told about what was called the *Voelkerwanderung,* the migration of whole peoples. But what happened then, in that distant past, was nothing compared to what has been happening in Europe in the last twenty years."

"What happened to your friend?" Katherine asked.

"To Ernst?"

"Yes."

"I don't know. I lost him in that field. And I never saw him again. He didn't get to England. That is sure. So the chances that he stayed alive are almost nil."

No one spoke for some time. We sat in a kind of silent salute to this man Ernst.

"That kind of horror," Theodore Stappler said and spread his arms wide as if to contain the totality of some unspeakable experience, "this country was at least spared. This whole continent."

We hadn't been forced to share the real horror that was European history between the wars, he went on. We had, as a nation, been spared the betrayals, the rottenness that reached out and touched and corrupted everybody, even those, in Germany, for instance, who didn't themselves commit any crimes but stood by, helplessly, so they said, passively certainly, while in their name crimes of the most unspeakable nature were committed. And even the victims, he said, even they were touched and drawn into the circle of corruption. As he knew, he cried out, yes, knew from his own bitter experience, how a man he had faith in, so much that he entrusted his own life to him, yes, and the life of one nearest and dearest to him, how this man could betray that faith, coldbloodedly, cruelly.

Now he was not impersonal. His whole body began to shake, he was so worked up, and when Katherine put her hand gently on his arm, he shook it off impatiently. Little beads of sweat stood out on his forehead, and she took a handkerchief and wiped them off, and he suffered her to do this.

But soon afterwards he regained his composure and was calm again and apologized to Katherine for his rudeness.

The more I observed him, the more enigmatic he seemed to become. There was the man of the world, suave and sophisticated, his manners polished, impeccable, and yet beneath that exterior he seemed emotionally highly charged, violent almost, and now and again, like a volcano, he erupted. It occurred to me that what he had said about the painting, about the quiet surface and the turbulent movement hidden below that surface, was in a way a description of himself.

"Let us have some coffee and liqueur," I said.

Katherine wanted to wash the dishes, but I declined her help this time and simply stacked them up in the kitchen and made some coffee.

When I came back into the living-room with the coffee and a small bottle of Benedictine, I found Theodore Stappler and Katherine Held sitting close together on the chesterfield. She was leaning against his shoulder with her eyes half closed, and his arm was around her and held her against him. From time to time his lips lightly touched her hair. It was an idyllic picture, and I hardly dared to disturb it. She looked so innocent, so lovely now; her long, dusky-gold hair glowed, and her body was relaxed. She seemed to have abandoned herself to him.

I felt for a moment – I don't know why, it was quite irrational – resentful, jealous even, as if I had wanted her myself and Theodore Stappler had bested me in a contest for her affection.

So I announced, rather brusquely, I fear, that the coffee was ready, and she opened her eyes slowly, languidly, as if she were returning from some far-off place, and slowly disengaged herself.

We drank coffee and Benedictine and talked a bit, but the conversation was rather desultory. There were no further emotional peaks. I'm not even sure what we talked about. I'm fairly sure that Katherine Held didn't say much. But after a while she slipped her hand very unobtrusively into Theodore Stappler's. I was sure then that she was very much in love with him, though the evidence admittedly was skimpy. It was nothing that she did, certainly nothing that she said, but she had the air of a girl who is very much in love. There was something about her attitude that was contagious, and I wished suddenly that there were a girl who would so abandon herself to me.

Theodore Stappler seemed to adopt, not so much the air of a lover, as the air of a protector toward her. But then, that might have been only my imagination. It was only that she seemed so innocent and he obviously so experienced, so obviously the man of the world. For him she was clearly not the first. And at one point I very nearly found myself saying, though luckily I restrained myself at the last moment, that I hoped he would not abuse her trust, that he would not betray her. I don't know why I should even have considered saying this, since Katherine Held's affairs were clearly none of my business.

In any case, I could hardly know what his real feelings toward her were. I could certainly not divine them. After a while I abandoned these speculations as vain and gave myself over to the glow of the Benedictine.

Around ten o'clock Katherine looked at her watch, sat up

with a start and announced that she would have to go home, because her father would start worrying about her. When I told her to phone him, she said that she would rather not.

So I roused myself reluctantly, and we got our coats and walked out into the bitter cold of the January night and got into my car, Theodore Stappler protesting but not too vehemently, that they could have taken a taxi.

She lived in the west end of the city and we had to cross the steel-girdered bridge, an ugly structure that had at first been built as a railway bridge. From below the bridge-deck the frozen river gleamed dully through the night.

The street she lived in was dark and quiet, and the snow there hadn't been cleared away but had become hard and packed, and the wheels rolling over it produced a dry, crunching sound.

She thanked me for the nice evening, politely, but she seemed abstracted. She whispered something to Theodore Stappler, but I couldn't catch her words, and then she was gone. For a moment the headlights of the car picked out her figure as she hurried onto the pavement. We waited a moment, until we were sure that she was in the house, and then I drove on again.

I didn't know where Stappler lived, but when I asked him, he didn't answer, and I had to repeat my question.

"I live," he said drily, "in a cheap little hotel with an imposing name. The Hotel Victoria! The Victory Hotel!" He laughed.

It was odd.

I had never heard of this hotel and asked him where it was. On Jasper Avenue, he said, but in the shabby part of that long street, around 95th Street.

He suddenly asked me to stop. The request took me by surprise, but his voice was so urgent, almost peremptory, that I immediately obliged him, and only then wondered what was the matter.

"You must forgive me, Professor Lerner," he said. He hadn't called me "Professor" since the early part of the evening.

"Are you all right?" I asked apprehensively.

"Yes, yes," he said. "I'm all right." He hesitated. "It – it is very early. The thought of going back to my room now is pretty terrible to me. I – this will sound ridiculous – I dread to be alone – especially after this civilized evening, for which I thank you."

He stopped, and I was still not quite sure what he wanted me to do. Did he want me to come to his room? But that seemed silly.

Did he want me to hold his hand and comfort him?

"My room," he went on when I remained silent, as if he knew what I was thinking, "is too awful. I can't invite you there." And then, as if taking courage, he said quickly, "Let me come back to your apartment. I must talk to you."

"Oh," I said. His tension had now communicated itself to me. "What about?"

"I'll tell you when we get to your apartment."

So I started the car again and drove home.

When we came into the apartment and I had turned the light on, I saw that his face was very drawn. He sat down at once and began to stroke his left temple with his fingers, as if he were trying to relieve a headache. And indeed he at once asked me for an aspirin.

Then he said, "You are very kind. I am imposing on you."

I answered politely that I was glad to be able to help him.

"You are very kind," he said again. "I knew you were a man who could be trusted."

"You haven't known me very long," I said. "How do you know that you can trust me?"

"I know. I have been long enough in the world."

He looked distraught. There was nothing now to remind one of the suave man whom I had first seen that afternoon.

"In any case," he said, "I must talk to someone because I don't know what to do."

"To do about what?" I asked.

He ignored the question. He seemed to be turning something over and over in his mind.

"You asked me this afternoon," he said at last, speaking very quietly, "why I came here, in the middle of a bleak and cold winter. I came here," his voice now dropped to almost a whisper, but he emphasized every word, "to settle accounts with a man I have been looking for for a long time. This man betrayed me. And not only me. There were others too. My mother was there, too. Indirectly, and yet also directly, this man is in part responsible for the death of my mother."

I felt myself stiffen, and I waited for him to go on.

"My mother," he said, "was killed in one of the – Nazi extermination camps. In Auschwitz."

"Oh, my God," I cried out.

Here it was, the whole horror of the recent European past, in this apartment, where on the whole I lived a peaceful, contented, relatively happy life. Here now were the old ghosts, and I was, whether I wanted it or not, involved.

"In this city?" I asked him. "He lives in this city?"

"Yes," he said, "in this city. But now that I have found him," he continued calmly, "I don't know what to do. It is an empty victory."

He fell silent and his eyes strayed to the painting he had so much admired before, and he sat there staring at the towering trees and the tangled underbrush.

"I promised myself that I would track him down," he said. "In moments of greatest darkness the thought of revenge kept me alive. He was the focus of – of my greater revenge." He seemed suddenly tongue-tied, unable to put the emotion that overwhelmed him into appropriate words. "I would confront him," he went on, "I would make him pay for that betrayal. That is what I thought. And now," he said sadly, staring at the wall, at the painting, as if he were searching there for an answer, "and now that I have found him I don't know what to do."

He looked at me quickly, and asked, "Can you guess who the man is?"

I wondered at this question. How should I guess? It was probably some recently arrived immigrant, I thought, who had managed to hide an unsavoury past from the immigration authorities. I had heard such stories.

"No," I said. "I have no idea."

He gave me a long look and then said very quietly, "Joseph Held. Katherine Held's father."

❦ IV

I THOUGHT AT FIRST THAT I HAD NOT HEARD RIGHT, AND THOUGH I was too surprised, stunned even, to say anything, my astonishment must have been written plain in my face, for he said, almost as if he were pleading with me, "Don't you believe me?"

"But," I said, "how is that possible? Wasn't he himself a refugee? Didn't he have to flee?"

"He did," he answered. "And he escaped by sacrificing us." And when I didn't say anything, he asked again, "Don't you believe me?"

I was, as I remember, evasive.

"I – I believe you," I said, but added, "What difference does it make whether I believe you or not?"

"It doesn't make any difference," he said drily. "But it does, also. Because unless I can talk it out, decide. . . ." He groped desperately for words, this man who talked so fluently and rarely seemed at a loss. "Unless," he went on, "unless. . . ." Again he stopped. "You must help me, Professor Lerner." It was almost a cry. "Or – or I'll go out of my mind."

But I was, curiously, annoyed.

"Don't call me Professor," I blurted out. I was at once aware of the absurdity of my objection and swung the other way. "My name is Mark," I said.

"Thank you," he said, grasping at this outstretched hand, as it were. "May I – may I call you Mark, then?"

"Yes, yes, of course," I said, at once touched and irritated.

"Thank you," he said. "In moments like these I am grateful for the informality of this country."

For the first time since we had returned to the apartment, he relaxed somewhat, and took out his cigarettes, lit one and offered me one, and though I don't usually smoke, I took a cigarette just to hide my nervousness.

Somehow, though I had resisted it, a bond had unquestionably been established between us, from the moment I had told him that my name was Mark. That was ironic, since my intention had been quite the opposite. For I had no wish to become involved with him, although, I reflected ruefully, my action in the cafeteria that afternoon belied my conscious intention. But now certainly the dust had been disturbed. But to what purpose, I could not say.

I was afraid. For I knew, even before I heard whatever it was he was about to tell me, that I would be called upon to pass some kind of judgement. And clearly, Theodore Stappler, obviously pursuing a course that he considered just, wanted me on his side. Did he want me to tell him in the end that he should carry out his revenge? But I don't, in principle, believe in revenge, though I hope I believe in justice. The truth is that I resented having become involved, although I knew that I could not now pull back, nor did I really want to.

I have since much pondered the whole question, to try to understand the ambiguity of my feelings. I cannot, in all conscience, deny that part of me does not like to become too involved with others. Brian Maxwell once suggested that I like the study of history because it involves me in the acts and sufferings of humanity but at the same time allows me to keep involvements at arm's length. I refuted his analysis at the time, but I am now prepared to grant it a certain validity. But it is also true that I shirk from involvements because, once involved, I am too involved. My whole being becomes involved; my nerves become frayed, my body tense. I sensed, sitting there and facing Theodore Stappler, that he would demand such an involvement. I therefore resented him, yet I could not, even at the moment, deny that a bond had been created between us. In an obscure way I identified myself with him.

Perhaps it is not so obscure, really. By an accident I had been born in a country in which, as Stappler had put it, it was possible without too much difficulty to be a decent human being, to decide what was morally right and to act accordingly, a country in which justice and law, though God knows often abused, were nevertheless very real. Yet if my grandfather had not come here, then I, too, would have been caught up in the European holocaust and I, too, might have fled desperately from country to country, as Theodore Stappler had done. And so, even as I resented his being here with me, disturbing the peace of my existence, causing old ghosts to walk here, I had also to accept him as if he were my more unfortunate brother. Part of me rejected him, but part embraced him. And so, indeed, it was to be throughout the whole of the affair in which he had so suddenly involved me.

But it was really, I thought suddenly, Katherine Held who had involved me, simply because she had not handed an essay in on time. But she, of course, was involved also, and in a much more profound way than I. For it was her father who stood accused. What, then, was the relationship between her and the accuser? It was not simply then a love affair.

"What about the girl?" I asked. "I may be wrong, but it seemed to me that there is a – a close relationship between you. And at the same time you are accusing her father of a most serious offence, of a crime. . . ."

He broke in. "I am accusing him primarily of a grave – how shall I put it? – of a grave moral sin. No court of law would now judge him. Perhaps no court of law could now judge him. But I can judge him, and. . . ."

"Is this permissible?" I interrupted him. "Is it permissible for you to act as judge in the matter?"

"Yes," he said, "and no. That is why I need another man, an honest man, to help me."

"To do what?"

"To find a way out of an impossible situation. I am aware that he was himself in a dreadful situation when he betrayed us."

"Have you already talked with him?"

"Yes." He nodded. "He said he could not act in any other way. He tried to – to. . ." his left hand, with the large signet ring giving off little flashes as the light caught in it, waved about in the air, "to vindicate himself."

"And?"

"I think it is impossible. It cannot be done." His voice, as he said those words, was harsh and clipped. There was something dreadfully final about it.

"I am concerned about the girl," I insisted. "She is my student." It seemed a trifling thing to say, we were so far from the atmosphere of a lecture room.

"Katherine?" he said, very softly.

"Yes," I said. "Does she know that you are accusing her father of a – a grave moral sin, as you call it?"

"No," he said. "She knows nothing."

"Nothing at all?"

"Nothing."

"But how is that possible?"

"Because her father hasn't told her and I haven't told her. When I first saw Joseph Held here, he pleaded with me not to say anything to his daughter."

"And?"

"I agreed. Though at the time I hardly knew her. That is one of the complications."

"And doesn't she sense that there's something wrong?"

"She does. But she thinks the objections her father makes, his dislike of me, are purely – what shall I say? – emotional."

He sat for a while in silence, smoking his cigarette. Then he said, "I never dreamed, of course. . . ," and broke off.

"Dreamed what?" I asked.

He was not to be hurried. Time and time again when I wanted him to get to the central issue, he altered the course of the conversation.

"It doesn't matter," he said.

"Dreamed that you would find the girl?" I pursued him.

"Perhaps," he said. "Always in my mind I saw the issue only between the two of us – Joseph Held and me. When I saw it, I imagined us alone – Joseph Held and me. Often I imagined us – don't ask me why – meeting in some desert. Only sand and sky. And nothing else. And there we would meet – the man and I. I would appear to him like a man who has come back from the dead. And when I thought of that, a great rage always came over me. Joseph Held had become something much more than a man. He had become the focus of all my rage. At such moments I thought – I thought. . . ." He got up from his chair and began pacing about the room, and his hands moved nervously, closing and opening, as if he were about to strike and then thought better of it. He stopped in front of me and looked down at me, where I sat, with a feverish look, but his voice was controlled when he said, "At such times I could have killed him, my rage was so great."

"The trouble with such dreams of revenge," I said, "is that

they overpower the personality. Ultimately they corrode it."

"Ach!" he cried out, and with a sweeping, almost contempt-uous gesture of his left arm seemed to dismiss my statement. Then, calmer, or so it seemed, he sat down again and lit another cigarette. Waving his hand slowly to extinguish the match, he said, "Of course you are right. In the abstract. Only it's easy for you sitting here in comfort and in peace to make professorial statements."

I resented that thrust. "Now look here, Theodore," I said and stopped. That was the first time I had called him by his first name.

He smiled. "I'm sorry," he said. "I didn't mean it personally. I only meant that such powerful feelings – such – well, you don't sit down and say, 'Is it really nice that I feel this way?' It's simply a fact."

"I realize that. I know that there are times when it is probably the only way to feel. It's only human."

"This is an academic argument," he said. "It doesn't get any-where. It is also a pointless argument, because it doesn't solve the problem."

I was riled. "Very well, then," I said. "Could you really have killed him?" I didn't want it to sound like a challenge, but that is how it emerged.

"Yes," he said at once. "At a certain moment, yes. Does that offend your professorial soul? And," he continued, leaning for-ward in the chair and pointing a finger at me, "it would have been right. Even though he was not the main offender. I knew that all the time. Still, it would have been right. It would have been just."

"A just murder," I said and felt suddenly very weary and sad. "How often have we heard that? And I assume you would have said your motives were pure."

"This is useless speculation," he said impatiently. "The fact remains that he injured me. I never touched him."

"And could you now?" I asked.

"What?"

"Kill him?"

"No."

"Why not?"

"Because – because when I met him again after – how long is it? – after nearly thirteen years, I found only a tired, middle-aged man with a little pot belly."

"And a daughter."

He gave me a quick look and the corners of his mouth turned down ironically.

"And a daughter," he repeated drily.

"So we come back to her," I said. "A very charming girl."

"Yes."

"She is in love with you."

He seemed taken aback. "She hasn't told you that?"

"No, of course not."

"Then how do you know? You seem very sure."

"I don't of course *know*. But I have that impression."

He didn't say anything, and his silence emboldened me, and I said, "You may think this impertinent. But you? What about you? Are you in love with her?"

"You Canadians," he said indulgently. "You like to have clear answers to everything. Yes or no."

"We allow 'maybe,' too."

"I'm too old to fall in love easily," he said.

"Well, then," I said. "She's to be used merely as a pawn in a game you are playing."

I had not intended to hit so raw a nerve. His response was violent.

He sprang to his feet and shouted, "No! That's a lie!"

"Forgive me," I said and added, "it's only that I don't like to see innocence used – or abused."

"I'll never use her," he said quietly. "You can be sure of that. It may be," he went on hesitantly, "that I thought of using her – at first. But not now. Certainly not now."

So I was partly right.

"Besides," he continued, "I am not playing games. I don't even want revenge any more. I want a kind of justice."

"What kind of justice?" I asked him. "You said yourself that no court can judge him now."

"I am the only one left alive who knows what happened. I want one other man to know. An impartial man. If possible I want that other man to confront Held, too. And after that – " he looked at me and his face seemed suddenly haggard – "after that perhaps I can have some peace."

"Who," I asked softly, but I knew the answer already, "who is to be that man?"

"You," he said, without a moment's hesitation.

Although I had expected this answer, I was annoyed by his tone of absolute certainty. He had cast me for a particular role, and it seemed that I had no choice in the matter.

"And what if I refuse?" I asked.

"You won't refuse," he said.

"How can you be so sure?"

"Because you have a conscience. You can refuse to judge, but you can't refuse to hear me out."

"You want an impartial man," I said. "But how can I be impartial? I will only hear what you say."

"That is true," he said. "You will be my witness."

Again that certainty, again that positiveness. I felt the blood rise into my face and said, without trying to disguise my annoyance, "I wish you wouldn't take everything for granted. I must give my consent first."

"Of course," he said. "But I am sure you will. Haven't you already? In all honesty, Mark, haven't you already?"

"But you want me to take your side." ·

"Of course," he said, "because justice is on my side."

"All right," I said. "But in the end, what do you want me to do in the end?"

"I don't want you to do anything," he said. "I want you to help me decide what I must do. I must confess something. . . . You won't be angry?"

"I don't know. I promise nothing."

"I decided that you would be my man even before I met you. That comes as a surprise!"

I bristled, especially because of the way he said "my man," as if I were his instrument.

"Indeed," I said. "But how is that possible?"

"Because Katherine talked about you. And what she said appealed to me. I knew that you would be my man."

Again I felt resentment because of the arrogant assumptions he made, but since I had already registered my opposition only to give in tacitly to his quiet, assured statement that I had already given my consent to play my part, I said nothing.

"I came to the University this afternoon," he went on, "to see you. Then luckily I met you by accident. Otherwise I would have come to your office."

"Did Katherine know about that?"

"Of course not," he said.

I laughed. For it was clear that, whatever I had done or not done, I would have become involved in the affair. Mark Lerner, Private Eye! How Bill Sommers would laugh when I told him.

"You are amused?" said Theodore Stappler.

"Yes," I answered. "In a way. Because I decided, when I saw you come into the cafeteria with Katherine, that I would somehow get to know you."

He threw his head back and laughed out loud. "It was fated, then," he cried and threw out his hands as if he wanted to embrace me and, a broad smile spreading over his face, he said, in a very ironic tone of voice, *"Mon semblable! Mon frère!"*

·V

ALL AT ONCE, THE TENSION BETWEEN US EASED. IT WAS AS IF AN unspoken conflict had been resolved. For the first time since we had returned to the apartment I leaned back in my chair, quite relaxed. Theodore Stappler, too, seemed to change. The tautness went out of his face. He began to talk about the weather, that innocuous, that wonderfully neutral subject. The cold was not nearly as bad as he had feared, he said, because the air was usually so clear and still. It was really quite exhilarating. Wasn't the city too provincial? he asked me, and I replied that it suited me, that the University gave me sufficient stimulation. He asked me then where my family was and I told him. So we talked for a while, very casually, like two strangers who had accidentally met in a hotel lobby and who would soon part again, each to go his separate way and quite forgetting what the other had told him.

I wanted, of course, to hear more about the circumstances that had led to his being here in the first place, but it was clear that he could not be hurried. I was careful, therefore, not to press him. I asked him if he would like some coffee and perhaps something to eat before he went home, and he accepted eagerly. It was then nearly midnight, and as it turned out, he spent the night in my apartment, for it was not until five o'clock in the morning that we finally went to bed. Until that time we talked. Or it would be more accurate to say that Theodore Stappler talked. He was, of course, as I have had occasion to note before, a very effective teller of stories. At one point I asked him if he had ever been an actor. The question seemed to surprise him. He loved the theatre, he said, and many of his parents' friends had, in fact, been actors, but he himself had never been more than a spectator. He read a great deal, he said, but the only thing he had ever studied systematically was medicine. Circumstances had forced him to break off his medical studies after three years, and he sometimes wished, he said, that he could return and pick up the threads again. Still, there was no doubt that he had a fully developed sense of the dramatic, and he could project the personality of others, mimic their speech and imitate their mannerisms. As when, for example, he described the big, jovial, middle-aged man with whom he had travelled west from Toronto.

"M'self, I live in Vancouver. I like it where it's warm." Theodore Stappler's usually mellifluous voice became gravelly. "This your first time in the West? I hope you like it. 'Specially now that it's so cold. Still, there's forchoons have been made there. In oil. Mind you, there's many has gambled and lost. But there's forchoons have been made there."

Theodore Stappler had followed me into the kitchen, where I was making sandwiches, and stood leaning against the counter and repeated softly, letting his voice go gravelly again, "There's forchoons have been made here."

The water on the stove was just beginning to boil, and I poured it into the percolator.

"Will you ever make a fortune?" he asked in his normal voice.

"I doubt it," I said.

"The jolly gentleman predicted that I would. 'I s'pose you'll try your hand at it too,' he told me. 'Cut yourself in on the boom. Shouldn't be hard. Man of your education and charm.' That's what he said." Theodore Stappler laughed. "I told him that I had come for a different kind of game, and he said, 'Oh, you're a big game hunter, are you? I think that's the wrong time of year to go hunting.' It took me a little while to straighten that out, although in a way of course I was a kind of hunter."

We took the sandwiches and the coffee back into the living-room and Theodore Stappler told me how he had walked into the station – it was now about five weeks ago, just before Christmas – past two rows of people waiting for new arrivals.

No one had come to greet him. He was not surprised, of course, for he had expected no one. Still, there was an air of expectation, of festivity, in the station, and he felt sorry for himself. A note of self-pity crept into his voice. It was not the last time that I was aware of it. For his temperament was a curious mixture of the ironic and the sentimental.

Now that he had reached what he believed to be the end of his quest, now that he was about to grapple with the ghosts of his past, he felt afraid. He didn't, of course, know with absolute certainty whether the man he sought was really here. His first impulse was to look through the telephone book, but something held him back.

He sat down on one of the long, polished, wooden benches. From the adjacent cafeteria a raucous juke-box voice chanted about love, and then a young girl with a little portable radio sat down beside him, and he heard a crooner singing glory to the new-born king, and then an announcer spoke about peace on earth and good will to men on behalf of a firm that sold tires.

The station emptied, and still he remained sitting on the bench.

"I knew," he said, "that I should at least look in the telephone book to see if Held lived here. But I was afraid. Afraid to find him and afraid that he wasn't living here at all."

And so he tried to postpone the moment of discovery. The station, he told me, had a somewhat dowdy look. There was nothing here that corresponded to his vision of a western frontier town, for that is what he had expected to find. He had had a vague idea of men, cowboys perhaps, perhaps an Indian or two, lounging casually, hands in pockets, chewing tobacco. But only a red-capped porter stood leaning against a wall, smoking a cigarette and talking to a taxi driver.

"I closed my eyes," he said, "and suddenly I heard a voice on the radio saying 'Edmonton, the Gateway to the North,' and I thought that I had come to the end of the world." He laughed. "I thought, you know, that I would go out of the station and there would be a great mass of ice and people walking about with frozen faces."

"Oh, my God," I laughed. "What a morbid picture."

"Of course," said Theodore Stappler. "I even went further. I thought that if the cold made my eyes water, the tears would turn to ice." He smiled. "I get some weird notions sometimes."

"Yes."

"So I decided to think of something else."

"What did you think about?"

"I thought of the Adriatic. Dark blue. And I thought of the warm sun of the Lido. From the Lido, you know, it looks as if Venice rises out of the waves. I didn't have a particularly good time the last time I was in Venice, but I always like to think back to the city. That summer I met a young girl there and I fell in love. Really. Passionately. If things had been different, I could have married that girl." He sat brooding about that for a while, and then gave me a sharp look and said, "You never married."

"No. As you see."

"Did nobody ever turn up?" It was a quaint sort of question, I thought.

"I suppose not."

"I think I would have been married by now if I had ever stayed in one place long enough."

"Perhaps you will stay here," I said. "And if you do, is there someone here?"

That was an unfair question to ask, I suppose. He didn't answer me but changed the subject. I was to observe that way of his often later on. Whenever he decided that he would not answer a question, he abruptly talked of something else, and it was impossible to broach the subject again until he himself was ready to take it up again.

So now he said, "I felt I had to talk to someone. And I turned to the girl who was sitting beside me on the bench – the one with the little radio – and made what I thought was a pleasant remark, but she looked at me as if I'd said, 'Let's go and sleep together,' and picked up her little radio and went away. That was my official welcome here."

He felt again utterly alone, he said, and at last he got up enough courage to walk over to the telephones.

"My hands trembled. But I found the page. There were two Helds in the book. One was listed as 'Held, Joseph.' I was sure then that he was here."

I now asked him a question that had been at the back of my mind for some time. "How did you know that he was here? In this city? And not in Winnipeg or in Vancouver? For that matter, how did you know that he was in Canada?"

"Oh, I knew he was in Canada. I found that out in London. He stayed in London for a few months and he registered there with the central refugee agency. They told me he was in Toronto. But when I got to Toronto three years ago, I couldn't find him. I asked around, but nobody knew anything. In a way I was glad. But then I found out when I least expected it. Casually. Almost by accident. From a fellow named Armand Krull. I sold encyclopedias with Armand. He taught me all I know about selling encyclopedias. How to make people think you are opening up a new world – for their children. People don't want new worlds opened up for them, but for their children, yes, for their children, yes. All the knowledge of the world right there, on one shelf. Armand and I worked together. One day I happened to mention that I was looking for a man called Joseph Held, and Armand remembered that he had met him. He asked around and found out where he was. And then I was in duty bound to find him. I wish in a way that I had never found him. But perhaps it is better that I did. Anyway, when I saw his name in the telephone book, a kind of cold terror overcame me. I felt almost paralysed, and I went back and sat down on the bench again."

It was nearly noon, he went on, before he ventured to leave the station, where he had felt warm and enclosed and insulated from the world. So also he had felt on the train as it traversed the vast distances of this land, almost as if he were hurtling through space on a timeless voyage.

It was well below zero. A brilliant sun, so far away that one could look directly into it, shone in a steel-blue, cloudless sky. It occurred to him that, if a man were suddenly transplanted to this place from Italy or the South of France and saw the blue sky and the bright sun, he might rush out coatless and hatless, only to be driven back by the slowly penetrating arctic air, for there was no wind, and to discover that the sun was quite impotent. It gave light, but no heat.

He walked away from the station, down a long street, past some shack-like wooden buildings that housed stores selling men's clothing and dry goods and furniture.

He stopped momentarily outside a pawnshop, he said, looking apprehensively into the window, at the worn watches and the old-fashioned gilded clocks, at dusty cameras and rusty rifles. The pawnshop reassured him. It humanized the place for him. He had made use of pawnshops before, he said, in several countries and in various cities.

Some of the stores had their wares, or at least part of them, displayed outside, in a manner which was familiar to him from some European cities in which he had been. He saw rubber boots dangling down, "swaying like mobiles," he said, and men's suits and overcoats suspended from hangers. That also pleased him. Especially, he said, the display-windows chock full of articles, shirts piled upon shirts, and shoes upon shoes. These displays, he said, gave him a feeling of abundant life. Because here were all these things, shouting out to the multitude that here was God's plenty, and that God's plenty was cheap.

He liked these stores better in a way than the more respectable department stores he passed later on. These, he said, were just dull. In one of them he bought some overshoes, some ear-muffs, and some warm woolen gloves, and so equipped ventured on. He stopped to have some lunch. Afterwards, exploring further, he noticed a boardwalk leading off the main avenue into what seemed at first a rather dingy alley. A little crude wooden sign was nailed up there, showing a pointed finger and reading PUBLIC LIBRARY. This sign he followed until, at the end of the alley there was suddenly a little square with the library on the left and something like a promenade walk beyond the square, and as he walked towards it, a marvellous vista of the winding, white, and frozen river suddenly opened up before him, and he looked across at the wooded valley and little houses stretching away on the other side. For some time he stood looking at the river and at the vast, clear sky, and then at last the cold drove him into the library. It was a charming little place, he said, and he felt as if he had come to an oasis.

He picked up a magazine from the rack, but he was suddenly so tired that he couldn't read.

"It suddenly struck me with enormous force that not a soul, not a single soul, knew me here."

"But surely," I said, "that was nothing new for you. You had been in so many cities."

"Yes, but curiously I always had some addresses. Wherever I was before there was at least someone I could call on. But not here. Except, of course, Held. I've never felt so utterly alone in the world, so completely cut off as at the moment when I sat down there with the magazine."

For a moment even, he felt disembodied, he went on, and the disembodied self seemed to be standing beside him and looking with astonishment at the figure of his fleshly self, sitting there in the public library of a strange and austere city. He felt desperately the need to establish some human contact. An old man was sitting beside him, studying intently some book on astrology, to judge by the zodiac illustrations.

But before he could say anything, make an innocuous remark

to establish some sort of contact, the old man turned his eyes full upon Theodore Stappler – dark eyes, said Theodore Stappler, lying in deep sockets – and said testily and in a loud voice that could be heard throughout the library, "No need staring, young fellow. It's all in the stars. All. Everything's there. All that's happened, and all that's going to happen."

Startled faces were turned towards the table where they sat. Then a patient librarian came over and, putting a hand on the old man's shoulder, drew him gently back, and he immersed himself again in his book.

It was, said Theodore Stappler, curiously unnerving for him. He thought that he should go out and find a room, but he couldn't bring himself to leave. It occurred to him that, as long as no record of his presence existed, he could do almost anything. He could even commit a murder, and no one need know that he had ever been here. He could leave as he had come, in secret and alone. The thought was chilling, and he could not endure it. He had, he felt, to establish his identity again, make his presence known. So he left the library and walked out into the streets again.

He decided that he would try to stay in a small hotel, out of the way somewhat. That would, in any case, save him money, and he did not intend to do much work here, if indeed any work at all. Nor did he know how long his stay would last.

He walked east on Jasper Avenue, keeping an eye out for a place that might be suitable. He had walked only a few blocks when the street scene changed with dramatic suddenness. The solid, if uninspiring, brick and stone structures, the hotels and the banks and the large stores, gave way to old wooden houses and shops, the paint cracked and peeling off. The people themselves seemed different, more shabbily dressed, lounging about even on this cold day outside pool halls, and standing in little knots in front of beer parlours, and then moving off, up and down and across the street.

Hesitantly, he turned back, and there, on the other side of the street, right on the dividing line between what seemed to be two different parts of the city, a green and red neon dragon above what appeared to be a Chinese restaurant caught his eye.

"I thought it was a splendid dragon," Theodore Stappler said with a smile.

Right beside it there was a more modest sign, and it said VICTORIA HOTEL.

It seemed an appropriate name. Besides, he said, he would sleep there protected by the dragon!

There were two doors, one leading into the restaurant and the other up a flight of linoleum-covered stairs to the hotel. The stairs were quite steep, and they reminded him in a curious way of the house in Venice where he had stayed during part of the summer of 1939.

The first room on the right of the landing was marked OFFICE. He walked in.

He saw a small man in his shirt-sleeves with his feet up on a decrepit-looking desk, his body stretched back in an ancient swivel chair. The man was dozing. When he became aware of Theodore Stappler's presence, he sat up with a start, yawned and rubbed his eyes.

"That was Sam," said Theodore Stappler. "A charming fellow in his own way. He looked in a curious way like a little dragon himself. He asked me what I wanted. I thought that strange. What could I want but a room. When I made that clear, he said, 'Number eight is free. Three-fifty a night. No visitors allowed in after eleven and no parties at any time.' I said I did not intend to have any parties. 'You got any luggage?' he asked. I said it was still at the station. 'You got to pay in advance, then,' he said. He asked me how long I was going to stay, and I said I didn't know. Then he gave me a card so I could register, and he watched me carefully fill it out. I hesitated a moment before I put down Toronto as my permanent place of residence, and Sam said, 'You're not sure where you live?' I told him I had lived in many places. 'You from England?' he asked. 'Yes and no,' I answered him. 'I lived there a while a few years ago.' 'You talk with an accent, like an Englishman,' Sam said. Then he went on with his interrogation. 'You from the old country?' he asked me. 'Which old country?' I said. 'Oh, you know,' he said, 'Poland, Austria, Hungary, Italy, Russia. Any of them.' I said that I had been in some of these countries. 'You're a reg'lar wanderer,' he said. 'Like me. You aren't Jewish by any chance?'

"I was taken aback by his questioning, and I should have been annoyed, but he seemend so – so human, and I so felt the need to talk to some one that I couldn't be angry. I told him that my mother was Jewish, that my father had been a Protestant, and that I was brought up in a Catholic country, and that some of my teachers had been priests. In a way then, I said, I was a little bit of everything. Everybody and nobody. Everything and nothing. This metaphysical bit of speculation amused him, for he cried out, 'The works! Like a two-scoop banana split with whipped cream on top!'

"Then he asked the same question you asked me this afternoon, 'What brings you here?' And he added, 'You got some prospects?' I said I had come to make my fortune. 'Doing what?' he asked. 'Selling knowledge,' I said. 'Encyclopedias.' He looked at me with great pity in his eyes and said, 'You'll be a long time making a fortune that way. I might make it faster betting on the horses.' With that he took a key from a large board that was behind his desk and walked around the desk to lead me to my room."

A bed, a table, three chairs, a chest of drawers, a sink in the corner. That was the room. But he found it acceptable enough. He did not, after all, expect to give parties there. He tested the mattress with his hand, and it seemed firm.

"The room is okay," Sam said, "The mattress is okay. The only thing is the walls aren't exactly soundproof. I got to tell you this right away. So sometimes you hear what's going on in the room beside you."

"That won't bother me," Theodore Stappler said to him.

Sam said he could have his luggage picked up for him if he had the stubs, and Theodore Stappler, glad that he didn't have to go back to the station himself, gave them to him.

And then he was again alone, but no longer quite unknown. He had, as it were, simply by talking to Sam, established his identity again.

Weariness overwhelmed him when he saw the inviting pillows on the bed. He took off his shoes and his coat, removed the faded pink flower-patterned bedspread and stretched out on the bed. He could hear the sound of cars and buses, but only faintly, because the noise was muffled by the double windows of the room.

After a while he fell asleep.

"And then I dreamed," he said. "The dream – the nightmare – was one that I have had for many years. It follows me wherever I go. It is almost always the same, in the general shape, I mean. Occasionally a detail varies. Have you ever been so – so afflicted?" he asked me.

"I dream," I said. "But my dreams don't recur. At least so far as I know."

"If they did," he said, "you would know."

He paused for a time and drank his coffee and smoked. And then he told me the dream.

The landscape was always the same, strange and yet familiar. It was evening, always evening, and there was something baleful about the evening. A deep red sun poured heat down upon a barren landscape. There were rocks like massive obelisks, and dried-up cactus plants, but also, scattered about here and there, a few green trees, like weeping willows. Suddenly huge black clouds appeared in the sky, like the outstretched fingers of a gigantic hand, and advanced towards the sun and threatened to engulf it. In this desolate landscape the figure of a man with a knapsack on his back and an alpenstock in his hand was stumbling from rock to rock. And as if, like Moses in the wilderness, he were looking for water, he struck each rock with his alpenstock and turned away again each time, for there was no water. He looked up into the sky and was terrorized by the cloud that was moving slowly towards the sun, and in his terror he sought refuge in the shadow of a red rock, but the rock threw no shadow, and so, stumbling on, at last he found a cave and crawled into the darkness of its black, gaping hole, and there squatted on the ground, his knapsack still on his back, his alpenstock still in his hand. Thus squatting, he pondered, but without any real hope, how he might ever get out of this desert, live again like a human being in a rational society, stop being agitated and terrorized by weird manifestations, cease to flee from rock to rock, grow roots anew, like the willow tree, and have his place again among men, in a universe that was not entirely unfriendly.

Then, all at once, he saw a woman silently approaching him, and his body grew tense as he watched. Her walk was stately and slow. She was a tall woman, and she wore a dressing-gown of black silk, embroidered with a silver-and-gold-threaded pattern of swirling and winding shapes that seemed to be abstractions of a dragon-like figure. Her face was elongated and extraordinarily pale and, when she came closer, he saw that it was his mother, and he shrank into himself and tried to crawl deeper into the cave, but he could not move, and he felt guilty because he was not elated when he saw her coming towards the cave.

Silently she came, and silently she stood before him. His impulse was always at that moment to run away, but he couldn't move.

He said, "I haven't yet found water, and I couldn't yet send for you or come for you. Why did you come?"

She only shook her head, mournfully. In the dream she never talked.

He said, "But you can see that there is nothing here but desert and rock. We can't live here. We'll die of thirst. Only the willow trees keep me alive."

His voice faltered under her sad gaze. She turned and walked away, without a stir, without a rustle, like a ghost.

A sharp, gusty wind had suddenly sprung up and blew the sand about, and he saw her fighting against the wind, and her dressing-gown was fluttering wildly in the hot breeze. Remorse overcame him, and he rushed out of the cave and ran after her and cried out to her, but the wind drowned his voice, and she walked so fast that he could not catch up with her. He threw off his knapsack and ran, but the distance between them kept widening. The wind whipped up the sand, and the massive black cloud-formation advanced towards the sun and blotted it out.

Then suddenly he found himself by the shore of a stagnant lake. Along the shore stood petrified trees, and from the lake itself gaseous fumes arose and poisoned the air. And he saw his mother in the middle of the lake, and he cried out to her.

Only the wind answered, and the fumes from the lake enveloped him, blinding and choking him, and, like a drowning man coming up for air, with arms flailing, he awoke from his dream.

The room was dark now, and he hardly knew where he was. Across the street there was a run-down cinema and the lights on its marquee flickered on and off. Staggering up from the bed, his body clammy with sweat beneath his clothes, he groped about to find a switch. He found it, and then the room was bathed in a pool of light, which at once dispelled the nightmare. By the door stood his two bags, like sentinels. There was the bed, crumpled, and there the sink, its chrome faucets glistening in the reflected light. There, in the mirror over the sink, he saw himself, his clothes dishevelled, his face looking haggard, for the nightmare had exhausted him. But at least he knew where he was. He got hold of his suitcase and took out a dressing-gown and went out of the room to take a shower. And when he felt the water flowing over his body, he calmed down and was soothed.

He went back to his room to shave. He was just beginning to

lather his face when he heard the door of the room next to his being opened, and two people entered it. He heard them talking, a man's voice and a woman's voice. Their voices rose and rose. They were quarrelling. Then the woman broke into loud sobs. He could not hear everything, but it became clear to him that it was a lovers' quarrel and that the woman was accusing the man of having been unfaithful to her. But the man protested that he loved her, and her alone. Then Theodore Stappler heard muffled noises, and then there was a long silence, until at last he heard the bed begin to creak softly in the other room. Thus their conflict had resolved itself.

"I felt happy for them," Theodore Stappler said to me. "And I thought if only I could so easily chase my ghosts away. Life," he said, speaking in his most rhetorical manner, "has no time for nightmares in its endless quest to reproduce itself."

He finished dressing quickly and went out to have his supper. The neon dragon glowed over the restaurant, in the darkness more splendid than before. Its open mouth and tongue were red, and its body and tail were green. In the window below there was a little tank in which goldfish swam, and a cardboard sign in the window bore the legend: TEACUPS READ HERE. MADAME SONORA.

In that restaurant he had his supper and struck up an acqaintance with the little waitress, whose name was Joyce. The meal he got was indifferent, but at least hot. He asked for wine, but the girl looked at him as if he were mad and said, "If you want something to drink, you gotta go to the liquor store and buy stuff and take it up to your room. But you can't come in a restaurant and eat and drink at the same time. That's the law."

So he drank tea and asked if Madame Sonora could read his teacup, but she only came in the afternoon.

He was still extremely tired and, after he had eaten, he went back up to his room. In one of the drawers he found a detective novel, which the last inhabitant of the room must have left there. So he read about murders and deceptions until he was drowsy and turned out his light and slept.

❦ VI

"THAT," SAID THEODORE STAPPLER, "IS HOW I SPENT THE FIRST day in this city." He leaned back in his chair and lit a cigarette. "Cities," he continued, lingering over the word, as if he were pondering over the meaning. "Strange what you remember about cities. Not always the things they are famous for, or the things that are most interesting. I remember the obscure bridge in Venice, the one we sold, my friend Ernst and I And this city will always be associated for me with that red and green dragon. Or my own city. The city where I was born and where I grew up and where I studied. Beautiful Vienna! Wine, women, and song!" The corners of his mouth turned downwards into an ironic smile. "What a lot of nonsense. Do you know what I remember most vividly about that city? What comes back to me in my dreams? Not the famous monuments. Not even all the wonderful and pleasant things. I think of these sometimes, of course. But the things that haunt me are cobbled streets, little winding streets that lead me to a dark wood. And I'm afraid. The air is brown because the light is going. That's a strange colour, I know, but that's how it appeared to me then and how I remember it. And I remember a friend saying to me, 'They're looking for you, Theodore. You'd better not stay at home any more. Don't sleep at home.'

"And from that day on I didn't. That was in March of 1939, a year after the *Anschluss*. Up until then I hadn't been too molested, even though I had belonged to a socialist student organization, which was of course illegal, and I was after all a Jew, even though only a *Halb-Jude*, a half-Jew. How absurd all this is, this racist nonsense, how mad, when you think of it."

"More than just absurd," I said. "Vicious."

He didn't pursue the subject.

"Perhaps they didn't bother me." he went on, "because my father's name was still a big name, even though he was no longer alive then. My mother and I were waiting to get a visa for the United States, but there were difficulties and endless delays. And so all at once there is this friend and he tells me that they are looking for me.

"I panicked. I didn't want to go home. I wanted to stay somewhere in the open. Somehow I thought that would be safer. And do you know where I went? To Schönbrunn. That used to be the place where the Hapsburgs had one of their great palaces. But there is also a zoo there. And so I went to the zoo. That day is also – what shall I say? – engraved in my memory. And three beasts there. A leopard, a lion, and a wolf. I came there just before feeding time. The lion roared with hunger. He had an enormous head. The wolf drooled. The leopard looked at me as if he wanted to block my way.

"Then I hurried home and told my mother what my friend had told me and we agreed that I should go underground. So from then on I slept in different apartments nearly every night. With friends, and at my uncle's house.

"But that was an impossible situation. It couldn't go on. If I had been alone, I would have done what some of my friends did – crossed illegally into France or Belgium. That was risky, but it could be done. The French and the Belgians were fairly decent about that. They closed their eyes to this illegal border-crossing and didn't deport people once they had got across the border. They even set up reception camps.

"But my mother – I couldn't expose her to such danger, and I couldn't leave her because my father had only recently. . . ," he hesitated, and it was a while before he said, "died," speaking very quietly, and so completed the sentence.

"My mother was therefore still in a great state of shock. Fate was very cruel to her at the end. And my own part in that fate was very terrible." His voice became harsh, almost a cry, and his eyes narrowed as he stared at me. "I tried to save her and only sent her into disaster. That is what I have had to live with."

"But surely," I said, "you can hardly blame yourself for whatever it was that happened. Don't you hold Held responsible? You accused him."

"Oh, yes," he said. "Held was a tool of evil forces. But I am also responsible. There was a moment when I could have acted but didn't. There are things that I must take upon my head."

That last was a strange phrase to come from him, and he spoke it solemnly, as if he had long thought about it. He stared down at the floor and then raised his head and our eyes met, and he held me. "I have never said this to anybody. I only rarely admit it even to myself. You are the first person to whom I have said it. But I knew it always."

The tension in the room had again become palpable. He was smoking cigarette after cigarette, lighting a new one on the butt of the old. I had a feeling that he was now moving closer to the central experience, to the moment which had clearly shaped his life from thenceforward. I knew of course that he had skirted it, that every time his story had taken him close to the moment he had drawn away, as if feared what he would have to reveal. Even now I thought that, having at last come to the precipice, he would yet draw back. He smoked in silence, inhaling deeply and then letting the smoke slowly out through his mouth and nostrils.

The silence became ominous and oppressive. To break it, I said that there was some liqueur left and asked him if he wanted some, but he shook his head impatiently and told me to leave it alone. Then, with an impulsive gesture — I had almost said a wild gesture, for so it seemed — he ground his cigarette into the ashtray, which was already full to overflowing. He hunched forward in his chair, then turned to face the painting that had so fascinated him from the very beginning, as if he hoped to derive the strength from it to say what he had to say. I realize that these are the motives I read into his gestures and into his looks. He may of course have been thinking about entirely different things. I don't know, for I didn't ask him, and he did not speak of it himself.

But all at once, outwardly calm, and in a very even voice, he began to talk about that central experience. He would try to recall it, he said, as objectively, as dispassionately as possible, before me — here he bowed his head to me, as he had done once before, as if in silent salute — whom he had chosen or whom fate had chosen — here the corners of his mouth turned down into a faint, ironic smile — to be his witness. But he felt toward me — "I say this quite seriously," he said, "quite consciously" — as if I were a younger brother of his, one who had been spared the agony, was not therefore directly involved, but would very much like to know exactly what happened and how it happened.

The change in his voice was remarkable. Except for two or

three moments, when the drama of the situation carried him away, the voice remained dry, matter-of-fact, at times was even a trifle pedantic. Clearly he was speaking in this way very deliberately because he feared, as he explained, that he might otherwise falsify the events about which he spoke.

He began first to speak of his mother. What stood out for him, what he remembered most vividly – it was absurd, really incomprehensible sometimes, he said – was her wedding ring, a wide, heavy, solid gold band which she wore, as is the custom in his country, on the ring finger of her right hand. It must be a symbolic memory, he said calmly. The ring was the bond that bound her to his father, to whom she had always been wonderfully faithful, even though he. . . . Here Theodore Stappler broke off. He would not, he said, allow himself to be led into matters not strictly relevant. But the ring bound her to the father, and so also bound the son to the mother. He was, after all, the only child.

"I only hope. . . I don't pray much, but I pray about that – you won't think this absurd?" He looked at me hesitantly, critically, as if to test my reaction.

"I certainly won't," I said. "Nothing you have said is absurd."

He nodded his head. "I pray that when. . . ." He broke off here and it took him a few moments to regain his composure – "that when her time came to die," he concluded, speaking so softly that I had to strain to hear him, "she did not think that I had broken my faith."

"But surely," I protested, very moved, "that is not possible. That can't be possible."

"Thank you for saying that," he said. "But hear me out."

After the death of his father, he said, she had always worn black dresses. She was a very beautiful woman. At least he thought so, he said with a wry smile. When he was a boy he used to compare her to the mothers of other boys, and he always thought her the most beautiful. He remembered how she blushed, almost like a young girl, when he told her so once. She had pushed him away playfully, protesting, but she had blushed. That blush he remembered, and how it spread up her rather high cheekbones, almost to the roots of her hair. She had black hair and black eyes, but her skin was very fair. She looked, said Theodore Stappler, like some of the beautiful women Rubens used to paint.

Visibly, he tore himself away from the picture he had drawn for me. At the time in question, he said, when he had been warned that he was to be arrested, they had already sold a great deal of their possessions because they were waiting for the American visas which kept on being delayed. But they were ready to leave at any time. They still had a large, luxurious apartment in a fashionable part of the city. They had not yet been forced to give it up. His father's name, said Theodore Stappler, still protected his mother, after a fashion, though it clearly no longer protected him. His father had, after all, been a great professor, a famous surgeon, and a Gentile to boot, an "Aryan." Theodore Stappler pronounced the word sneeringly, as if it were a curse.

"My father was, you see, a member of the master race!" he said. "How absurd it all is. In retrospect even more absurd than it seemed at the time."

I couldn't help noticing how often he used the word "absurd." It ran, like a kind of *leitmotif*, through his story. But then, of course, he was right. The world he described was utterly absurd, insane even, representing as it did the complete triumph of the irrational over every rational and humane instinct.

Theodore Stappler's friend had been right. For one night – he was still staying away from home at night, sleeping at friends' apartments – a group of uniformed thugs came looking for him, authorized to arrest him because of alleged activities against the state, although he was not active in any organization any more. Theodore Stappler smiled wryly when he told me this.

They ransacked the apartment when his mother told them that he was not at home. They began to interrogate her, and for a moment she thought that they would arrest her. A photograph of his father, which showed him in colonel's uniform, happened to be standing on one of the tables in the drawing-room where the interrogation was taking place. They asked her who the *Oberst* was, and she told them.

"And then," said Theodore Stappler contemptuously, "the leader called the dogs away.

"That was ironic," he said, "because my mother was passionately anti-militaristic. But my father was very proud of the fact that he had been a colonel at the age of thirty-two, toward the end of the first war, and he always liked it when people called him *Oberst*. My mother didn't like it. She always said that she hadn't married a colonel against the wishes of her family, but a fine surgeon. She had married a healer, not a destroyer." He shook his head sadly. "Yet it was the soldier who saved her that night, and not the healer. But that was only right. In a world gone mad, that was absolutely right."

As soon as they had gone, she phoned the friend with whom Theodore Stappler was staying, in fact the professor of dermatology in the University, a man of about sixty, a very close friend of the family. She was remarkably calm. He was on no account to come home, she said. She would come and see him in the morning.

When she came, they held what Theodore Stappler referred to as a council of war. The situation was clearly intolerable. It was only a matter of time before he was caught. He must leave at once. But he refused. He would not leave without her.

What, then, she asked, did he propose to do? She would rather he left the country by himself than run the risk of arrest and of being thrown into a concentration camp.

He told her that he had something in mind and, when she asked him what it was, he said that a few days ago a friend of his had told him about a man who might be able to arrange some things. This man evidently had some connections with people in fairly high places. The state, said Theodore Stappler to me, was corrupt through and through and, by bribing certain officials, this man could get people across the border into France. His friend had told him that he would get him in touch with this man. He would know for certain this afternoon. If that plan came to nothing, he was prepared to go alone.

His mother agreed.

That was, he remembered, a Tuesday. In the afternoon Theodore Stappler saw his friend.

"I've spoken to the man," his friend told him. "He thinks he can arrange it. He wants to meet you tomorrow in the Café Sturm. At three o'clock. Go in and ask the waiter for Joseph Held."

Theodore Stappler interrupted his tale and turned to me. "I am telling you this story," he said, "and as I talk, I keep thinking that I am telling you a bad dream or a cheap detective story. But that was the atmosphere we were living in. Those things were commonplace. Here was one of the great centres of European civilization, and here was the distinguished wife of a great professor of surgery in one of the world's great medical schools, and she was made to act this tawdry part in a degrading drama."

I wanted to say that, even if she had been the wife of one of the poorest of the poor, she shouldn't have been made to play this part, but I refrained.

He went on to say that the Café Sturm was a small café in an obscure section of the city. He took a tram car there. It was a beautiful day, and the city seemed serene and peaceful, in spite of the many uniformed men about. Thuggery was mostly reserved for the nights.

Theodore Stappler arrived at the café ten minutes before three and asked for Joseph Held, as he had been instructed to do. But Held had not yet come. He normally sat in the back, the waiter said and led Theodore Stappler to a seat away from the windows. There, in semi-darkness, he waited with growing impatience. Joseph Held did not arrive until a quarter to four.

"That bothered me," Theodore Stappler said to me. "For I was about to trust my life and my mother's life to this man, and he was not punctual. I realized then, as I do now, my unreasonableness. After all, many things can happen to delay a man's coming. And I was, as you can imagine, very impatient. Still, there was some doubt in my mind."

But at last a smallish, but very trim-looking man entered the café and spoke to the waiter. He was the only waiter working at the time. The waiter pointed to the back, and the man made his way to the table where Theodore Stappler sat waiting.

"Are you Mr. Kessel's friend?" he asked.

Theodore Stappler nodded and told him his name.

The man held out his hand. "My name is Joseph Held," he said and removed his grey hat.

They shook hands, and Held sat down.

Theodore Stappler noted that his face was a bit puffy, and that he was beginning to lose his hair, and was combing what was left of it rather carefully, especially at the top where a few strands were made to camouflage a largish bald spot.

He beckoned to the waiter and ordered *Kaffee mit Schlag*, coffee with whipped cream. He didn't say anything until the waiter brought it, and then he took a careful sip so that the black coffee would come through the whipped cream and be flavoured by it. Then, to Theodore Stappler's great annoyance, he smacked his lips.

"I am told," he said at last, looking very carefully all around the café, "that it is hot."

"In those days," said Theodore Stappler to me, speaking very pedantically, as if he were talking about something that had happened thousands of years ago, "in those days people were talking in whispers and in home-made codes. Completely absurd, of course. But the absurd had become standard behaviour. So I simply nodded and said that it was indeed hot, and that a certain lady and her son would very much like to take a holiday. In a foreign country, if possible."

He said that this was a good idea and that he understood the circumstances, more or less. And wasn't it a shame, he said, that the price of everything had gone up, and that just the other day, at least so he had heard, train fares had gone up enormously.

For a moment Theodore Stappler felt panicky, for he suddenly realized that he was wholly at the mercy of this man. What if he was not honest? What if he was an agent? Here they were, at the back of a long and narrow little café, with the door a long way off, and he wanted desperately to get away. But he forced himself to remain calm.

How much, he asked casually, would it cost to go, say, to France?

Held pursed his lips and seemed to make a silent calculation. "For one or two?" he asked.

"For two," said Theodore Stappler.

"Oh," Held said, and then named a sum roughly equivalent to two thousand dollars.

Theodore Stappler was appalled. "Isn't that rather steep?" he asked then, for he had not thought it would cost so much.

"Well," said Held, taking a long sip of coffee, "that all depends. People will do a lot for their health. And France is an expensive country. Italy, for example, is cheaper. Much cheaper. That is because Germany has special arrangements with Italy. But then, of course, once you are in Italy, where are you? It's a dead end. You can't go anywhere from Italy. France, on the other hand. . . ." He completed his sentence with an expressive gesture of his hands, which seemed to indicate that unlimited opportunities awaited the travellers once they were safe in France.

"But," Theodore Stappler insisted, "why is it so expensive? Who is making all the money?"

Held became visibly annoyed. "If you have no money," he said curtly, "you shouldn't think of taking holidays abroad. Go down to the Danube and take a swim."

Even as he recalled the conversation, I could see the anger mounting in Theodore Stappler's face. He flushed. Little veins stood out in his throat, and the fingers of his left hand tapped nervously against the arm of his chair.

"I almost left him there and then," he said. "And I wish to God I had. But I couldn't afford to. This little man, this – this arrogant – oh, what's the difference. I had no other way to turn. So I placated him. I hadn't meant anything, I said, but surely I had a right to ask."

"Look, my dear sir," Held said. "Everything is expensive. Everywhere I turn, hands are stretched out. Everybody has to be buttered up. You understand that, don't you? People these days expect large tips. Look here," he went on and dropped the absurd home-made code in which, until now, he had conducted the conversation, "we have to secure ourselves. As it is, there is hardly any risk. But how do you think this is done? By magic? You are old enough to know better." He picked up his cup and sipped his coffee.

"Don't think I'm making a fortune," he said. "Nearly three quarters of what you pay me goes into other pockets. Some gentlemen are sitting in offices, getting rich on the misfortunes of others."

"I looked at him," Theodore Stappler said to me, "and I couldn't help saying to him that he had evidently connections with these gentlemen. I suppose he took this as a kind of moral condemnation on my part, and I suppose that was what it was, although God knows I was in no position to be righteous. Anyway, he gave me a very dirty look and said, 'Listen, young man!' Up to that point he'd always called me 'sir.' 'Listen, young man. Don't lecture me. I'm saving people! Do you hear? I'm saving people!' I've often thought about that since. And in a way he was right. He was dealing with unscrupulous men, that was certainly true. But if the result was that he could save us, and others, too, even though it cost a lot of money, then who was I to complain? I could hardly expect him to be a great and selfless hero." Then Theodore Stappler added very softly, "I'm the last man to make such a demand. Of anybody. Because when my moment came. . ." His voice trailed off and he didn't complete the sentence.

I found myself reflecting that the most terrible thing about the kind of situation he was describing – complete social upheaval and the tearing away of all moral sanctions, a situation not unfamiliar to me from my own study of European revolutionary history – the most terrible thing about such a situation was that simple, black and white distinctions between good and evil were all blurred. There was just a grey range of evils, all of them morally corrupting.

"Well," I said. "I suppose you were annoyed with him because he wanted to elevate his action into something you didn't think it was."

"Probably," said Theodore Stappler. "But I have to say to his credit that he never claimed anything like that until I implied that he wasn't much different from the dainty gentlemen who were sitting in offices and getting rich and fat on the misfortunes of others."

"And now, after all these years," I asked him, "do you still think so?"

He considered his answer for a long time, then shrugged his shoulders and said, "In absolute terms – yes, I would have to say yes. But of course things don't happen in a vacuum, and the more I think about this particular moment, when we sat together there in that little café, the less sure I am. After all, didn't I come to him? Wasn't I in need? Is it realistic – I mean looking at the world the way it is – to expect a man to put himself out, perhaps to take risks, to sacrifice himself even – for people he doesn't even know? For strangers? He wasn't a saint. But there are some things one has a right to expect, and there. . . ." He broke off. "You said you had some liqueur left. I think I would like to have some now. If your offer still stands."

"Of course," I said. "Gladly."

I went to get the bottle – what was left of it, at any rate – and two glasses.

He lifted the glass and sniffed the liqueur and then took a little sip.

"Well," I said. "What happened then? What did Held do?"

"For a moment," said Theodore Stappler, "I thought he would break off our conversation and leave me sitting there, because he picked up his hat and I thought he would go. But then he seemed to reconsider, because he said, 'For the last time, do you want to talk business?' and I said that I did."

"All right, then," Held said. "Do you have the money?"

"With me?" Theodore Stappler asked him. "Right here?"

"No, no. I mean, can you raise it?"

"Yes. I think so."

"All right, then," said Held. He was now very business-like. He would have to get half the specified amount two days before they left; the other half would have to be paid when they were on the train. Those, he said, were the conditions. Could Theodore Stappler accept them? Could he meet them?

Theodore Stappler nodded and thus gave his assent.

"I take it," said Joseph Held, "that you want to leave as soon as possible?"

Again Theodore Stappler nodded.

"All right." He spoke very matter-of-factly, precisely to the point. "We leave Saturday at noon. Can you be ready?"

"Yes."

"There will be five others in the party. With you and your mother seven people altogether. With myself that makes eight."

He had not thought about it before, but now suddenly the realization that Held himself would be with them reassured him. This fact seemed to make the whole venture safe, and he suddenly felt, he told me, as if a heavy burden had been lifted from him.

He gave expression to his satisfaction, and Held said, "Of course I go with you. That goes without saying. How else could the thing be done?"

"Then you – you guarantee our safety?" Theodore Stappler asked him.

"All I can say," Held answered, "is that I have already taken sixty-five people across. If anything goes wrong, well, I am there, too. We are all in the same boat. I will not jump out. (*Ich werde nicht herausspringen.*) I'm an honourable man. (*Ich bin ein Ehrenmann.*)"

These last words, said Theodore Stappler, Held spoke almost defiantly, as if to answer the last lingering doubt Theodore Stappler might have.

His tone became again matter-of-fact, precise. The train, he said, got into Saarbrücken about three o'clock on Sunday afternoon and remained there for about forty minutes. There Held would meet his contact man and get last minute instructions. Then the train would move on again, and they would get out at a village not far from the French border. Here they would be picked up by an official and would be taken across. It had worked nine times before, Held said, rather proudly, and Theodore Stappler could rest assured that it would work again.

And so the matter was arranged.

"We will meet again tomorrow, if it is at all possible," Held said. "Here. In this café. At the same time. You will then give me half the money. If you ask me why I need the money, I will tell you that I have to bribe a very high official of the secret police here." He had now altogether abandoned any attempt to camouflage the arrangements. "He clears the way for us. As soon as he gets the money, he telegraphs instructions to his man in Saarbrücken. That is how it is done."

Held picked up his hat, paid the bill and, when they stepped out of the café into the bright sunshine, Theodore Stappler felt curiously elated. Everything seemed all right. Next week at the same time he would be walking along Parisian boulevards with his mother. The thought, he said to me, excited him. It was a moment of exhilaration he would never forget.

"Of course," he said, "it is easy to see now, with hindsight, that we wouldn't have been safe in Paris for very long either. In just over a year Paris – that wonderful city – would be conquered, and the German armies would be goosestepping through the city. But that I couldn't know then. I couldn't even have imagined it. I would have refused to imagine it. We had been in Paris so many times – my father loved Paris and we went there nearly every year – it was the city where he had taken my mother on their honeymoon. I was sure that everything would turn out all right. For a moment – the sun was so wonderful – I nearly felt like embracing Held. He was making this possible. It was costing money, but we had money – we were well off – and it was all worth it to breathe clean air again. I shook Held's hand and thanked him as if he were our great saviour."

Held smiled, said Theodore Stappler, obviously pleased and flattered. Before they finally parted, Held said, "When I see you tomorrow, I will give you the railway tickets. I have reserved four sleeping compartments."

"But how did you know that I would agree?" Theodore Stappler asked him.

"I didn't," said Held and smiled again, and Theodore Stappler noticed for the first time two gleaming gold teeth in the upper row of his front teeth, "but there would have been others if you hadn't been able to come." Then he tipped his hat and turned and was gone.

For a moment, Theodore Stappler said to me, he was stunned.

It was clear, since there was no reason to doubt what Held had said, that he and his mother might just have missed this chance, but they hadn't, and a sense of great relief overcame him. Again he was sure that all would be well.

Then he took a tram car again and went to his uncle's place, where he had agreed to meet his mother.

"Everything is settled," he cried as soon as he came in. And breathlessly he told her about the arrangements.

When she asked how much it would cost and he told her, somewhat hesitantly, she merely nodded. She took everything very calmly. In a way she seemed abstracted, Theodore Stappler told me, as if all this had nothing whatever to do with her.

He was not too worried about that. Ever since his father's death she had been like that, he said. Withdrawn, aloof. Much of her immense vitality, her vibrant interest in the world and in society, had gone out of her. But that was not surprising. What was heartening for him was that she had withstood the double shock – her husband's death and the death also of her world, so that suddenly, inexplicably, absurdly, so it must seem to her, she was an outcast in the city she had loved – that she had, then, withstood this double shock without completely collapsing. But he hoped, was sure, in fact, that once they were in France, she would recover her spirit. That was why he could not think of leaving her here alone, for he was certain that, if he were to go by himself, as she had urged him to do more than once, she would withdraw completely into the world of her private memories and so pine away and die.

When he told her that they were to leave on Saturday, she merely nodded and said that she would do everything he wanted. His uncle – his father's brother – then joined them. He was very upset. He kept shaking his head and saying that the world was no longer a place he understood. He wished he had not lived to witness the day when his own sister-in-law would be forced to leave the city of her birth in such ignoble circumstances.

"Poor Uncle Paul," Theodore Stappler said. "He was a decent man. But I knew also that he had been among hundreds of thousands, perhaps millions, who had rejoiced at the union of the German-speaking peoples. A fine euphemism, that! But he had strong nationalistic, not to say chauvinistic feelings, and he was after all a good, hundred-percent pure Aryan! I will say this for him. He was beginning to see where things were heading and what was happening. An ideal that could lead to the expulsion of his own sister-in-law must be evil. He loved my mother. I am sure of that. But he was quite powerless to do anything. And I think I was harsh with him then. I told him that he could not wash his hands of what was happening. That he was, in his own way, responsible. That he had willed it. And do you know what happened? The poor man broke down altogether, started to cry, and kept asking me to forgive him. It was embarrassing."

"And did you?" I asked.

"What?"

"Forgive him?"

Theodore Stappler shrugged his shoulders. "Words," he said. "Words. What difference could it make?"

"But surely it could make a difference to him," I said. "There was a shock of recognition on his part. He saw. And he wanted you to know."

"I suppose so," said Theodore Stappler, but he was clearly impatient. "That is a matter we could talk about and debate all night. But it would only take us away from the main point."

"True," I said. "But since the matter came up, let me ask you if you consider the matter of forgiveness to be merely a form of words."

"I don't want to be drawn into that discussion," he said curtly. "Some things a man can forgive – forgive himself and forgive others. But some things he can't."

"You believe, then, that some things are unforgivable?"

"Of course," he said, looking at me with his eyebrows knitted together. "There is no question about that. As far as my Uncle Paul is concerned, my mother-herself terminated his display and saved me from joining him in some kind of emotional bath. She said coolly that Uncle Paul should not make a scene. 'All the Stapplers,' she said," and here Theodore Stappler smiled ironically, for obviously he included himself among them, " 'are given to theatrical gestures.' What had happened had happened, she said, and great displays of emotion on their part wouldn't change anything. She had given Uncle Paul money – it was safer with him – and she asked him to give me what I needed."

Theodore Stappler met Joseph Held again the next day at the Café Sturm. He handed over the money in a paper envelope, and Held put it into the inner pocket of his coat, without looking at it.

"Aren't you going to count it?" asked Theodore Stappler.

"No," Held answered. "I trust you. After all, you trust me. I could take this money and I could keep it. What could you do if I didn't show up on Saturday? Nothing."

That was, of course, true, and Theodore Stappler had thought of it, but he had also realized that there was no way out. If Held wanted to defraud him, he could do so. That was a risk he had to take.

"I am an honourable man," said Held. "*Ein Ehrenmann.*" These were the same words he had used the day before.

"It seemed to me then," Theodore Stappler said to me, "that he was reminding me of the turn our conversation had taken when I first met him. He spoke defiantly, as if some of the things I'd said were still riling him. Then he gave me the train tickets and we parted."

His Uncle Paul drove them to the big, cavernous station. He embraced and kissed his sister-in-law and then his nephew, and they got on the train and went into their compartment. Held was already on the train. He and another man shared the compartment next to them. Held knocked on their door, came in for a moment, shook hands with Theodore Stappler, who in turn introduced him to his mother, and then he left again. Held was obviously nervous, but that seemed understandable enough.

"My mother," said Theodore Stappler, "asked me what I knew about this man, and I told her that I knew little about him, except that my friend had told me that he was reliable, and everything so far seemed to indicate that he was."

When the train pulled out of the station, he noticed that his mother's eyes were full of tears. She stared out of the window. The city receded, its high buildings, the steeples of its churches, the city where she had played a distinguished role as the wife of a distinguished man.

"Her lips trembled," Theodore Stappler said, "and she was hardly able to control herself. She turned to me and said, 'What would your father say if he could see us leaving like thieves in the night?'"

Theodore Stappler's voice nearly broke as he recalled this moment, and he hurriedly picked up the liqueur glass and took a sip of his Benedictine. He put the glass down again, and then sat very still, hunched forward in his chair, his elbows on his knees and his hands supporting his chin. A brooding silence settled over the room, and it seemed a very long time before he resumed his story.

✤ VII

THE MEMORY OF THE JOURNEY ITSELF, HE CONTINUED AT LAST, was in many respects vague, and the details were blurred. He remembered that for long periods, even during the day, his mother insisted that the window-blind of the compartment be drawn. She complained of a headache and several times she asked him to wet a handkerchief, which she then applied to her forehead. Then sometimes she would talk to him, almost compulsively, recalling incidents from his childhood, little things of no importance any more, of how he had come home crying one day because he felt that he had been unjustly punished for something another boy had done, of how excited he had been when his father once brought him a stuffed toy animal, which happened to be a lion – things he had himself forgotten, trivial things not worth remembering, and yet she recalled them. So far as Theodore Stappler could remember, she spoke only about things that were long past – she never discussed recent events. Only the past seemed to have any real meaning for her. He tried to arouse her enthusiasm for Paris, a city he knew she loved, but she said only that she wished she didn't have to go to Paris. She didn't really want to see Paris just then, she said. It would be too painful.

Occasionally, and for only brief periods, she would look out the window at the neat countryside, the fruitful fields ripening under the late spring sun, but then she would draw the blind again. Once she went into the dining-car, but for the rest contented herself with sandwiches and coffee, which Theodore Stappler bought for them when the train stopped at a station.

Toward the evening Joseph Held knocked on their door and came into the compartment. Again Theodore Stappler noticed that he was very nervous, but he thought that the reason for this nervousness was the extremely aloof manner in which his mother treated him. That was quite unlike her, Theodore Stappler said to me, but it must have been clear to Held that she regarded the whole matter with the utmost distaste and that she was not particularly pleased to see him.

Held tried to make small talk, but every subject he broached died after a few sentences. It was clear, of course, why he had come, and Theodore Stappler could have cut the whole painful business short if he had simply handed Held the rest of the money.

"But for some reason," Theodore Stappler said to me, "I didn't want to give him the money until he asked for it, and he obviously felt embarrassed, probably because my mother sat there so – how shall I say? – stiff, I suppose. Finally he asked me if he could see me alone in his compartment. And so we went there and I gave him the envelope with the money and then I went back. My mother looked at me and said, 'IS he honest?' But what answer could I give her, except to say that I thought so."

That night neither of them slept much. Theodore Stappler said that he would doze off fitfully only to be jolted awake again, and he had weird dreams. The toy lion of which his mother had reminded him turned into a real lion and attacked him, and he woke up all in a sweat. The night seemed endless, and it was a blessed relief when day broke.

And now it was Sunday, and early in the afternoon they would be in Saarbrücken and a few hours later, if things went according to plan – and he did not for a moment doubt that they would – they would be across the border of France and on their way to Paris.

The train stopped, and he got out and bought coffee for his mother and himself, and some buns, but neither he nor his mother felt like eating very much, although his mother seemed very calm, much calmer, in fact, than he himself.

Intermittently throughout the day church bells rang as they passed through the quiet villages. And then they moved into the Saarland, and he remembered the massive chimneys of the factories and the enormous slag heaps, which looked like huge scabs on the hills.

They arrived in Saarbrücken on time. There would now be a wait of about three quarters of an hour.

"I was very tense," Theodore Stappler said to me. "There were a lot of people at the station, and I wished we didn't have to stay there. The thought of staying there for a while made me even more tense. I looked out of the window, and there was Joseph Held. He walked along the platform. I watched him. Then suddenly he looked quickly over his shoulder. Almost as if he wanted to make sure that nobody was following him. At least that was the impression I got. I don't know why, but I was suddenly suspicious. I knew he was going to meet someone and make the final arrangements and get final instructions. He'd told me he would do this. Probably it was only my tension. Anyway, I suddenly decided to follow him and see where he was going." He stopped. "I wish now I hadn't," he said then very softly. "I should have stayed with my mother and with the others. I would have shared their fate, and that would have been better."

The smoke from his cigarette rose up towards the ceiling in a thin blue column, and he seemed to watch it intently.

"I told my mother that I wanted to have a look around, and she said, 'Don't stay long.' I said, 'I'll be back soon,' And those," said Theodore Stappler, giving me one of his long, long looks, "were the last words we ever spoke together, my mother and I."

He went on to say how he ran onto the platform and pressed forward, threading his way through the crowd. For a moment he lost sight of Held but then picked him out again as he made his way through the station into the street, and he followed him.

Outside, the city was in a frenzy. Excited crowds were lined up on both sides of the road, and evidently some sort of celebration was going on. Theodore Stappler was not surprised. This kind of mad, absurd enthusiasm, he said, was part of the pattern of life in those days. (Again his voice took on a remote, detached quality, as if he were describing some weird tribal ritual that had taken place thousands of years ago.)

Held stopped for a moment and looked at the crowd, and Stappler stopped, too. Then all at once they heard, and then saw, waves of planes, bombers and fighters – the same perhaps, Theodore Stappler said, smiling, which he encountered a year later at Dunkirk – roaring over the city, wave after wave, flying low over the city. And then, in the distance, the first column of marching men. The column approached, serried ranks of men, marching, eight deep, and looking to him callous and brutal. Though not so to the thousands who lined the streets and waved banners and flags, and cheered, and repeated, as if in the grip of some overwhelming hypnosis, the same slogans, over and over, and the marching men waved their banners slowly and rhythmically in time to the mind-less chanting. And behind the marching men, oblivious to the cheering, there came tanks and armoured cars, rumbling darkly, the drivers granite-faced and helmeted, looking even more like puppets than the marching men.

Held watched for a few minutes and then continued on his way. He turned off the main street, but even the side street was full of people, all in gay holiday mood, some stumbling drunkenly, others laughing and joking and shouting in hoarse voices, as they flowed up and down and across the street.

Held seemed to pursue a kind of zigzag course through the crowd, though whether out of necessity or by design Theodore Stappler did not know. It seemed to him that Held would never stop walking, though in point of fact Theodore Stappler saw, when he consulted his watch, that they had been walking for less than five minutes. Nevertheless, he was almost ready to turn back, since he knew that his mother would be worrying if he didn't soon re-turn, when Held stopped in front of a sidewalk café, hesitated, and then sat down at one of the tables.

Theodore Stappler remained where he was and observed him. After about five minutes, "one of the devil's men" appeared. (That was the phrase he used – "one of the devil's men.") He wore the black uniform of the élite guards, with the gleaming death's-head insignia on his cap, and immaculately polished black jackboots. (To this day, Theodore Stappler said to me, interrupt-ing the flow of his story, he could not look even at an ordinary pair of riding-boots without a feeling of terror.) This man, he continued, sat down at the table, facing Held.

In a way that encounter was not unexpected, for Held had clearly indicated that something of the sort would take place. But when Theodore Stappler actually saw the beginning of the trans-action, he felt that there was something obscene about it. And suddenly, as if driven by some uncontrollable impulse, he wanted desperately to know what these two men were talking about. So he walked cautiously on, crossed the street so that he would be behind Held's back, and sat down at a table directly behind Held. The officer in the black uniform now faced him.

Here I interrupted him. "Was that a daring thing to do?" I asked.

"No," he said, "but in any case that never entered my mind.

I doubt it, though. The man didn't know me. And if Held had seen me – well, what of it? What could he have done?"

Once seated, he strained to hear what they were saying, but they were talking in low voices and only a stray word or two of no significance drifted over to him. In any case, it was Held who was doing most of the talking. Theodore Stappler assumed that Held had already handed over the money and that he was now discussing the details of the border-crossing. He wondered why it was Held who was doing so much of the talking and why the other was sitting there in a kind of sulking silence.

A waiter came up to him, and he ordered a beer. Suddenly his attention was drawn to the street. Two men were carrying a banner which said "Down with France!" They were dancing down the street with it, and behind them a crowd of shrieking boys and girls pressed on, and they danced, too. and shouted "Down with France!"

When Theodore Stappler turned again to face the black-uniformed officer, the man seemed to him even more sullen than before. Suddenly he spoke. "You will take them off the train," he said, and the menace in his voice was palpable. "We will be waiting there, on the platform. But *you* will bring them out."

Theodore Stappler heard these words. He froze with fright. For he realized that this officer, this devil's man, was talking about their group, about him, about his mother and the others, who were now quietly waiting for the train to move on towards the French border, and that their venture was evidently doomed to failure.

Held said something. Theodore Stappler couldn't hear what it was, he could only see the officer dismiss it with a derisive gesture of his hand. He looked contemptuously at Held, and then quite unexpectedly, frighteningly, he hit the table with his fist and said in a loud voice, so that Theodore Stappler heard it distinctly, "They can't get across. You were told in Vienna that you would have to take them off the train. Now do it."

"My heart nearly stopped when I heard that," said Theodore Stappler to me. "For a moment I didn't know what to do. Then my only thought was that I had to get back to the train. I had to warn them. I had to try to get them off the train and out of the station. The full horror of Held's action was not yet clear to me. It hadn't penetrated. It was not until much later that day, after everything was over, that it suddenly dawned on me that he must have known all along that we would not get across. He must have known in Vienna. At least by the time we got on the train. Perhaps that's why he was so nervous. But why he did it, in what trap he was himself caught, I didn't know. I still don't. It's a mystery. There was some kind of deal. He betrayed us so that he could save his own skin."

At the time, however, there was no time for speculation. He pulled himself together, quickly threw some money on the table and left. He mingled with the crowds. He wanted to run, but he was afraid that he might draw attention to himself. But suddenly he was aware that he didn't really know where he was going. He seemed lost in a gigantic labyrinth. He turned corner after corner, but he never arrived at the main street that would have led him back to the station.

He became desperate, but he was afraid to ask for directions, lest somehow he draw attention upon himself. It was hot and humid. His shirt clung to him, and perspiration ran down his face and into his eyes and stung his eyes until they hurt. He broke into a trot and then suddenly felt a pain in his side and couldn't go on, and stopped and leaned against the grey wall of a house.

Someone stopped and asked him if he was sick, and he said, no, no, it was all right. But the voice of a human being that seemed concerned comforted him, and he said that he had lost his way. He wanted to get to the station, he said, and the man said he was going the wrong way, he was moving away from the station instead of towards it, but he said it wasn't difficult to find the way to the station, and he showed him exactly where he should go. Then Theodore Stappler thanked him and moved on.

He looked at his watch and saw that the train was due to leave in fifteen minutes, and he began to run and felt the pain in his side again, though not so severe as it had been before, but in any case he paid no attention to it but kept on running. Then he came to the main street again, and here the crowd was so dense that he had to slow up, and then at last he saw the station and looked at his watch and saw that he still had ten minutes left. Unless, of course, Held had already been there before him.

He began to run again, pushing his way through the crowd. As soon as he entered the station, he saw that it was filled with uniformed men, soldiers, policemen, and stormtroopers in their brown shirts, and he was suddenly afraid. It was, said Theodore Stappler to me, impossible for him to describe the dreadful panic that came over him.

I thought back to the moment when we had first hit the beach in Sicily, and I understood what he meant. For I, too, had known fear and even panic. But I was in the company of friends and comrades, and we had drawn strength and sustenance from each other's fear and so had conquered our fear. But he was utterly alone, dependent solely on himself.

I looked at him as he sat there, in my comfortable apartment, his face now almost ashen-white, drawn in remembered pain, and I knew all at once that he had failed to rise there in that station, that his fear had conquered him, and that it was this knowledge he had had to live with since that day. I knew and my heart went out to him, and I leaned forward and touched his knee lightly with my hand. He seemed to understand what I meant by the gesture, for a fleeting smile crossed his grave face.

"I was also afraid once," I said.

"Everybody is afraid," he answered harshly. "But that is not an excuse."

"You judge too harshly," I said.

"Wait," he said.

It seemed suddenly to be unbearably hot in the apartment, and I became aware of sweat under my armpits and at the back of my neck, and I wished he would get the thing over with and tell me at once the brutal facts which I already surmised, already knew in my heart, as one foresees the destruction of a tragic hero and sits in horrid fascination and longs to cry out a warning, but knows it would be pointless.

"I know now, knew of course very soon after," Theodore Stappler continued his account of that crucial event, "that I had five minutes to run out on the platform and rush to our carriage and get six people off the train. It would have been enough time. But I did nothing. I stood paralysed. Because a policeman stood at the gate leading to the platform and I was afraid. Yet when I finally moved, he didn't even attempt to stop me.

"But listen, Mark!" he cried out to me. "Listen! When I finally moved towards him, he didn't do anything to stop me. He just moved aside and let me go past the gate. But it was too late. Because when I got on the platform, I saw a group of policemen coming through another entrance, and they were led by the same

officer who had sat with Held, and with them there was Held himself. They were ahead of me, and so cut me off from the carriage.
And Held walked with them, he led the way. He walked with
them!"

Theodore Stappler's voice rose and he was quite beside himself. He jumped up from his chair and began to pace about the
room, like a caged animal. He closed his hands and opened them,
closed them and opened them. And then he stopped by my chair
and seemed to tower over me, and his finger jabbed the air and
pointed towards me, as if he were trying to accuse me, as if I, in
fact, were Held, although it was also clear to me that his fury was
really directed against himself as much as against Held.

"The traitor!" he cried. "He walked with them!"

I tried to calm him, and I touched him gently on the arm, but
he brushed my hand aside.

In a low voice, hoarse with emotion, he went on to tell how he
had watched them march along the platform, and when they came
to the carriage where his mother and the others were, Held stopped, and the detachment stopped, too, but Held alone entered the
carriage, to carry out the last step of whatever infernal bargain
he had made. Outside, on the platform, the policemen waited.

Time passed. The train should already have left, but clearly
there had been orders that it should not leave. What was happening inside the carriage?

Quickly, as if they sensed that there some sport afoot, a crowd
gathered. They joked and shouted and jostled against each other.
Men picked up children and sat them on their shoulders, so that
they might see better whatever it was that was about to happen.
And Theodore Stappler stood at the back of the crowd and
watched helplessly.

All at once Held appeared and got off the train, and behind
him the others. Theodore Stappler's mother came last. As soon as
they were all on the platform, and as if by a prearranged signal,
the policemen surrounded them and began to push them on. One
of the women began to scream hysterically and nearly fainted,
but one of the policemen propped her up and half dragged her
along the platform.

The crowd, suddenly aware that people were being arrested,
began to shout and hoot at them.

One of the policemen put his arm on Theodore Stappler's
mother, but she shook him off with such an imperious gesture that

he withdrew his hand in surprise. And she walked on between two policemen, with pride and with her head held high, and when Theodore Stappler saw this he tried to cry out, to shout to her, but his throat was so constricted, as if a man's fist were choking it, that he could make no sound. Only a weak moan came from him.

Did she see him there, standing on the platform? He would never know. For suddenly he felt himself go limp; his knees buckled under him, and he dragged himself to the back and leaned against the stone wall there and closed his eyes and prayed that the earth would open and swallow him up.

Then they were gone.

There was a blast from the engine whistle, and the train began slowly to move on towards the French border and to Paris beyond.

The crowd dispersed. And Theodore Stappler heard, vaguely, as if in a dream, a man say to his child that this was how spies were caught, and that that was how the country was protected. Now these people would not be able to take their secrets and give them away to their nation's enemies.

Then, in a sudden rush, Theodore Stappler ran out of the station, into the street, thinking that perhaps he might yet see them. But they were gone. And forever after he would have to live with the knowledge that he might have saved them or at least might have shared their fate.

"But could you really have saved them?" I asked him. "Would you not have been found?"

"Not necessarily," he said. "I did after all save myself. We could have hidden somewhere. I don't think they would have gone searching for us. Not at that time. But all that is idle speculation. I didn't do anything. I just lost my nerve and stood by while all this was going on."

The account of these events had completely drained him. His face looked pale and drawn. He walked slowly back to his chair and sat down and buried his head in his hands. And so he sat, for a long, long time.

I wanted to say something, but I could think of nothing that would not seem fatuous. For nothing I could say would alter a particle of what had happened on that hot and desperate afternoon. And sympathy, I sensed, was the last thing he wanted at this moment. I sat helpless, not knowing what to do, when suddenly a line of poetry that I had heard or read once, but whose source

I could not immediately recall, forced itself into my consciousness. *After such knowledge, what forgiveness?* I almost said it aloud but checked myself at the last moment. For God knows, I did not want to judge them, neither Theodore Stappler nor Joseph Held.

❧ VIII

NOW AN ODD THING HAPPENED. I FELT SUDDENLY A SENSE OF relief, a slackening of a nearly unbearable tension. I suppose, having anticipated the catastrophe, the final act of a tragedy, I was glad it had come at last. What he had darkly hinted at earlier on in the evening, I now knew. The curious thing also was that Held, though one of the chief figures in the affair, had nevertheless receded into the background for the time being, and Theodore Stappler himself had taken the centre of the stage. I did not want to set myself up as a judge – there were in any case too many things I didn't know – but nonetheless, and with a kind of ironic persistence, the question recurred to me: "How do we judge them?"

That was a question I often asked my students, when complex personalities and their actions were under discussion. Then we debated the question, weighed one set of facts against another, dispassionately, some of the less sophisticated students becoming indignant because a historical personage was not behaving in true Sunday School fashion, others defending his weaknesses, but with a patronizing air, as if to say, "Of course he acted weakly, but we must be charitable," yet clearly implying that *they,* had the call come to them, would have behaved differently. We are all heroes in our mirrors, or think at least that, when our moment of testing comes, we would not miss the chance to give a true, perhaps even heroic, account of ourselves.

Yet Theodore Stappler was an amazing man. For more quickly than I would at first have thought possible he had himself under control again. I was, to be sure, aware of a continuing inner turmoil, because of the studied way in which he tried now to appear casual and the way he used irony as his shield.

"Now then," he said. "What do you say now? Theodore Stappler, the hero!"

"I might have acted in the same way," I said.

"Of course," he answered. "But you didn't."

"But perhaps only because I was lucky," I said.

"No," he said. "I was lucky."

"Oh?"

"Of course," he said, quite matter-of-factly, as if he were speaking of something universally understood and accepted. "Most people never have a chance to show what is in them. They live, of course. Fairly simple lives, most of them. Blameless, I suppose. Little sins, here and there. But I had an opportunity. There was a moment, don't you see?"

"Like Charlotte Corday," I said.

He looked at me, puzzled. Then he raised his eyebrows, and suddenly the connection dawned on him.

"Oh," he said, "Katherine is writing an essay about her. For you."

"Yes."

"But what has Corday to do with me?" he asked. "I didn't want to kill anybody. On the contrary. I could have tried to save people. It might have come to nothing. But I could at least have tried."

"I wasn't thinking of that. I was thinking of the opportunity. Of the moment."

It was clear. He wanted to be a hero. And yet I would never have guessed it when I first met him, and when he talked so urbanely about some of the things that had happened to him. But I have known such men. There was in our company a man whom everyone regarded as a potential winner of the Victoria Cross. He was always talking about it, was always seeing himself in the role. Duffy Macdonald – that was his name. He did in fact win the M.C. And was later killed. But that was after I had myself been wounded and was back in Canada. I heard afterwards from one of our men that his death wasn't really necessary, he had taken a greater risk than was essential, but it was a brave death nonetheless, and it was mentioned in dispatches.

"Yes," said Theodore Stappler, speaking very slowly, as if he were revolving something in his mind, "the moment. If I could only have it again."

"Five minutes," I said. "That's not much."

"Oh, I could find excuses. All the excuses in the world. I know all the excuses. I've rehearsed them and paraded them before me a thousand times. But deep down. . . ." He tapped his left index finger against his heart and shook his head sadly. "Look at your watch, Mark," he said then, "and watch the little second hand go round five times. I have done that. Often. And when you do that, you will see that five minutes is a long time. A long time, Mark, and much can be done in that time."

Sympathy, I saw, was the last thing he wanted. He judged himself, and judged himself harshly. Whatever Held's responsibility, he did not shirk his own. That was clear, and it aroused my admiration. But how ironic, I thought, that he should have travelled thousands of miles in order ultimately to encounter himself. In his own eyes he had behaved like a coward, and his vision of himself was forever tarnished. The rescuer, the saviour, had, in the moment when it most counted, been paralysed by fear.

Ultimately, however, it seemed to me, as a man not directly involved and looking at these events, if not quite dispassionately, at least with a measure of objectivity, that both Held and Stappler were themselves victims, as much indeed victims of the affair as the people who had actually been arrested. That observation, I thought, ought to be recorded, ought to be made clear. For that situation, in which the victims themselves are made to seem responsible for their fate, seems to me one of the really obscene corruptions of our brutal century. No matter how corrupt Held might have been – and I was not yet, I felt, in a position to judge the matter with any degree of finality – no matter how corrupt, then, he might have been, the agent that infected him, the source of the corruption, came from outside.

These opinions, then, I voiced. Theodore Stappler nodded his head very slowly and said that he agreed with me. But there was yet something, he said, speaking now as victim – he smiled ever so slightly when he said that – speaking now as victim – he repeated the phrase and gave it more emphasis – that he would add. And that was, he said, that even in the worst of circumstances, when everything had been taken from a man, one thing still remained with him, was his and could not be taken from him, and that was the power to choose his own way even at the last. To choose, that is, to bear himself as a man, even if he became a victim.

"You are romantic," I cried out.

He merely shrugged his shoulders, as if to say that the label hardly mattered. Then abruptly, as if he were deliberately cutting short this theorizing, he took up the thread of his story again.

He staggered back into the station, he said, and sank down on one of the long wooden benches. He was too numb to think about anything, and he did not know then, nor did he now, how long he sat there. He remembered comforting himself with the thought that perhaps his mother and the others would be released and would return to the station. At last this hope became a conviction and his heart leaped up every time someone came into the waiting-room. And then he would give way to dark despair when he saw that the familiar face he sought was not among the newcomers. He toyed vaguely with the idea that he should go to the nearest police station and ask to be arrested. But what purpose would be served by that?

After that, he told me, he must have dozed off, for the next thing he heard was a voice, hoarse and shrill, telling him to get out of the waiting-room. And a rude hand shook him awake. A man in a porter's uniform stood there and said to Theodore Stappler that if he wanted to sleep, then, God damn it, let him go elsewhere.

So he stumbled out of the station. It was dusk, and the air was hot and humid. He found breathing difficult. He had now almost abandoned hope, but despair had not taken its place. There was only an immense void inside him. What happened to him was now of no importance. This feeling, he said to me, he was to experience again a year later, lying near the beach at Dunkirk, with the bombers roaring out to sea and back again.

He began to walk, since that was the only thing he could do. He walked mechanically, aimlessly, like an automaton, on and on. People passed him – the streets were still crowded – but no one paid the slightest attention to him. He had, of course, no idea where he was going, since the city was completely strange to him. It was, he said, as if he had strayed onto a friendless shore, without any prospect of finding his way back.

Night was coming on, and he thought vaguely that he should find himself a lodging somewhere, but he could not bring himself to go into a hotel and ask for a room, because he could not bear the thought of four walls enclosing him.

So he walked on and on, through narrow streets, through unlit streets, retracing his steps, or so it seemed, for now and again he would recognize some landmark – a sign, a house, an inn – that he had passed before.

At last he could walk no more. His legs refused to carry him, and he slumped down in the doorway of a large, grey tenement building in what was clearly a poor neighbourhood. The stone work of the house was crumbling. The gutter was full of refuse, bits of paper, dog excrement. The street was dark and empty. Only a pale light, cast by a bare electric bulb, lit the doorway of the house. He had lost all sense of time.

Suddenly a man walked up to the house and saw him there, although Theodore Stappler, his head resting on his chest, did not see the man. But the man touched him with his foot, the way, Theodore Stappler said to me, one would touch the body of a dying dog in the gutter, and he felt a deep sense of anger and outrage, and roused himself. But as soon as the man saw that Theodore Stappler was not drunk, he apologized. The city was full of drunks, and they cluttered up the streets, he said.

"Are you not feeling well?" he asked, and his voice, said Theodore Stappler, was, astonishingly, full of solicitude. He was a little man, about fifty, with a pinched-looking face, and he wore a grey cloth cap. As long as he lived, Theodore Stappler said to me, he would remember that man.

"I don't know to this day," Theodore Stappler said to me, "what came over me. But I told him that I was a fugitive, *ein Flichtling,* and that the police were looking for me. I think I really wanted him to turn me in, although I certainly didn't do anything deliberately at that moment, I can tell you that. But he just asked, 'Why are they looking for you?' I didn't answer him right away, and he asked 'Political?' and then I told him what had happened, very briefly. He looked at me, and seemed to think hard, and then he looked away and then he looked at me again, and looked and thought and looked and thought, and then said, 'Come with me.' I went with him. I didn't ask him where he was leading me. I didn't care. I just went where he led. It could have been to a police station. I half expected that. But we walked only about half a block, to another tenement house, and he opened the door and started climbing the stairs."

They went up the worn stairs to the third floor. The man had a little two-room flat there. A woman opened the door. She was even smaller than the man; her face was thin and on the side of her nose there was a large red wart. She looked a little like a witch, and she eyed Theodore Stappler gravely and suspiciously. Then the man waved her into the other room, and Theodore Stappler heard them talking in excited whispers.

When the man came back, he said that Theodore Stappler could stay the night, but that he would have to sleep on the floor. And when Theodore Stappler asked, in astonishment, why they were doing this, the man answered that he hoped someone would do this for him if he were ever desperate and in need of help. And he added that he believed in the brotherhood of man.

In the meantime his wife had brought out a large loaf of black bread, and the man then cut large slices off the loaf and sprinkled salt on them and passed them, first to Theodore Stappler and then to his wife, and they all ate the bread.

"It's a bad time to get across," the man said.

"Why?" asked Theodore Stappler.

"Because they got soldiers all over," the man said. "Something terrible is going to happen."

"What?"

"War," the man said. And when he said that, his wife shuddered, but said nothing.

The man sat brooding silently, with his elbows on the table and his hands clasped together, and then suddenly, as if seized by a fit of inspiration, he began to talk. He said it was ordained that the wicked would be destroyed, but that the righteous must suffer also. Only in the end the righteous would inherit the earth, and the wicked would perish.

The words now came from his mouth in a steady stream and grew ever more apocalyptic. The details of what he said Theodore Stappler had long forgotten. But the face, pinched-looking, at times distorted with anguish, and the mild eyes, which took on an intense glow as he talked – these, said Theodore Stappler, he would never forget. Only one detail, one image, out of the torrent that came from the mouth of that little man, he remembered. At one point in what seemed an interminable apocalyptic sermon, the man said that an eagle would come from the sea and that the eagle would have twelve feathered wings and three heads. But Theodore Stappler could not remember whether the man explained what the eagle would do, or indeed whether he had anything to say about its significance.

The man stopped as abruptly as he had begun. And then he asked, very matter-of-factly, where Stappler had come from and, when Stappler told him, he said that he had better go back, since there was absolutely no chance right now that he could get across the border. He asked no further questions, offered no further advice, but said it was time to go to sleep now.

His wife went into the other room – their bedroom – and came back with a pillow and a threadbare blanket.

She said, and these were the first words she spoke to Theodore Stappler, and very nearly the last, too, that she hoped he would not mind sleeping on the hard floor, but there was no extra bed, and he thanked her and said it would be all right.

He slept fitfully. From time to time he heard the bed creak in the other room, and once or twice he heard the man moan in his sleep. He was glad when the dawn came.

For breakfast they had coffee, which was mostly chickory, and dry black bread, and then the man said that he would take Theodore Stappler back to the station. When Theodore Stappler offered money to the woman, she drew back, as if in horror, and the man admonished Theodore Stappler and said that to take money for an act of brotherhood would nullify the act.

"He walked with me to the station," Theodore Stappler said to me, "and there said good-bye to me. I bought myself a third-class ticket and I sat on a hard wooden seat all the way back, all through the day and the night, and part of the next day. I didn't really believe that I was going back, you know." And when he saw the hazy outline of the city's outskirts, he went on, he thought for one wild moment that he was seeing the suburbs of Paris. But when he stepped off the train, without any luggage, a sudden panic gripped him, for he knew of course that he was back again, alone.

It had been raining. The streets were wet. He took a taxi to his uncle's house. The maid, when she opened the door, stood staring at Theodore Stappler, as if he were a ghost that had returned to haunt the house.

She stammered, "*Wo ist die gnädige Frau?*" She meant, of course, his mother, but he didn't answer her. He was too overwrought. He just pushed past her and crossed the hall quickly and went into the living-room, into the *salon*, hoping to find his aunt there, at least. The maid came after him and said they were both out, the *gnädige Frau Doktor* and the *Herr Doktor*, and so he sat down on one of the sofas to wait, and the maid, obviously sensing that something was terribly wrong, withdrew, trembling and tearful.

Around suppertime his aunt and his uncle returned together. He heard the excited voice of the maid talking to them in the hall, and then his uncle, as if not believing that he had indeed returned, and evidently without his mother, flung open the double doors leading into the *salon*, and stood there, speechless, as if he were seeing some fearful apparition. His aunt gave a little cry when she saw him and swayed, as if she were going to faint, but caught hold of the back of a chair and steadied herself.

At last his uncle said, in a dry, hoarse voice, "Where is your mother? *Wo ist die Lotte? Was ist ihr geschehen?*"

And then Theodore Stappler told – "babbled" actually was the word he used – his story.

They listened in silence and with mounting horror. When he had finished, his uncle mumbled, "*Das kann ja gar nicht wahr sein, das kann ja gar nicht wahr sein*, it can't be true, it can't be true," over and over again.

His aunt burst into uncontrollable sobs, and then, when she had got herself more or less under control again, she turned to Theodore Stappler and cried out, "Couldn't you do something?"

Her words, Theodore Stappler said to me, cut deep, for he felt that her implied accusation was just, in spite of the fact that his uncle intervened and asked bluntly, "What could he have done?" There was in any case, he went on, no point in going over possibilities that were now merely academic.

He went to the telephone and spoke in succession to a number of people who, he said, had some influence and might be able to do something.

Next morning they found out that his mother and the others had been tranferred from Saarbrücken to Frankfurt, pending further investigation into the whole matter. His uncle thereupon engaged a lawyer, who held out some hope that he might be able to arrange for the release of Theodore Stappler's mother.

In the meantime Theodore Stappler tried to get hold of Joseph Held, if indeed Held had returned to the city. But the friend who had arranged their meeting in the first place, and who felt therefore a kind of responsibility for what had happened, discovered that Held had not returned to the city. In fact, he had given up his apartment some two weeks earlier. His family – his wife and small daughter – had also left the city. No one knew where they had gone. They had certainly left the country. Some of their neighbours said they had gone to France, and some said they had gone to England.

The days dragged on and Theodore Stappler hardly ever left the apartment of his aunt and uncle. On some days everybody was hopeful. The lawyer said that everything was arranged and that she would be released any day. But nothing happened. After two weeks had gone by, his uncle suggested to Theodore Stappler that he should go to Italy and wait there for further developments. He could do nothing here and he was in constant danger of being arrested. But Theodore Stappler did not want to leave.

For nearly another week he vacillated, and at last he decided to go. He hoped, he said to me, he really hoped that he would be arrested on the border.

He left. He was not arrested and so crossed into Italy, where his life at any rate was for the moment safe. In Italy also he got the first letter from his mother. His uncle sent it on to him. She was allowed to write one letter a week. This first letter was re- markably cheerful. She was happy, she wrote, that he at least was safe. That news had reached her through his uncle, and she could hardly describe her feelings when she had heard that he was safe. Whatever was in store for her, she wrote, she could bear. She was not alone. Those whom she loved, both those who were alive and those who were dead, were constantly in her mind and in her heart. She hoped that he, her son, would always do things of which he and those who loved him could be proud.

He knew the letter off by heart, he told me, for he had read and re-read it countless times. He had it still.

Theodore Stappler looked at me searchingly and said very quietly, "The only thing I have done is keep alive. Perhaps," he added ironically, "in our time that is something to be proud of. But it isn't much."

His uncle wrote reassuring letters, too. It couldn't be long. Everything that could be done was being done. Mr. So-and-so, a highly influential man, was pulling strings; the Dean of the Medical Faculty was using his influence; even the *Rektor* of the University had been approached and had promised. . . . But nothing hap- pened.

Then the war broke out. For a little while her letters still reached him, but not regularly any more. And then they stopped coming altogether.

❦ IX

"AFTER ALL THAT," THEODORE STAPPLER SAID TO ME, "YOU CAN imagine how I felt when I arrived here and when I looked in the phone book and found Held's name. Everything, the whole past, rose up to haunt me. I thought I had remembered everything. But only now I know how much I had in fact forgotten, and in some ways I wish I'd left them where they were. But I suppose one can't do that anyway. They rise up, these things, in the most unexpected places and in the most casual way, too. A chance word, an insignificant gesture, and the door is unlocked, and you have to enter the cabinet again, where the skeletons are." He stopped and lit a cigarette and sat smoking in silence for a while.

"For two days," he continued, "I hardly moved from my room. I thought I was losing my nerve, you know, and I didn't know how to prepare myself for the encounter. I talked to Sam. I went out to eat and took little walks, I went to the movies nearly every night, but I didn't even dare to ask where precisely Held lived in this city. Once or twice I nearly gave a taxi-driver the address so that he could drive me there and I could at least see the house, spy out the terrain, but at the last moment I always drew back."

"You were afraid?" I asked.

"Yes."

"Of what?"

"Who knows? Of many things."

"Of Held?"

He hesitated. "No," he said. "Not really. What could he do to me?"

"Were you afraid of what you might do to him?"

Theodore Stappler did not answer me at once. He furrowed

his brow and then closed his eyes and rubbed them with the thumb and forefinger of his left hand.

"Do you mean," he asked me then, "that I thought I might – what shall I say? – hurt him? In a physical sense?"

"Yes," I said.

"No," he answered, firmly and without hesitation. "I wasn't afraid of that. There were times – I told you that before – when I could have been violent with him. Could even have killed him."

"To kill a man," I said. "That's an enormous deed."

"It has been done," he said, with irony. "At a certain time I could have done it. If I'd met him on the street there at Saarbrücken, I could have killed him. And even in London a year later, or even two years later, I could have done it. But I knew that now, after so many years, I couldn't do it."

"You think, then, that you could kill a man in anger?" I asked.

"I'm not much drawn to this kind of theorizing," he said.

"But this is more than theory. I take it there were times when you were contemplating. . . ."

"Not consciously," he said. "I never sat down with a piece of paper to work it out! Certainly I couldn't kill a man for something relatively trivial, even if my blood boiled. I sometimes get angry about trivial things, absurdly so sometimes. But I could never kill a man for a trivial offence. But this isn't trivial. The offence is grave. It was a great betrayal. It was a matter of life and death. He became a tool of the death-bringers. He walked with them. He did their bidding."

"I know. And even before I know what made him do it. . . ."

But here he interrupted me and his voice was harsh and completely without pity. "Nothing can excuse such an act," he said. "A man's action must be his own. And he can always refuse to act. Even in the worst of times. He has that choice."

"Even if it means his own death?" I said.

"Of course," he said, "even if it means his own death. I'm not saying he could have prevented the arrest when it actually occurred. But perhaps we needn't have been there at the time. I'm convinced he knew in Vienna what was going to happen, and he let it happen. He didn't have to turn himself into their tool. He didn't have to walk with them. That damns him."

"You are very harsh," I said.

"Why?" he demanded. "Why am I harsh?"

"I don't know what pressures, what threats were used against him. What you demand is a kind of – what shall I say? – heroism, or at least a superior sort of conduct that. . . ."

"I demand integrity," he said. "He himself insisted on it. He kept saying he was *ein Ehrenmann*."

"But when pressures are put on them, some men can't withstand these pressures. They are weak. Can we condemn a man for weakness alone?"

"Ah," said Theodore Stappler, "that's one of the ways that lead to hell. There's such a thing as criminal weakness. In one sense, everybody who commits a crime is weak. Weakness can explain many things, but it can't excuse them."

"But once we understand the reason for an action, isn't it easier for us to comprehend the action itself and perhaps even to forgive it?"

"That depends on the action," he said. "Some things can't be forgiven. That is my position."

He leaned forward in his chair and fixed me with his eyes, and then, with a violent gesture, he shot a finger at me, as if I were a particularly stubborn witness, and said, "You see the trap you are leading me into!"

"How?" I asked, quite astonished.

"You want me to say that all is past. Therefore everything can be forgotten. Written off."

"By no means," I protested. "I don't want to write anything off. I'm merely trying to understand."

"Yes, so that then you can forgive the action. 'Forgive' is one of your favourite words, isn't it?"

"I'm not ashamed of it."

"Ah, yes," he said, and for a moment I thought he was almost sneering at me. "You can afford the luxury. The issue is academic for you."

"You're absurd," I said, deliberately using the word he was so fond of. "But at any rate, what has it to do with me? I'm not, as you say, involved. And I'm certainly not trying to lead you into any trap."

"Oh, but you are."

"How?" I asked, now feeling quite exasperated with him. "How am I leading you into a trap?"

"Because if I say that I forgive him, if I explain it all by saying that there were tremendous pressures brought against him, that all is now past and should be forgotten, and if not forgotten, at least forgiven, then how easy would it be for me to forgive myself. Because I, too, you see, was under enormous pressure!"

That argument, I confess, I had not thought of. He was a subtle dialectician. He had been afraid once, had let an enormous opportunity slip by, and he could never forget that. Nor could he forgive himself. In a very real sense, I could see, Held hardly mattered to him.

"I take it you must go on torturing yourself forever," I said.

"I'm not torturing myself," he retorted sharply.

"What then?" I demanded. "What are you doing then?"

"What is done," he said, "can't be undone."

"That's not an answer," I said.

He shrugged his shoulders. "We're talking around the issue," he said. "What's the point? It's not leading anywhere. You keep asking these absurd questions. Could a man kill another man? Could I specifically kill a specific man? Could I do it now? And if not now, could I have done it at some time in the past? Could I forgive a man? Was he weak perhaps? Was I weak? . . ." He made a sweeping gesture with his left arm, as if he were dismissing all these questions and the problems they raised. "I never thought about all that," he continued. "I had to find a certain man. And then I found him. And then of course I had to go up to his house and ring his bell and say, 'Here I am. My name is Theodore Stappler.' And that was the most difficult thing of all."

He did eventually gather up enough courage. Twice he went to the house where Held lived. But he could not bring himself to walk up to the door and ring the bell.

The third time he managed it. It was past seven o'clock in the evening. It was very cold out, but there was a full moon and a clear sky and the street was quite bright. The house itself, he told me, seemed dark and forbidding to him, but he forced himself to walk up to the door, yet hoping all the while that no one would be home, so that perhaps he could flee again.

I interrupted him here to ask why he had not telephoned first, but he answered brusquely that he had never even considered doing that. It was not fitting, he said. It was an odd phrase. "It was not fitting." The encounter had to be personal, he went on to say. It had to be face to face.

I thought of these two men meeting suddenly, in the desert, alone. For so, he had told me, he had always imagined it. And so in a way it had happened. For they met here, in this northern city, in the middle of a pitiless winter, with the indifferent moon gazing down from the cold, clear sky, thousands of miles from the place where the original tragedy had played itself out.

He stood for a long time, he said, his finger on the doorbell, but not daring to press the button. At last he touched it, and drew back. Was almost going to run away, like a little boy bent on mischief. But could not move. Could not lift his feet. For a moment it seemed that no one was going to answer. Then suddenly the light went on in the hall, and the door opened.

A young girl was standing there, and looked at him, and said, "Yes?"

For this he was not prepared. It destroyed the picture of the meeting as he had imagined it. Between him and the man there was now this girl.

He felt his knees go limp, almost buckling under him. He tried to speak, but no words came.

"Yes?" she said again. "Is there anything I can do for you?"

Still he couldn't bring himself to say anything.

He sensed that she was becoming alarmed, and he thought for a moment that she was going to slam the door in his face, and he knew that he must prevent her from doing that, because he felt that he would not have the courage to come again, if he did not finish his business now.

So he found his voice. "Does a Mr. Held live here?" he asked.

"Yes," she said.

"Could I see him?"

"He's not at home," she said.

"Then can I wait for him?" he asked.

The request seemed to take her by surprise, for she drew back, as if she were going to close the door.

"I've come a long way to see him," said Theodore Stappler.

"Oh," she said.

He felt he had to explain further, and so he said, "Yes, I knew him well quite a long time ago, but we've been out of touch for many years. Someone told me he was here, and since I happen to be passing through the city. . ."

"Oh," she said, still rather doubtful, "Couldn't you come back? He should be home in about an hour."

"I came by taxi," he said. "I have no car here." He must stay, he felt. He could not let himself be driven off, or he might never come again. "It's very cold," he said, appealing to her sense of mercy. And indeed it was cold, and his ears were beginning to bite from the cold.

"All right," she said then, very abruptly, as if she had made a sudden decision. "Come in."

She stepped aside and allowed him to come into the house. He walked into the hall and she closed the door behind him. Then she turned to him, and he saw her properly for the first time, since with the light behind her, her face had been in shadow before. She looked intense, even a little frightened. All at once he became aware that there was no one else in the house, and now he understood her reluctance to let him come in.

She opened the door that led into the living-room, and beckoned him to sit down on the chesterfield. Then she excused herself. She had to go out soon, she said, and had to get ready. But he was welcome to wait here. And with that she withdrew.

The room oppressed him. The furniture was drab and over-stuffed; the chesterfield and the upholstered chairs were limp and soggy, and the grey carpet looked worn, its colour faded. Heavy, brocaded drapes were drawn across the far wall where the windows were, and it seemed to Theodore Stappler as if he were enclosed in an airless room with no exit, no way to escape and, as usual when he felt trapped between four walls, he began to sweat. He rushed to the window and drew the curtains back a bit, and the sight of the glass and the dull-gleaming snow outside, which after a few moments became visible to him, calmed his nerves, and he went back again to the chesterfield and sat down to wait.

A book lay on the chesterfield. He picked it up. It was about the French Revolution. (Here Theodore Stappler looked me full in the face and smiled.) A bookmark stuck out of one of the pages and, when he turned to it, he found there an account of the murder of Jean Paul Marat. And so, as he sat waiting for Joseph Held, he read about Charlotte Corday and of how she had gained entry into Marat's house under false pretences and had there stabbed him to death in his bath.

After a while he heard the girl coming down the stairs. She went first into the kitchen, or so at any rate he supposed, for he heard water running, and then the door opened and she came into the living-room.

He noticed at once that she had changed the slacks she had worn when she let him in, for now she had on a green, high-collared dress, and he thought that she had also brushed out her hair, for it looked smooth and silken.

"My father won't be too long, I hope," she said. "I've put some water on for coffee. I hope you care for some."

He thanked her and said she was very kind, though there was no need really for her to go to any trouble.

It was no trouble at all, she said.

He remembered thinking what a pity it was that this fresh-looking, young, and striking girl was Held's daughter. He had, of course, thought that she was Held's daughter from the moment he had laid eyes on her but was sad now to have this confirmed. He would now not be able to deal with Held (though he still had no idea what he would do when Held finally stood before him) when they were at last face to face, without thinking of the girl. The fact that she existed, that he had seen her, made Held less abstract, less the symbol of the betrayal, more simply a man who had fathered this girl who, presumably, had affection and love for him. It made everything much more complex. He wondered also about the girl's mother, Held's wife. Where was she? Perhaps, he thought, she was out with Held.

"You said you'd come a long way to see my father," said the girl. "Where've you come from?"

"From Toronto," he said. It suddenly struck him that he had not yet introduced himself, and so he got up and said very formally that his name was Theodore Stappler, and she in turn told him her name was Katherine Held.

They talked for a few minutes about inconsequential things – about the weather, about Toronto where, she supposed, her father and Theodore Stappler had met. No, he said, they had first known each other in Europe, in Vienna, to be exact. Oh, she said, then that *was* a long time ago. More than a dozen years ago. Even longer than that, he said. Nearly thirteen years ago.

"Oh," she cried out. "Then you must be a friend of my father's. I didn't realize that." Her voice was suddenly very warm and welcoming.

"I felt very embarrassed," Theodore Stappler said to me. "I felt I had cheated her, forced my way in, and now she was under a totally false impression. I'd come under false pretences. I was hot under the collar, and I almost told her, 'No, we're not friends. Quite the contrary,' but I didn't do it. I couldn't do it."

He was saved, he said, when she announced that she would go

into the kitchen. The water must be boiling by now. Did he mind instant coffee? He said he didn't, and she said laughingly that that was what he was going to get, whether he liked it or not.

She came back, carrying a tray with two cups of coffee, a cream and sugar set, and a plate of biscuits.

She was a very poor housekeeper, she said with a smile. She simply didn't have time. Nor indeed the interest. That ever since her mother died – thus casually did Theodore Stappler learn of the fate of Joseph Held's wife – more than three years ago, her father had had a rough time of it, eating meals that were prepared in haste and most of whose ingredients came out of cans.

They both laughed at that, and then Theodore Stappler said he was sorry to hear that her mother had died. Yes, she said, after a long illness. They had come west partly because her father was a rather restless man, but partly because the climate was drier here than in the East, and her mother had long been suffering from a bronchial condition. It was none the less a dreadful blow, the girl said, especially to her father, when her mother died. He had been terribly dependent on her, in spite of the fact that she had for so long been ill.

Her eyes were downcast when she told him about these happenings, and her voice was low. Then, turning directly to Theodore Stappler, she asked him if by any chance he had known her mother.

No, he answered her, no, he had only known her father.

"I thought back," said Theodore Stappler to me, "to that dingy little café, the Café Sturm, where I first met him, and then I could see him walking with them down the platform in Saarbrücken to the carriage, where my mother was waiting for me to return and where others were waiting, too. And I saw him again going into the carriage alone, to play his awful part."

It was difficult to reconcile the picture he had of Held with the impression the girl conveyed of the devoted husband, dependent on his ailing wife, shattered by her death, and now suffering the poor housekeeping of a young daughter.

"I'm sure," the girl said, "that my father will be very glad to see you. He's so lonely now. And he hardly has any friends here."

He merely grunted, quite non-committally, feeling again embarrassed, and trying desperately to think of something to say, so that they could get onto a different subject.

But she persisted. "Did you ever come to visit us?" she asked.

"I was only a little girl, and I wouldn't remember, of course. No, but if you had," she went on, correcting herself, as it were, "you would have known my mother."

"No," he said, "I never came to your home."

"And what brings you here?" she asked. "To this city?"

Once again that question.

"Everybody asked me that question," said Theodore Stappler to me, "as if it was a standard question. But when she asked me this question, my hand began to shake and I had to put my cup down because I was afraid that she would notice how wrought up I was. Why had I come? How could I tell her? I didn't know what to say. I felt the blood rush into my face, and I think I stammered something about World-Wide Encyclopedias, and about going on to the coast, to Vancouver after I had finished my business here, and I said something about Vancouver being a beautiful city, or so I had heard, and something about a balmy climate. . . . I don't know exactly what I said. I remember feeling ashamed because of the deception."

Then suddenly, mercifully, he went on to tell me, his eye fell on the book that was still lying where he had put it down and he said that someone seemed to be interested in Jean Paul Marat and Charlotte Corday and in that bathroom affair.

"Bathroom affair!" she laughed, and the laughter broke the tension, and he could start breathing easier again.

"And then," Theodore Stappler said to me, "I heard your name for the first time, because she said, yes, she was interested in the bathroom affair, she was as a matter of fact writing an essay for Professor Lerner." His eyes twinkled rather playfully. "And then," he said, "she began to talk about you." And he added emphatically, "At length."

I felt myself blushing, but I didn't say anything.

"Aren't you interested in what she said about you?" he asked.

"Mildly," I said, clearing my throat. "But perhaps it's better if I don't know."

"You're too modest," he said. "She spoke about you with enthusiasm. She admires you. Tremendously. For a while I thought that here was a student infatuation. That a student had fallen in love with her professor."

"Nonsense," I burst out.

"Honestly," he said. "I thought that."

"But now you know better."

"I don't know anything any more," he said, rather sharply, I thought. "But I liked what she told me about you," he continued after a pause. "As a matter of fact I decided that if it was possible, I would try and meet you."

"Really?" I said. "You're making that up."

"No," he said. "Why should I make this up? What point would there be?"

"Why should you have wanted to meet me?"

"To talk with you." He seemed to grope for words. "I – I had an instinct – what shall I say? – a hunch. I'm alone here. I don't know a soul. And I'm a man who needs people. I have to talk to people. I can't keep things entirely to myself. And here I am, involved in an affair about which I couldn't say anything to anybody – until now. I knew I would have to talk to someone or else I would. . . ." He spread his hands out wide, though what he meant by the gesture I didn't quite know.

"So you picked me," I said lightly, "out of a hat."

The ancient mariner, I thought suddenly, stopping the wedding guest and pouring out his tale.

"Not out of a hat," said Theodore Stappler. "I liked what she said about you. A man of conscience. Of conviction. Of principles."

"Oh, no," I cried out. "Is that what she said?"

"More or less."

"And you thought she was infatuated, was in love with me!"

"And why not? Can't a girl fall in love with a man of conscience and of principles?"

His tone was so clearly ironic that I didn't know how to take him, and so I said irritably, "I suppose she could. But God help us! God help the man!"

"Well, well," he said, "I believe you are angry."

"Nonsense," I said. "A man of conscience and of principles! How dreadful." I suddenly thought of Bill Sommers. If I told him what I had just heard, he would die laughing.

"There's nothing wrong with such a man?" said Theodore Stappler, still with that ironic twist that gave an ambiguity to his words.

"Nothing," I said. "But to fall in love with such a man for no other reason. . . ."

"I believe you like the girl," he said.

"Oh, come now. I hardly know her. She is one in a class of

forty or fifty students. I've spoken to her a few times and until tonight never for longer than half an hour. But what is this, anyway? What have I to do with it all? *You* have involved me. This evening. And until this evening I never thought of the girl at all."

"Not at all?" he interrupted. For whatever reason, he evidently enjoyed the spectacle of seeing me dangling in a somewhat uncomfortable position.

"Well, hardly at all. I thought of her. But certainly not seriously. I think of many things. But it's you, I thought, *you* who're involved. You're in love with the girl."

He seemed to shrink into himself. "I wish you wouldn't say that," he said then quietly. "Understand me. I don't wish to deny anything. But I don't know what I feel for her. I can't know. Things are too confused. There's her father. Always her father."

"What has she to do with her father?" I asked. "I thought you were enlightened. Are you transferring the sins of the fathers to their children?"

"Of course not," he retorted sharply. "At least I hope not. But it is absurd to pretend that the past isn't going to rise up to haunt us."

"You say you haven't told her anything about what is between you and her father?"

"Yes."

"Why don't you? Why don't you tell her the truth?"

"No," he said, "not yet."

"Will you ever tell her?"

"That I don't know."

"Why?"

"Because I can't face it. Because I'm afraid of what will happen. Perhaps because I'm a coward. But the situation is unbearable. It's impossible. It can't go on. It's like a boil. It must burst. Sooner or later it must burst. And I'm afraid of what will happen when it does." He stared out into space, unseeing. "I wish I could run away," he said then, in a barely audible whisper. "But if I do," he went on softly, as if he were weighing all these possibilities, "if I do she'll think that I have betrayed her. And if I stay, I will have to make her unhappy in another way. That's my choice."

"Then you do care," I said. "You do care about her."

He turned his face to me. It was grave and almost solemn, and in some obscure way I felt ashamed for having pressed him to reveal his feelings. "All right," he said, "all right. I do care for her. Of course I care for her. But why do you harp on it? What is it to you?"

Suddenly I found myself on the defensive. "I – I certainly don't want to pry. But you have involved me, and I have a right to establish certain things."

"Well, all right," he said, very much calmer.

And then he quickly moved back to that first encounter, when he sat talking with her and waiting for the arrival of her father. In fact, he said, their conversation had grown so animated and he was so charmed by her that for whole stretches he quite forgot what he had come for.

But this idyll, if indeed it was an idyll, came suddenly to an end. For the bell rang, and she got up and said, "There's my father."

The moment had at last come. Face to face. But not alone. There was now the girl, too.

When she said, "There's my father," Theodore Stappler felt himself go rigid, as if suddenly his body had been turned to stone. He also rose, so that he would meet the man standing. And so, rigid, he waited.

Had she noticed this change in him? I asked, but he said he didn't think so.

Katherine went out of the living-room. She left the door open, and he heard the front door creaking on its hinges, as she let her father in.

Then he heard her say, "There's someone to see you."

"Oh," said Joseph Held, "who is it?" He pronounced the "s" very sharply. His speech, as Theodore Stappler would soon find out, was rather heavily accented, though his English was very precise, very correct, and in some ways even elaborate.

"You'll be surprised," she said.

"Who is it, then?" he asked, half entering into the game of guessing who his visitor might be.

"A man you knew many, many years ago," she said.

There was a silence that seemed to last for eternity.

Theodore Stappler, standing, waiting, was almost ready to go out into the hall, but before he could do this, Held asked, "What has he come for – this man?"

"To see you," she said. "He's in the city for only a short while, and then he's going on to Vancouver. Someone told him you were here, and he thought he would look you up. Isn't that nice?"

"Do you think," I interrupted Theodore Stappler's narration, "that he knew who it was? Did he know it might be you?"

"Oh, I don't think so," said Theodore Stappler. "But I think he prepared himself, out there in the hall, for whatever was coming. He is a man of great self-control in any case. That I soon found out."

Joseph Held now asked his daughter what the name of the man was, and she answered, "Theodore is his first name. He told me his surname, too, but I didn't quite catch it."

"I see," said Joseph Held, and there was again a long silence.

"I have to leave," said Katherine to her father. "And so I'll just stay for a minute."

"Will you be out late?" her father asked her.

"I don't think so," she said. "I'll be back before midnight."

Of course, Theodore Stappler said to me, the whole thing, from the moment Katherine opened the door to the moment Joseph Held came into the living-room, could not have taken more than three or four minutes, but it seemed as if at least an hour had gone by.

The man who finally came into the living-room was the rather short man Theodore Stappler remembered, but he was no longer very trim. He had a little pot belly and he was now quite bald. Only a fringe of hair was left on the sides. His round face, which Theodore Stappler remembered as puffy, was now puffier still, and had a yellowish, unhealthy pallor. He looked in general very tired, almost listless, as if all spirit had gone from him. His brown suit was rumpled, and the jacket hung loose.

So they faced each other at last, Theodore Stappler and this tired, pot-bellied, middle-aged man.

Joseph Held looked at Theodore Stappler intently, brows furrowed. He gave no sign of recognition. And indeed, Theodore Stappler did not think that Held recognized him, for he would not have recognized Held immediately either, if he had met him casually.

At last Held smiled a little and said very politely, "With whom have I the honour to speak?"

Behind him stood his daughter. She came forward and now was in the middle, beside them both, between her father and Theodore Stappler.

Theodore Stappler said to me that he felt a shudder go through him, because it seemed, for a moment at least, as if the girl was about to place herself in front of her father to shield him from a blow that was about to fall and so take that blow upon herself. He knew, of course, that it was absurd of him to think so, since the girl could have no knowledge at all of what was between him and her father. But nevertheless he thought, if only for a fleeting second, that she was protecting her father.

"You must forgive me," she said to Theodore Stappler, "but I couldn't tell my father your name, because I didn't quite catch it when you told me before."

Theodore Stappler's throat was dry, and his knees began to tremble and when he spoke his voice was dry, too. "My name is Theodore Stappler," he said.

The name did not seem to register at once. Or else Held managed ruthlessly to keep himself in check. Certainly he betrayed no emotion.

In any case, their attention was diverted, because Katherine Held said, "Of course. Mr. Stappler. Mr. Stappler says he knew you in Vienna. . . . But you must excuse me. I must leave now. I'm already late." She turned to Theodore Stappler and said how nice it was to meet him and that perhaps they might see each other again. And then she turned and left the two men alone, and soon after they heard her leave the house.

And now they were really alone. Standing face to face. Theodore Stappler and Joseph Held.

"When he heard your name," I asked, "did he know at once who you were?"

"No," said Theodore Stappler. "I don't think he did. I'm pretty sure he didn't. Not at once. But he was obviously trying hard to remember, he was trying to place me. And finally he asked me, again very formally, very politely, where he had had the honour of meeting me. So I said to him, 'Don't you remember? We met in a little café – Sturm I think it was called.' I knew of course perfectly well that that was the name of the café. It is certainly a name I shall remember as long as I live. As soon as I spoke the name of the café, I could tell that he knew, too, because he seemed to sway a little, and his eyes stared at me – they were large and there was panic in them. I swear there was panic. But he caught himself very quickly, he steadied himself, I suppose he was trying to prolong some kind of illusion for a while longer. Anyway, I don't know why he still pretended to be in the dark, but he repeated in a puzzled sort of voice, 'Café Sturm? Café Sturm?' and I suddenly felt tremendously angry, and I almost lost control, and I think I could have done something violent, but all at once I thought of the young girl, of Katherine, of this man's daughter, and of what she would say, what she would do, if she suddenly came in and saw me do violence to her father, and that thought — what shall I say? — disconcerted me, restrained me. So she did protect him after all."

"What did you do then?" I asked.

"I said to him, 'In Saarbrücken also. . . .' And then, of course, he couldn't pretend any more. He looked at me with the same panic in his eyes, he was frightened, and he repeated the name of the city, three or four times. Then he looked away from me, did everything to avoid my eyes. He still tried desperately not to give himself away. At all costs he tried to keep calm."

But once Theodore Stappler had made it impossible for Held to pretend that he could not remember him, once the word "Saarbrücken" had been spoken and had set off the dreadful echoes, Joseph Held said hoarsely, "I remember."

For some time yet Joseph Held stood as if transfixed to the floor. All colour seemed now to have gone out of his face. The skin was leathery and waxen. Deep grooves were in the face. Only the eyes burned and showed that the head was not a death mask but belonged to a living man. The mouth was tight, a straight line. And then, like a snake, the tip of the tongue moved slowly across the parched lips, and then, hoarsely, the voice formed words, but the man was not speaking to Theodore Stappler, he was talking to himself, murmuring some words in German, but Theodore Stappler was so totally absorbed that he would have known even if he had heard nothing at all, like a deaf man watching someone speak, what the lips of Joseph Held were saying.

Joseph Held, speaking in German, said, "*Ich glaubte, dass die alle tot sind.*"

And a shudder went through him when Theodore Stappler answered him in English, "But you see that we are not all dead."

Held looked at him for a long time and then said, "No. Not all. I am glad of that, too."

"You swine!" Theodore Stappler cried out.

Held cringed, as if a whip had struck him across the face.

Theodore Stappler turned to me. "It may seem strange to

you, but I was sorry, as soon as the word 'swine' was out of my mouth, that I had used that word. That I had lost my temper. It was the only moment of violence between us."

"It doesn't seem strange to me," I said.

"But after my outburst I felt calmer. 'You wish that I was dead, too,' I said to him. 'You wish that, don't you?' He held up his hands in a kind of horror and said, 'No, no.' His voice was hardly audible. It was almost as if a corpse were speaking, when he said, 'No, no. I am glad that you have come.' I told him then that I didn't believe him. And of course I didn't. How could he have been glad? But then in a curious way, in an obscure way, perhaps he was."

At any rate, Theodore Stappler went on, Joseph Held shook his head in utter resignation, as if to say that it really didn't matter whether Stappler believed him or not. "You will please allow me to sit down," he said.

"You are my host," Theodore Stappler said to him. "This is your house."

Held sat down, but Theodore Stappler remained standing. And when Joseph Held beckoned him to a chair, with a halting gesture of his hand, Stappler ignored the gesture So he forced that tired, middle-aged man, old beyond his years, to look up to him, but he wished that the man would not seem quite so defence-less. He did not want, he said to me, to wrestle with a shadow, with a ghost.

Held said, "For many years I have sat and waited. I thought somebody would come. Surely, I thought, somebody must come. You or one of the others. I wished that somebody would come and at last I would be rid of – oh, God, I don't know, I don't know . . . . I see that you don't believe me. But I wanted to be rid of this burden. Somehow. . . . I don't know how."

Theodore Stappler didn't answer, and when I interrupted the account to ask whether he believed what Held had said, he shrugged his shoulders and said that he didn't know what to say. He was frustrated, he said, because things had turned out to be so very different from what he had expected. For the pitiable man, sitting there on the chesterfield, shrunk into himself, he could feel no hatred, but no compassion, either. The image of the man who had walked along the station platform in that faraway city to betray the people who had trusted their lives to him seemed the image of another man entirely, and it was increasingly difficult for Theodore Stappler to relate the two.

As if to convince his visitor, that sudden apparition that had emerged to confront him out of the dark and distant past, as if to convince him that what he had said was true, Joseph Held almost pleaded with him. "I could have changed my name, you see," he cried out.

"You went far enough away," Theodore Stappler answered him. "You never thought that anyone would find you."

"*Man ist doch nur ein Mensch*," Held mumbled. "I was afraid. Of course I was afraid. I used to wake up in the middle of the night. Especially in the middle of the night. And even more so after the war when people began to come to Canada from Europe. From the camps. The survivors. I was afraid. Of course I was afraid. How could it have been different? I was selling real estate in Toronto. Just as I do here. We have to live and I cannot practise the law here. Then I started to be afraid to go out. To knock on doors. Because I always thought that someone from that time – from that place – from that train. . . ."

"And so you left Toronto," Theodore Stappler said to him. "You ran away, thousands of miles."

"But I didn't change my name," Held cried, as if that in some way vindicated him. "I am here. And you have found me here."

Whether by design or not, Theodore Stappler said to me, Held paralysed him, and made it impossible for him at the moment to contemplate any action. But he was suddenly also aware that he did not really know what he wanted to do, that his plans had never gone beyond the initial point of the initial encounter, of the two meeting each other, in a deserted place, all alone. But if ever Theodore Stappler had contemplated force, the reality of the confrontation made even such a contemplation pointless. He felt, Theodore Stappler said to me, a sense of frustration greater than any he had experienced before, for he thought that he should do something but did not know what, and so he remained silent, standing there and looking down at Joseph Held and waiting for him to make some move that would point the way toward action.

At last Held spoke again. "You think that I am – *verdamm*."

"If you say so."

"Yes," Held said. "Yes. I say so. Sometimes I think. . . Oh, God, it doesn't matter what I think. Sometimes I think – in the night I wake up, all in a sweat, because these people, they come to me. Your mother. . ."

"Oh, for God's sake, shut up," Theodore Stappler cried out. "Damn you, anyway. You want me to feel sorry for you, don't you? That's what you want."

"No," Joseph Held said. "That would not help me in the least. It would do me no good. But perhaps only if you understand. If you would only listen to me, I could explain. . ."

"Every traitor can explain," Theodore Stappler said harshly, and again it was as if his words were lashes, and Held drew back and raised his hands to his face, almost as if he wanted to protect himself from physical blows.

"I could," Held said then, speaking haltingly, "if you would only allow me, I could explain why I. . . ."

"I don't want to hear your explanations," said Theodore Stappler.

"But listen," Joseph Held pleaded with him. "Let me explain why I did. . ."

"To make money," Theodore Stappler said, speaking as coldly, as icily, as he could. "That's why you sold yourself, and that's why you sold us."

"No," Held cried out. "No. If that is what you want. If you want me to pay you back the money. . . ."

"I wouldn't take any money from you," said Theodore Stappler. "How could you wash away the deed by giving me money?"

"But listen," Held said.

"I want to ask a question," Theodore Stappler said, quite disregarding Held's urgent pleas. "Isn't it true that you knew already in Vienna, when we boarded the train, what our fate would be?"

If ever Theodore Stappler had been in doubt about this matter, that doubt was now dispelled. Held said nothing, but the horror in his face was unmistakable. Then he closed his eyes and covered his face with his hands. So he sat, for a long time, without moving, without speaking. Theodore Stappler's question remained unanswered, at least in words.

At last Joseph Held raised himself, with great difficulty, it seemed, from the chesterfield, struggled to his feet, and now again the two men stood face to face. Held took a step forward until the faces of the two men almost touched each other.

"I tried," said Joseph Held in a hoarse whisper, "I tried to save my child."

For this, Theodore Stappler was not wholly unprepared. He had, in fact, expected Held to advance some such explanation. But he had already, so he told me, rejected such an explanation before it was made. It was merely, he said to me, a kind of rationalization of the most obvious sort.

"I take it, then," I said to him, "that you did not believe him when he said he wanted to save his child."

"The issue was entirely irrelevant," Theodore Stappler said to me. "It could make no difference."

"But could it not at least be taken into account?" I asked. "Could it not to some extent mitigate his action?"

"His action – his betrayal," said Theodore Stappler, speaking in his driest, most pedantic manner, "must be judged entirely by itself, entirely on its own."

"But no man ever acts in isolation," I said. "We don't live in a vacuum, in an atmosphere of moral absolutes."

"That," he answered, "is my position," and repeated, as if to drive home his point, "The action must be judged entirely by itself."

I could see that I would not be able to budge him from this position. I therefore asked him how he had answered Held.

"I told him what I have just told you, that I rejected his explanation," Theodore Stappler said.

"And what did he do?" I asked.

"His face went almost white," Theodore Stappler answered. "His hands began to tremble, and his body swayed from side to side. I thought his knees would give way under him and that he would collapse. And I tried to reach out my hands to help him, to support him, but I couldn't do it. It is terrible for me to say this, but I couldn't reach out my hand to him. If he had died there, on the spot, I couldn't have reached out my hand to him. I would have let him perish like a dog."

I shuddered when he said that. But it was, in an odd way, a shudder of admiration, paradoxical as this might seem. There was, in Theodore Stappler's manner, in his directness, a kind of ruthless moral honesty. He waited, looking at me, and evidently expecting me to make some sort of comment. I had the feeling that he wanted me to come to his defence, to exonerate him, to say that his action had been right. But I said nothing, because I could neither approve nor disapprove.

Theodore Stappler waited, his eyes fixed directly on mine,

pinning me, as it were, against the wall. He seemed to enjoy my discomfort, or else to try to force me to speak, but I braced myself, felt my stubbornness rising in me, made myself meet his eyes, even though I had a strong desire to avoid his fixed stare, and remained silent.

He broke the silence and said, almost sneeringly, "You think I was a beast?"

"No."

"You think, then, that I was right?"

"No."

"What, then?"

"I don't know."

"Ach!" he exclaimed, the tone of his voice so nearly contemptuous that I was furious, though I tried to contain myself. "You professors," he went on, in the same contemptuous manner, "you are so objective, so. . . so aseptic, so. . . God knows what, that you will take no stand at all."

"You don't want me to take a stand," I said. "You want me to agree with you – and without any reservations. And that is what I won't do. Because Held, I think, was also a victim. Like you, and like – well, the others. Your mother and the others."

"You mean there is no difference? Between betrayer and betrayed there is no difference?"

"No, no," I said. "That's not what I meant, that's not what I meant at all."

"But you are willing to find excuses for him. You are willing to have so many shades that there is no colour left at all." He leaned forward, as if he were about to pounce on me.

I began to squirm in my chair. I felt uncomfortable. I felt as if I were rapidly losing all my bearings. "Not necessarily," I said, speaking very cautiously, for I was aware that I was wading through a moral pigsty, where all was dirt. "Only I think that in the end there are others much more responsible than Held. There was also what you called the devil's man."

"I haven't forgotten," said Theodore Stappler, his inexorable eyes still fixed on me. "But there is nevertheless Held."

The issue clearly could not be settled. It could never be resolved.

"What happened then," I asked, "when Held nearly collapsed and you couldn't reach out your hand to help him?"

Theodore Stappler lit a cigarette. He exhaled slowly and

watched the smoke rising towards the ceiling. "Oh," he said, very calmly, "he recovered. Without my help."

Then suddenly he grew excited. With a furious gesture he stubbed the newly lit cigarette in the ashtray. "And do you know what?" he cried. "The worm turned! Yes, he turned! And he said to me, 'Let me ask you one question, Mr. Stappler. You were not there when I came back. Did you know that I was coming with them? And if so, why didn't you tell the others? Why didn't you warn them?' That is what he said to me. And what could I say? He, Joseph Held, he had the nerve to say that to me! *He* had the nerve to ask *me* why *I* didn't save the others! *He!*"

For this sudden and violent outburst I was not prepared. He seemed to have completely lost control of himself. And, after all, it was amazing. For the charge that he had not acted in a heroic manner, that he could have saved the others but had been, at the crucial moment, afraid and had only, in a sense, saved himself, was precisely the charge he had brought against himself, here, in this very room, within the last two hours or so.

Of course, I understood him in a way. It is one thing for a man to examine his conduct and find it wanting, even to admit his own weaknesses, and it is quite another to have his enemy point the finger of scorn in order to feel absolved of his own transgressions. And Held, of all people! I could understand Theodore Stappler's anger.

"What did you do?" I asked him.

He did not answer at once. I sensed that he was embarrassed because he had let himself go. He leaned forward and pulled a fresh cigarette from the package that lay on the coffee-table, and I noticed that his hand trembled when he lit the cigarette. After a few puffs he seemed to have regained his composure, and he now answered my question in an even, deliberate voice.

"Nothing," he said. "Nothing. I did nothing. What could I have done? He had no right to say what he did. But I was not going to justify myself before him. Still, he paralysed me. Because, you see, in a way he robbed me of – of my fury, of my indignation. He took it away, you see. He took away my indignation. Or at least a part of it. And I could see that he knew it, because he smiled at me in that kind of – well, patronizing way, you know, and I suddenly recalled that that was the way he smiled when we first met – in that dark little hole of a café."

"Are you sure you aren't reading things into that smile?" I asked.

"No, no. He knew that he had scored. He's a lawyer, after all. Or was."

"Then you think he asked you deliberately?"

"Oh, no. I don't think so. Not at first. But he realized that I was vulnerable as soon as he. . . ." He broke off and sat staring down at his hands.

"But why couldn't you say you'd gone into the station by accident, by a stroke of luck, and so. . . ."

"No," Theodore Stappler interrupted me. "I couldn't say that. Never. I just couldn't say it. I would have felt like the meanest of worms. No, no, I couldn't say that. Held and I are sailing in the same rotten boat."

He was outwardly very composed now. Slowly he leaned forward, stubbed his cigarette in the ashtray, and then sat back again. He locked his hands together and put them against his chin. Then he pursed his lips.

"I said before that whoever else stood behind Joseph Held and pushed him, even compelled him to act, there was nevertheless Held. He cannot escape his own responsibility." He spoke very softly. "But I," he said, speaking every word very clearly, very precisely, "but I was also there."

He got up abruptly and began to walk slowly up and down the room, as if I were not there at all. He stopped once in the middle of the room, staring long and hard at the tangled roots of my Emily Carr, and then he walked over to the painting and began to examine it closely and very methodically, his face nearly touching the canvas.

After a while Theodore Stappler turned around again and stood with his arms behind his back. "I was furious," he said. "Furious, I tell you. What right had he? But of course, even a rat will defend itself. Then Held got up and I had the clear feeling that he was no longer afraid of me. But I was wrong there. I was wrong. His voice gave him away. It was trembling. He said to me, 'Before I came you were here with my daughter. Did you. . .?' I knew at once that he was afraid to ask me, and I knew why, too. Because, you see, I could have said something that couldn't be reversed. Obviously he didn't want his daughter to know anything about those awful events. I knew it then, and I know it even better now. Once she knows, he won't be able to go on living. He wouldn't be able to face her. He would kill himself first."

Theodore Stappler fell silent and sat brooding, and I asked him if he meant that literally, and he said, yes, he did. He was sure, he repeated, that Held could not survive such an exposure. Katherine, said Stappler, was everything to her father. If life now had any meaning at all for Held, it was because of her.

"He finally got the question out," Theodore Stappler said. "He asked me, 'Did you say something to her?' I didn't answer him at once. I let him hang there, in suspense. He was sweating, and he mopped his face and the back of his neck with a large white handkerchief. But he gave himself away. At that moment I knew that I could dominate him through his daughter."

Theodore Stappler's eyes grew strangely hard and fierce. Hatred burned in them. I felt a sudden antagonism toward him. I was physically revolted, and I thought I would be sick. I put my hand up to my mouth. He saw the gesture.

"You disapprove?" he said.

"I feel sick. I feel like vomiting."

"Of course," he said. "I understand."

"You wouldn't," I said. "You wouldn't really use her?" I thought of her suddenly, how she had sat in my office and had told me of her desire to help some abandoned human beings, and here all the while this threat hung over her.

"Not now," he answered. "I wouldn't do it now. But at that moment. Certainly. I felt triumphant when I realized that I could have Held in my power. And why not? I had come all this way. Why? Surely to do something. I had come for revenge. What else? And he had paralysed me. He had taken my indignation – robbed me of it. We were two rats, each in his corner. Only now I found a – a way. . ."

I closed my eyes and felt the room swaying before me. I tried to understand him, tried to grasp the tangled web of his motives, his confusions, his frustrations.

"Then at last," Theodore Stappler went on, "I told him that I had said nothing to her, and he gave an enormous sigh of relief, of gratitude for all I know, and mopped his brow, and stammered, 'Thank God, thank God.' After a while he said, 'Mr. Stappler, let it be between you and me. Whatever you want from me, I will do. But don't let her know. Don't let her know.'

"I didn't answer him. I didn't commit myself to anything. I just said, 'We will see.' And then I went to the door and opened it and went out into the hall. There was nothing more I wanted to do there. I just wanted to get out, to get some fresh air, to be alone. He followed me like a dog with his tail between his legs. I put on my overshoes and my coat, and he just stood there looking at me, and I couldn't stand it. I couldn't stand myself. I was sick, I was disgusted, with myself, with Held, with the whole world. Then he began to plead with me again. Again and again he asked me not to tell her anything. I never answered. I said nothing, not even 'good night.' I just pulled open the front door and staggered out into the night, and I ran away, and once I stumbled and fell down in the snow and got up and ran and ran, the way I had in Saarbrücken on that cursed day."

X

"THE STREET," HE SAID, "WAS DARK AND I WAS ALL ALONE THERE. I was confused and I ran until the cold air got into my lungs and I couldn't run any longer and then I stopped and I was so confused that I didn't know where I was. I – I have to tell you that even though I was alone, there was no one in the street, still, for a few minutes when I first ran from the house I had the clear impression that somebody was running behind me, was following me. It was a kind of hallucination, I suppose. But I was sure that he was running behind me and that I was running away from him."

"Who was it?" I asked.

"I don't know. It was never clear. You see, I was alone, and at the same time I also thought there was someone else. It was strange."

"You didn't think it was Held, did you?"

"No. Definitely not Held. Somebody. I didn't know who. Just a – a man. But anyway, I was running away. I was fleeing. For a wild moment I even thought he was beside me, had caught up to me in fact. I thought I even saw him. He wore a brown coat – I saw that distinctly. But not his face. I never saw his face. It was a weird experience." Theodore Stappler put his hands up to his eyes, as if he were brushing cobwebs away. "Strange," he said, "what tricks you play on yourself. There was nobody, of course. I was all alone, in a dark and deserted street with snow on the ground."

"Well," I said, half playful, half serious, no doubt, thinking about all the ghosts of the past that were haunting him, "perhaps you weren't alone after all."

"What do you mean?" he asked.

"Nothing," I said, for I did not want to pursue this subject, "nothing really."

"Out of the darkness suddenly two lights came towards me," he continued. "And do you know," he gave a curious little laugh, "I didn't realize at first that it was a car. Just two yellow eyes came rushing at me out of the darkness. But I recovered from the first shock in time to recognize a taxi and I began to wave my hands about and he drew up to the curb and stopped, and I can tell you that never before has the inside of a car seemed so friendly to me. I got in beside the driver and it was warm in the taxi and the seat was soft. I could let myself relax. I could have stayed in that taxi all night. I didn't want to get out. I just wanted to stay there. I didn't want to speak, I didn't want to think about anything. I just wanted to stay where I was. So long as I was in the taxi, I could pretend that I was in limbo. I wasn't anywhere. In fact, when we stopped in front of my so-called hotel, the victory hotel!. . ." He chuckled softly, and repeated the phrase, "The victory hotel! Anyway, when we stopped in front of the hotel, I didn't make a move to get out until the driver said sharply, 'Hey, mister. This is it.' He was suspicious, I think, because I didn't say anything during the whole ride, though he tried to get a conversation going. But I just didn't want to talk. They must get lonely, these taxi-drivers, especially at night. I was almost going to tell him to keep driving, but at the last moment I decided not to. He was already getting impatient, and I don't even think he would have done it. So I crawled out of the taxi, and I gave him a fifty-cent tip just to make him feel ashamed or embarrassed because I was sure that he thought. . . Oh, well, what's the difference. God knows what he thought.

"I got out of the taxi and ran up the stairs to my room and I tore off my coat and my tie, just to breathe easier. That room – it felt terrible to be there. So bare. Like a cell. I wanted to rush away again, but where was there to go? So I turned out the light and lay down on the bed and tried to forget what had happened. But Joseph Held was there with me, in the room, inside my head, and I couldn't shut him out. I couldn't shut out what had happened. It kept turning and turning in my mind, and I tried to sort it all out, to come to some conclusion. To see where I stood now. To try to understand how things were, and what I should do next.

"I felt that I had come to a dead end. In a way we had reached a stalemate, Held and I. In a curious way we had found each other out. He found my weakness – by accident perhaps. But he found it. And I found his.

"But that was not how I imagined it would be. In a sense I was defeated. I began to think of what I should have done, how I should have acted. I should have been strong, I should have humbled him. I had that right, you know. At least so I thought. I think so now. But always, no matter how I started, no matter how I twisted, I always ended up in the same narrow alley, and I had to go up this alley and at the end of it there wasn't Held, there was just Stappler. Theodore Stappler. I myself, facing an emptiness."

"Well," I asked, "is there no way out? Do you have to go on? Can't you shut the door, after all these years?"

"I thought of that, too. And I wish in a way I could. I even thought that I would pack my bags and steal away. I thought I should do it. Held would never know. He would live all his life thinking I would come back again. Maybe tomorrow. Maybe next week. Maybe next month. He would never have any peace. And that would be a kind of torture. But I rejected it. It didn't satisfy me. Not now. I had come all this way. And for what?

"And then I would again be furious, and yet helpless, and there is nothing worse than that kind of – of impotent rage. *You*," he said suddenly, vehemently thrusting a finger at me, "what would you have done?"

And thus confronted, point-blank, I was much less sure than I had thought. The further pursuit of Held, whom I also saw as a victim, seemed to me a sad, almost a pointless endeavour, and yet, having come thus far, how could Theodore Stappler be expected to terminate the affair without, so to speak, having brought it to a proper kind of climax? Except, I thought, that the confrontation itself was a kind of climax. A bit ambiguous perhaps, climax becoming anti-climax, but even so a kind of resolution. And so I said again, more firmly than before, that he should close the door, because I could not see, I said, how he could ever accomplish anything that would not at once turn to gall.

He nodded his head, as if in agreement. He did not, I noted, accuse me of a Jove-like attitude, as he had done once or twice before.

Indeed, he said, looking at me, and yet curiously past me, if he had known then what he knew now, he would have left at once, that very night.

But the same demon, the same devil, he said, who had first

put that poison in his ear, whispered to him again as he lay there on the bed, tortured by self-doubt, that he should get at Held through Held's daughter. A charming girl, devoted to the father. Why not get to know her, cultivate her? He was aroused and excited by the thought. It was a delicious thought.

How, I asked him, could he be sure of doing that? He knew nothing about the girl, after all. For all he knew, she might have been engaged to someone, or if not, what was there to guarantee that she would be interested in him?

These considerations, he said, with an impatient wave of his hand, never entered his mind. Or if they did, they only added spice. He was sure of himself, he said, and smiled confidently, and now was all at once the dandy-like figure that I had first seen that afternoon.

Once he had thought of this new plan, he felt elated. He was no longer tortured. All his problems seemed, for the moment at least, to have solved themselves. The question of whether he should pack his bags and run away was now irrelevant. And what was more, what came as a blessed relief, he said, was that he did not have to think of himself any more. He could now think of the girl, of Katherine Held.

"Come now," I said. "You weren't thinking of her. You were still thinking of yourself. You were simply going to use her as a tool. A decoy to catch a man." I despised him.

"Of course," he said, quite matter-of-factly. "But what I mean is that I no longer had to circle round and round the vomit, like a dog. I had made a decision and it seemed for the moment to solve my dilemma. It led me out of the *cul de sac*. Or so I thought. Of course it didn't. It led me deeper into it. But I couldn't know this at the time. I didn't think the matter through. I was too elated. I jumped up and walked around my room – my cell – and laid my plans and I got more and more excited. I put my tie back on and went down to the restaurant and ate with great relish, thinking all the time of my campaign. I would make Held sweat and I would watch the spectacle. He could never know what I might say to her. And that would be my revenge. To see him sweat."

"And when you had used her," I said to him, "what then? What were you going to do then?"

He shrugged his shoulders.

"You were going to toss her aside," I said. "Like a lemon that's been squeezed dry, eh?"

"The trouble is," he said drily, "that you never think about these things at the time. You're – well, driven on. Possessed, I suppose. Half the time you don't know what you're really doing. Until suddenly you see, and then it's too late."

"Then it *is* too late?" I asked.

"Yes," he said, "yes, in a way it is. That's why I'm sitting here talking to you. Why do you think I'm telling you all this?"

"I don't know," I said.

"Because I feel the need to talk to someone," he said. "I must tell someone. . . . And then perhaps I'll know what to do."

He was a pathetic figure, too, I thought. A man obsessed, caught in a net of circumstances, all entangled, and desperately trying to get free.

"Do you mean," I asked him, "that I should tell you what to do?"

"No, no," he said quickly. "There's nothing you can say to me – except," he added, in a dry, ironic tone, "to moralize and to look properly shocked whenever my conduct doesn't come up to whatever it is you think proper."

I felt myself blushing and was about to defend myself, but he held up his hand. "Don't answer me," he said. "I'm grateful to you all the same. Just for listening. I've been honest with you because I want to be honest with myself."

"Look," I said. "I don't want you to come up to any proper standards. I don't want to play the judge. I've told you that."

"I know," he said. "But you can't help it anyway. You judge all the time. And in a way that's right. That's right. That's how it should be. But I won't see you again after this," he added enigmatically, "and so I speak to you without fear of shame." He looked away from me, towards his feet.

After a while he continued, speaking in a dry tone, to tell me how he went about making contact with Katherine Held. The first thing he did the next morning, he said, was to phone down to the University to find out when and where I lectured on French history. That information was not, of course, hard to come by, and two days later, on a Thursday, he came down to the University and waited outside the lecture-room. When the bell rang and the students came out of the lecture-room, he did not at first see her. She was one of the last to appear because she had stopped to talk to me. At last she came out. In the hall she stopped briefly and talked for a moment to another girl and then went on alone.

She walked out of the building, hesitated, and then, before he had time to duck, for he was not yet ready to reveal himself to her, was in fact still wondering what would be the best moment to make the plunge, she turned, pushed the doors open again, and practically bumped into him.

She gave a little cry of surprise, and then looked at him with wide-open eyes, as if he were some kind of apparition.

They were standing there, blocking the way, and so they stepped to one side. He was extremely embarrassed, Theodore Stappler said to me, almost as if he had been caught breaking into her room.

"What are you doing here?" she asked. It was, he said to me, half a question and half a challenge.

He told her, facetiously, that he was a tourist, after all, and that he had come to see the sights of the city.

"And did you find what you came looking for?" she asked him.

"Yes, indeed," he said. "I found what I was looking for. Especially now."

She didn't say anything but just looked at him, and he got the clear impression that she knew he had come to find her.

So her told her it would be wrong to say he hadn't hoped he might run into her.

"And you did," she said. "Run into me."

Now that he had, by some lucky coincidence, indeed run into her, he said, perhaps they could go to some place where it was easier and more comfortable to talk.

She seemed to be trying to make up her mind, but as she stood there, somewhat indecisively, Theodore Stappler said to me, he suddenly got the impression, though there was nothing really to go on, that she had expected him.

Without saying anything, she turned and led the way out of the building and he followed her. She didn't talk to him as they walked but contrived somehow to keep a step or two ahead of him. She led him across the campus, to the tuck shop, where they found an empty booth and sat down, and then he went to the counter and got two cups of coffee and brought them to their table.

"How odd," she said, "that you should run into me."

"Yes," he said. But suddenly, he didn't know quite why, he got the impulse to tell her the truth. "I didn't run into you," he said quietly. "I came to find you."

She only raised her eyebrows, but once again he had the distinct impression that she wasn't really too surprised.

"I apologize," he said. "I hope you're not angry."

"Angry?" she said. "No. I'm not angry. I'm amused."

"Why?"

"Because you went through these extraordinary — manoeuvres," she said. "Almost like some — no, I'm not going to say it."

He waited for her to say it nevertheless, but she never did, and he never did find out exactly what she had in mind. But she laughed and her laughter, he said to me, embarrassed him, because he felt that she regarded his approach as somehow melodramatic, and he was sorry that he had not persisted in his original light-hearted explanation — that he had come to look at the University and had met her by chance.

When she asked him why he wanted to see her, he had to go on with a more or less romantic pose. "I wanted to see you again," he said, "because I had so little chance to talk to you the other night. I was sorry you had to leave so quickly. I enjoyed talking to you. You were so charming."

"Are you flattering me?" she asked.

"No," he said. "It's the truth."

"We have a telephone," she said.

"I don't like to telephone," he said.

She changed the subject abruptly. "How did my father look to you?" she asked. "After all these years. He has changed a lot, hasn't he?"

The question put him on his guard, and he said non-committally, "Of course. Time has passed and we're all older."

"Yes," she said. "He hasn't had an easy time. He was never really successful here, you know. His profession wasn't of much use to him. He couldn't do much with it."

He wondered, he told me, what she was driving at. Had Held told her anything, and was she now trying to work up sympathy for him? But that seemed unlikely on the face of it. Held would move heaven and earth to prevent her from knowing anything about the real reason why Theodore Stappler had sought him out.

"He never felt at home here," the girl went on. "He was always very restless. In the last year or so his heart has been giving him trouble."

Theodore Stappler mumbled that he was sorry. She sipped her coffee slowly and kept looking at him, he said to me, as if she were turning some things over in her mind, and then at last she said, almost as if she were challenging him, "I thought you were my father's friend."

He sought refuge behind a non-committal, "How do you mean?"

"That was the impression you gave me when you first came to our house."

"That is not what I said," he countered. "I merely said I knew your father." Then he added, "Did your father not confirm that?"

"My father said he hardly remembered you. He said you'd once been a client of his."

"Yes," Theodore Stappler said, "I suppose I was that."

"My father also said," she went on, "that you hadn't been quite satisfied with the way he handled your case."

How much, he wondered, had Held actually told her? In any case, it was clear to him that whatever he had told her had been enormously distorted.

"Well," he answered, very cautiously, "it is possible to put the matter that way."

"What exactly was involved in the case?" she asked. He got the clear impression that she was really trying to get him to reveal things she didn't know, and he in his turn decided to try to find out exactly how much she knew.

"It all happened a long time ago," he answered her. "In another country and in another place. It's all very complicated."

"My father said something about money. . . ."

"Money was involved," he interrupted her, "but it is not of the first importance."

"My father is an honest man," she said.

"I have no doubt," he said.

"If it is at all possible," she continued, "he will repay you. He told me that."

"He must have misunderstood me," Theodore Stappler said, "if he gave you the impression that I came for money."

"Why did you come?" she asked.

"For no particular purpose," he said. "As I told you, I happened to be passing through the city. I had heard that your father was here and I thought that I would call on him and clear the matter up once and for all. Write an end to it. I will confess to you that it bothered me – your father's handling of my case."

"A lawyer and his client can be in disagreement," she said.

"My father told me that he couldn't act in any other way. He had to act the way he did. He said he coudn't handle your case in any other way."

"That," said Theodore Stappler, "will always remain a matter for debate. But I don't want to pursue it – certainly not with you. Why should you be involved? You were a small child when it happened. I don't want to drag you into the affair."

He turned to me and said that he was, of course, not frank when he told her that. For he meant to involve her.

"I hope to see your father again," he said, "and I hope we will be able to settle the matter. But please tell your father that he must not think that I want any money. That is the last thing I want. . . .

"I bear no grudges," he continued after a while. "No grudges at all." Once again of course he was less than frank with her. "I am alone here," he said, now playing openly for her sympathy. "I have some business to do here in this city that will keep me here a week, perhaps two, perhaps even longer. I get very lonely."

He went on, he told me, to paint a gloomy picture of long and lonely evenings in provincial cities, with nothing to do except perhaps go to a movie now and then. That was why it was such an unexpected pleasure for him when he met her the other evening. It was not often, he said, that one met a young and beautiful girl with whom it was possible to carry on an intelligent and spirited conversation. He had to see her again. And that, he said, was the real reason why he had gone out of his way to find her. He didn't want to talk about dreary legal entanglements that were long past and forgotten. It was the present he cared about.

He would be most pleased, he said, if she would agree to have dinner with him some evening.

"And she agreed?" I asked.

"Of course," said Theodore Stappler.

I thought I detected a kind of self-satisfied leer, but that may have been merely my imagination playing tricks on me. There was, however, an unmistakable smugness in that "of course," as if one of Don Juan's conquests had been questioned. Theodore Stappler clearly saw himself as irresistible, and I knew, of course, that his involvement with Katherine Held had moved considerably further from that point, though exactly where it stood now I didn't know.

"She agreed," Theodore Stappler said. "Now I almost wish she had refused, but at the time I was naturally very pleased because the first step of my plan was working out perfectly. I would call for her, and her father would see us going off together, and I knew he would go through hell, and that was exactly what I wanted." He paused for a few moments, and then said slowly, "I couldn't know where all this would lead me. The plans one makes are always so neat, so perfect. And then what really happens. . . . Well, it is all very different."

So they arranged to meet the following evening. He was to call for her at six o'clock.

All that day, and all the next day, he walked about in a curious state – a mixture of excitement, elation, and fear. He felt like a hunter, who could see his prey approaching the trap and was now only waiting for the inevitable end. When the time came at last he took a taxi to Held's house, wondering whether Held himself would be there. He asked the taxi-driver to wait, and when he rang the bell, Katherine opened the door. He helped her on with her coat, asking off-handedly if her father was at home. She said no, he wasn't. She seemed to him rather distracted. Her face looked pale, but he thought it was the black dress that made it look so.

He took her arm, and they got into the taxi, and he told the driver to take them downtown. She sat looking straight ahead, and she seemed suddenly very aloof. When he asked her where she wanted to have dinner, she said it made no difference to her, and he said that perhaps she might like to eat at the Macdonald Hotel, and she nodded her head.

There were few people in the large, panelled dining-room and, after they had given their orders to the waiter, and she still sat there very quietly, he asked her why she was so downcast. Had it anything to do with him? Was she sorry that she had accepted his invitation?

She was slowly turning the glass of water that the waiter had poured for her, and it seemed to him a long, long time before she answered, very hesitantly, that her father had been very upset when she told him.

He ought to have been pleased, he said to me, because this was, after all, exactly the effect he had hoped to achieve. But he found that he wasn't really pleased at all, but on the contrary, rather annoyed. That was a strange reaction.

"Aren't you old enough to make your own decisions?" he asked her.

That remark seemed to touch a sensitive nerve, for she said rather aggressively, "Of course. That's not in question. But I –

don't want to hurt my father – needlessly. He has no one now. And besides. . . ."

"Besides what?" he asked, when she didn't finish her sentence.

"Well, let me be honest," she said. "I – I was rather taken with you when I first met you the other evening. I know I shouldn't say that. It's not playing the game right." She smiled. "And then when you came looking for me, I thought that was rather – well, perhaps a bit unusual. But I was also pleased."

"Well," he said, "I'm at least glad to hear that."

"But then, you see," she went on, "when I told my father he said that – "

It was a while before she could make herself go on. Or so it seemed. "He told me," she said at last, "that you were not an honest man, that you were – " She gave him a long, long look. "Well, I'll be honest, that you were a – a coward and – well, I won't repeat any more of what my father said."

Theodore Stappler turned to me. "That," he said, "was the last thing I expected. It took me completely by surprise. I was unprepared, although I should have expected some kind of counter-move on his part."

"And what did you do?" I asked him.

"I asked her what charges her father had brought against me. Evidently he had told her that I had run away and left him alone at a time when he needed me to be present, and that now *I* accused *him* of not having acted properly, and that I had come to collect money he had spent at the time in the interest of my case. These were fantastic distortions, and for a moment I was so angry – the waiter had just brought our soup, but I could hardly hold my spoon – I was so angry that I nearly told her there and then why I had really come, why I had searched for him, but I stopped myself in time. I had my own cards to play, after all. A coward – well, of course. I could be accused of that, though Held of all people didn't have the right to – well, no point going into that matter." He made an impatient gesture with his hands. "But more. Whatever else it was he had accused me of, it was really too much. But still I realized in time – just in time – that if I made counter-accusations, I would lose her sympathy at once. He would deny everything I said, anyway. It would be just my word against his. And naturally she would believe him. And why not? Who was I? Some stranger, blown in by the wind. A nobody who went around the country selling encyclopedias. But still, evidently I had made some kind of impression on her. She *was* pleased that I had called on her, if in a slightly unorthodox fashion. I didn't want to destroy whatever impression I had made. I had to win her confidence if I were to have any chance at all, and so I just said that she would have to judge for herself what I was.

"So that was how the evening started," he went on after a few moments. "A pretty strained note, to put it mildly. But after that things eased a little. We found it very easy to talk to each other, and toward the end of the dinner we were talking as if nothing had happened earlier on. Who knows, the thought that she was dining with a disreputable character might even have been faintly exciting to her. She drew me out about my past, and I made things sound – well, I suppose 'romantic' is the word. The dreariest things, if they are far enough away in time and if they happened in distant places can sound exotic enough.

"We finished our meal, and I asked her if she wanted to go to a movie. She agreed and we walked out of the hotel. It was cold and I took her arm. She drew close to me, perhaps even a little closer than was strictly necessary. At least I got that impression. It may just have been the cold. Then we sat there together in the dark theatre, and after a decent interval I found her hand, quite by accident, you understand."

"Of course," I said, and we both laughed.

"It was an awful picture," he said. "Dull and boring. After a decent interval I drew her somewhat closer to me, and that felt pleasant. So we sat close together, the coward, the. . . God knows what, and that young girl. I was sorry when the picture was over and the lights went on, because for a while I'd forgotten, well, almost forgotten why I was really there. And when we walked out I felt depressed because I didn't want to deceive the girl, and yet what could I do? I didn't want to tell her what I had really come for. And now I suddenly knew even less than before what I should do."

He lapsed into silence. Then he went on again. "We went into a restaurant to have some coffee and talked again. She was so spontaneous – so, in a way, innocent – that the thought of using her in some kind of, well, diabolical scheme was suddenly impossible for me to contemplate. I decided that I wouldn't go through with it, that I would terminate everything. I wouldn't use her. And I would have done it, I swear I would have left the very next day, if Held had not. . . ." He interrupted himself. "But let me tell you everything in order, because if I tell you everything in order, then perhaps in the end I'll know what to do."

He went on to tell me, then, how they arrived again at the house, and how, even as Katherine fumbled in her bag to find the key, the door was suddenly and, so it seemed, violently opened, and Joseph Held stood there, his face red, his hands clenched.

"Mr. Stappler!" He very nearly bellowed the name, he was so furious.

He seemed to be barring the way to Theodore Stappler. So sudden and unexpected was the action that Stappler himself did not know what to do. He very nearly turned to slink away, since he felt in any case uncomfortable, not to say guilty, about the motives that had led him to establish contact with Held's daughter.

But it was Katherine Held who saved him. For she was plainly shocked and outraged by this reception. Theodore Stappler could tell that by the tone in which she said, "Father!" And then she pushed past her father and, in a clear gesture of defiance, held out her hand and pulled Theodore Stappler gently into the house. Then she closed the door.

But Held was not to be so easily put off. He now appeared calmer. He turned to Stappler and said that he did not want him to abuse his daughter. But though he spoke softly now, there was still a menacing undertone in his voice. Katherine clearly sensed it, for she answered sharply and said that she had not been abused, and that she was old enough to look after herself. Held said stubbornly that whatever she might wish, he did not want to welcome Theodore Stappler into his house.

All at once she stiffened and said coldly that Mr. Stappler was *her* guest and that, as long as she lived in this house, she would have the right to invite her own guests.

He felt, Theodore Stappler said, hot under the collar. The situation had taken a grotesque, absurd turn, and he wanted only to get away and never to come back.

He said that he was sorry, that he did not wish to cause dissension between the father and the daughter. He thanked her for a very pleasant evening and said, with as much dignity as he could muster, that he hoped she would not believe anything too slanderous that was said about him. He said that pointedly. And, using the phrase that Held himself so liked to use, he said that he was an honourable man. He hoped she would believe him, all the more so since it was likely that he would not see her again.

And with that he went past Joseph Held and opened the door and walked away.

He was now really determined, he said, to terminate the whole affair, since it was clear that he had not found his way out of the *cul de sac* but on the contrary had only gone deeper into it. What he had imagined had turned out to be very different when he was actually trying to carry it out. And there was no pleasure, no satisfaction, only annoyance, especially when he thought that his name was being blackened by Held and yet he could do nothing about it. So the final victory seemed somehow to be Held's, although, said Theodore Stappler and shrugged his shoulders ironically, it was a hollow victory. Really a stalemate, he said. Two hollow men, he said, pointing at himself with one hand and gesturing with the other vaguely into the distance, had run into each other and there was some noise, and then a great void, a nothing.

Deflated, he went back to his room. Further pursuit seemed pointless, and he began, listlessly, to pack his bags.

He would undoubtedly have left the next day if there had not been a telephone call for him from Katherine Held the next morning.

He did not at first suspect, when Sam called him to the phone, who could possibly want to speak to him, and he thought at first that it was all a mistake. But then he heard her voice, timid, uncertain, as if she were not quite sure she was doing the right thing.

She had to speak to him, she said. She wanted to apologize for what had happened last night. Her father was excited. He didn't know what he was doing, she said. She felt very badly, and so. . .

He was quite stunned, and when her voice trailed off and she was evidently waiting for him to speak, he didn't know what to say and could only stammer that it was not necessary for her to apologize, that he did not hold anything against her. Then, because he could think of nothing else to say, he asked her to meet him again, and he was surprised when she seemed eager to agree, and they arranged to meet that very day at noon to have lunch together.

"So it began," said Theodore Stappler and crossed his legs and looked at me. "My real involvement. Against my will. Against my better judgement. But. . . ." He shrugged his shoulders. He was very calm now. "Held obviously made a great mistake. His action turned her against him. It was the last thing I would have thought of. But there you are. And what can you do? Well, we met, and again we found it easy to make contact. And after that, everything was easy. She began to talk about her father, and again she apologized for him. You know – she was sorry and all that. I told her I didn't want to know anything about that. What was between her father and me shouldn't concern her. As far as she was concerned, I said, the matter should be closed. And when she began to be more insistent, asking me again and again what had happened and what she could do to smooth things over – well, I just repeated again what I had told her before, and then I said that I didn't want to talk about it, and I told her not to ask me. Like Lohengrin, you know," he said and smiled broadly. "*Nie sollst du mich befragen.* Don't ask me who I am or where I come from – that sort of nonsense. I was firm. So we talked about other things. Then we arranged to meet again on the weekend.

"What is there to do in this town? One eats. One goes to the movies. One sleeps. We went to see a picture, and afterwards I asked her to come to my room, since I didn't want to be thrown out by her father again. She agreed. It all seemed the most natural thing in the world. We sat and talked and flirted and held hands, and then I put my arms around her and kissed her. But nothing more. Not that evening. We just sat together, and it was all very nice and very peaceful. I was very restrained.

"We met again. And then again. I've been with other women, but there was something particularly – what shall I say? – exciting, I suppose, about her. For me at least. I don't know quite what it was or why I felt that way. It's hard to say exactly what I mean.

"We lay together on my bed – she took off her dress so it wouldn't get all crumpled up . . . . You smile? But it's really true. Anyway, I felt wonderful. It was a very beautiful moment. She was very soft, and I wanted the moment to go on and on. I must sound very sentimental. And I was of course – very sentimental, I mean. Because I did something which I can't understand even yet. I hadn't thought it out at all. But suddenly I asked her if she could ever imagine marrying a man like me. It wasn't quite a proposal, of course, but it was close. It could be taken seriously. Her heart was beating against my hand. Like a little bird's. And suddenly I asked that question. . . . I would do it again, you know. I would do it again. But I regretted the words as soon as I had spoken them. That very moment."

"And she said yes, I suppose, she would only be too delighted to marry a man like you."

"You needn't be ironic, Herr Professor," he said. "As a matter of fact she didn't. She was surprised, of course. But not more surprised than I was at myself, I can tell you that. She said I must be joking, and I had to assure her that I was not. I had to do this in self-defence, you know. And I wasn't of course joking. I was quite sincere. At that moment certainly, with her beside me on the bed. But the implications – well, that is another matter. Perhaps," he went on, talking more to himself than to me. "perhaps I thought that I could somehow undo – somehow get out. . . ."

He stopped.

"Yes?" I said, prodding him.

"Well," he said, "I had come all this way to wrestle with the ghosts of the past. And slimy ghosts they are, God knows. Well, I found the ghosts, but something else, too. Something very simple and in its own way very pure. A —a lyrical relationship. At least for the time being. And so perhaps something might be saved, and a new start made. But of course," he concluded sadly, "that's all a dream. An illusion, really. . . . But we have gone on, these three weeks or so, like two romantic lovers sharing some kind of secret. And now it can't go on very much longer. Lohengrin must say who he is and what his prospects are, and above all why he came. And this Lohengrin certainly didn't come to rescue a pure and innocent young girl.

"And yet – to make the relationship honest, the past has to be revealed. . . . But what then? I would triumph over the father once and for all. Or would I really? In any case the triumph would be hollow, completely hollow. I don't want it. And then, what of the pain I would cause her? What would it do to her? Why should she be crushed? I could, of course, break the whole thing off and leave without any explanation. This would cause her a different kind of pain. And then I would confirm everything that her father said about me – that I am unreliable, that I am a scoundrel."

"But if you were very deeply in love with her," I said, "if you really felt passionately, would there be any choice? Any real choice? Would you give a damn about the consequences?"

"You try to make the thing too simple," he said.

He rose abruptly and signified clearly that he did not wish to pursue the subject any further.

"It's very late," he said. "I apologize for keeping you up so late." He looked at his watch. "My God! Five o'clock. And you have to get up early."

"Please," I said. "You needn't apologize."

"I must get a taxi," he said.

"I tell you what," I said. "It may be some time before you can get a taxi. Stay the night. This chesterfield can be turned into a bed."

He seemed to hesitate.

"It's really no trouble," I said.

So he consented. I went to get some linen and some blankets, and together we made up his bed.

"You have been very kind," he said. "I had no right really to barge in and involve you."

"Not at all," I said.

"But I neeeded someone to talk to, and you have been of great help."

"Well, it's nice of you to say so. But I don't see in what way I helped. At times I thought. . . ."

"No, no. You helped me. I had to put some things in order. And you helped me. I see my way clearer now. Not yet clear. But clearer, anyway."

I left the room to let him undress, and then I looked in again after a few minutes and was astonished to find that he had fallen asleep. I turned out the light and went into my bedroom.

But, unlike Theodore Stappler, I could not sleep. I was too exhausted. His presence was everywhere. It enveloped me. I could hear his deep breathing, almost as if he were sleeping beside me.

At six o'clock I had still not fallen asleep, and so I got up and sat down and picked up a book – on Robespierre, as it happened – and read. At eight o'clock I made a pot of coffee and boiled an egg. I had breakfast. All the while he slept.

I left the apartment at half-past eight and drove over to the University to give a lecture. Afterwards I felt so exhausted that I could not go up to my office and instead drove home again.

Theodore Stappler had left. There was a note on the coffee table. He thanked me for all I had done and said that he would take the liberty to get in touch with me again.

I stretched out on my bed and after a while I fell asleep. At one o'clock the phone rang.

"Herr Professor," said the familiar ironic voice.

"Yes," I mumbled.

I was still drowsy, but even so I was at once aware of the changed tone in his voice when he said, "You must come to see me. I have something to tell you." The voice was firm, imperious even, and I was annoyed and was clearing my throat to refuse, when he said somewhat less abruptly, "It is very important for me. Please come."

The "please" mollified me.

"Well," I said, "if it is important to you. . . ." I tried to put an ironic edge on the words, but he missed the irony.

"It is important," he said. "I must see you."

"Well, if you must. . . ."

"At four oclock," he said, without even giving me a chance to finish my sentence. "In the restaurant with the dragon, just below the Hotel Victoria. I'll be waiting for you there."

Again I felt annoyed with him, with his easy assumption that he could summon me without taking into acount whether or not I could really spare the time. But yet I had no intention of refusing him, and he seemed to know that I would somehow find the time, even if it meant postponing other important matters. The fact that he knew this annoyed me even more. Yet I could not refuse, and I could not even register my annoyance.

"You will come," he said.

And I answered, almost meekly, "Yes."

❦ XI

WHY DID I SO READILY CONSENT TO COME TO HIM? WHY DID I NOT simply say that I was busy and wouldn't be able to see him that afternoon? I could then have withdrawn gracefully and washed my hands of the whole affair. But of course I couldn't do that. For he had involved me, subtly and in a sense against my will. He had disturbed the order of my life, and I found myself once again resenting his intrusion. Then, too, a part of my consciousness whispered to me that the events of the past had perhaps best be forgotten, had perhaps best be covered by merciful and forgetful snow. Yet there he was, this stranger who had suddenly burst in on me, and he wouldn't allow it. He dug it all up, like a dog suddenly uncovering a mouldering bone.

What now? I felt that in an odd sort of way Theodore Stappler wanted my approval. I realize that this is an arrogant assertion, for what difference could it make to him whether I approved of his actions or not? I knew that nothing I had to say would in any way change his mind. He would do whatever he decided to do. And yet he wanted my approval. I was sure of it. Or else why had he told me so much? Why had he chosen me as his confidant? Somewhere in that vast and indifferent world which he inhabited, he had to find someone with whom he could share his burden and, whatever the reason, he had chosen me. By accident, simply, because a young girl had decided to write an essay about a peculiar assassination.

I wondered what more he had to tell me, and I came to the conclusion that it must have something to do with the decision he now had to make. I began to feel restless. I could think of nothing except Theodore Stappler and Katherine Held, and the pathetic figure of her father hovering in the background. I tried to read some essays I had brought home with me, but I could not concentrate and stopped reading.

At three o'clock I left my apartment and drove downtown. I didn't want to arrive early, and so I parked my car and went into one of the large department stores and strolled about aimlessly for half an hour, looking at things, and then I went out again and drove the several blocks to the Hotel Victoria.

All through the day the sky had been darkening, and now it was all overcast, and snow flurries were beginning to drift down. There would be a lot of snow. In the dull light of the afternoon the city seemed to have drawn into itself. The clouds seemed suddenly low, so that I had the feeling that I could reach out my hand and touch them. When I got out of my car, the buildings on either side of the street seemed to have moved nearer to each other and I felt for a moment as if I were enclosed in an enormous room with a massive grey ceiling and sombre, red, impenetrable walls.

The neon signs were already on, and the green and red dragon, of whose splendour Theodore Stappler had spoken the night before, now beckoned to me. Only I didn't think it very splendid. It was just a commercial, tame-looking, neon dragon.

I walked into the restaurant and looked about for Theodore Stappler, but he was not there. And this surprised me, since it was now five minutes past four, and the urgency with which he summoned me had made me expect that he would be waiting for me. I went up to the cashier and described Theodore Stappler to her and asked her if she had seen him. She knew him at once and said that he had been in the restaurant only about ten minutes ago but had suddenly left. She didn't know where he had gone.

I decided then to go into the hotel and see if he had perhaps gone up to his room. I walked up the linoleum-covered stairs, into the room marked OFFICE, and there at once I recognized Sam, looking exactly as Theodore Stappler had described him, sitting in his shirt sleeves, with his feet up on a rickety wooden desk, as if indeed he had not moved from this spot since the moment Theodore Stappler had first walked in a few weeks ago.

"Yeah," he said, hardly looking at me. "Anything I can do for you?"

I told him that I was looking for Theodore Stappler.

"Oh, him," he said. "He isn't here. He went down to the restaurant a little while ago."

"I was supposed to meet him there," I said, "but he isn't there, and the girl at the cashier's desk said that he'd left."

"Well, I've been sitting here all the time, and he hasn't come back up again."

"You must be Sam," I said.

"Yeah," he said. "How do you know?"

"Stappler told me about you," I said.

"Say. Are you a friend of his?" he asked.

"Well – yes, in a way."

"What do you mean, in a way? A guy is either my friend or he isn't my friend. Is that guy a friend of yours?"

"I suppose. I haven't known him very long."

"You know, I've been wondering. Exactly what does this guy do for a living?

"I think he's selling encyclopedias," I said.

"Sure," said Sam. "Only this is a helluva time to sell encyclopedias. In the snow and in the ice and just after Christmas and New Year's at that. Everybody's broke."

"Well," I said, "I think he's just scouting around. If he sees that there are good prospects around here, his firm might send him back again. At least that's what he told me."

"That guy tells a lot of stories," Sam said. "I kinda like him, though. He comes in here to pass the time o' day and we talk. I'm still trying to figure him out, though. Well, it takes all kinds, I guess. . . . Siddown, will ya? He's bound to come back pretty soon. Where can he go?" He looked out the window. "It's snowing pretty good now," he said. "So he'll be back."

I sat down.

"You know this friend of yours real good?" Sam asked.

"I don't really know," I answered. "I do and I don't.'

"Say, what is this?' said Sam, with a show of great indignation. "You and he brothers or something? Why'n't you talk like ordinary guys? You do and you don't! You know, when he first got here he told me he was everybody and nobody. What kind of a deal is that? You don't take old Sam like that. I wasn't born yesterday."

"I don't want to take you," I said, quite unprepared for this sudden outburst.

"What's your name, anyway?" he asked belligerently, as if I

had just been brought into a police station and he were interrogating me.

"Lerner," I found myself answering meekly. "Mark Lerner."

"Yeah?" he said, as if he didn't quite believe me. "Lerner, eh?"

Footsteps coming up the stairs spared me further interrogation, at least for the time being.

"That's not your friend," said Sam. "That's Number Six. I can tell by the way he walks up the stairs. Guys like him oughta pay more. They damn near wreck the building."

"Number Six" came into the office. Morosely and without saying anything, he held out a large hand, took the key Sam gave him and stalked out again, silently, like a bear.

"Big talker, Number Six," said Sam. "He hasn't said ten words since he's been here. Over a week now." He turned his attention on me again. "Lerner," he pondered, "Mark Lerner. I didn't meet you some place by any chance?"

"No," I said, "I don't think so.'

"What do you do?" he asked, and added, "For a living, I mean."

"I teach at the University," I told him. "I teach history."

"History?" he repeated. "Like what happened, eh? All about those dead kings and those screwy battles. Man, did I ever hate that stuff when I was in school. I could never remember nothing. Who needs it, anyways?"

I shrugged my shoulders and smiled at him.

"You know," he said, "you guys with all that expensive education, you should tell us what's going to happen – tomorrow or the next year. The future. That's what I want to know. Like f'r instance, who's going to win on the Woodbine in the third. That would be something really worth knowing about. Listen," he continued, with sudden, great animation. "You got three days racing, see, and you figure on betting six races each day. Eighteen races. Now you put four bucks on the first race, and you win. You just let that money ride. You get it? You just let it ride."

I nodded, to signify that I had got it.

"Well, then you just keep betting, see, and you call winners on every race. Seventeen more times you bet and you win every time. But you just keep letting your money ride. You just plough your winnings right back again, and you keep calling those winners. You know how much you make for yourself in those three days?"

I said I didn't know.

"Fourteen million bucks," said Sam triumphantly, "give or take a million, depending on the odds. That's Sam's method!" he exclaimed and hit the table with the flat of his hand. "You know what the odds are of pulling off that kind of a deal?" he asked.

He waited dramatically.

I could only shake my head.

With a great flourish, he opened a drawer in his desk and pulled out a worn and raggedy newspaper clipping. He read with all due solemnity. "A hunnert and twenty-four million, two hunnert fifty-six thousand six hunnert and sixteen to one."

He carefully stowed the clipping away again. "How do you like that?" he said.

I said that I would settle for winning on an Irish sweepstake ticket. A mere hundred thousand or so.

"Oh, sure," he said. "In a pinch I would settle for that. But if you could work the other!" He mused silently for a while, and then continued, sadly, "The only trouble is that I would lose the dough anyway. It doesn't matter how much it was. I'd lose it. On the ponies the next time or in a bunch of crap games. I could never hang onto any money, if you know what I mean. You take my brother now, he can hang onto money like he was a leech or something. Matter of fact, you give him a dollar, he can squeeze an extra cent out of it. For me the dollar is worth ninety cents to start with."

"A lot of people seem to have that trouble," I said.

"Not my brother," said Sam. "He started with nothing, and now he owns this joint and that Chinese restaurant downstairs."

"He's not Chinese, though," I threw in facetiously.

"You kidding?" he said. "Do I look like a Chinese? My mother never slept with nobody except my old man. At least I don't think so. Naw, he's Jewish and he hires himself a Chinese cook. He makes out okay." He put a cigarette in his mouth, and then began frisking his own pockets, searching for a match.

I happened to have some matches, and I lit one and held it out for him. He took two deep puffs from his cigarette, held the smoke and then exhaled it slowly from his mouth and nostrils and watched with a kind of fascination as it curled lazily up towards the ceiling. Then, casually, he asked, "You Jewish by any chance?"

"Yes," I said.

"I thought so," he said. "Where you from?"

"Toronto," I said.

"What d'you know?" he said. "That's where I'm from. I lived there until two years ago, but then my brother needed somebody to run this joint for him, so I came up here. I was broke, anyway, so what did I have to lose? Was you born in Toronto?"

I said that I was.

"I wasn't," he said. "I was born in the old country. Poland. I don't remember nothing about it, though. I was still wetting diapers when my mother brought me here. My old man'd come out first, like. He was getting fed up with the old country. He was sick right up to here with being a sitting duck in pogroms and all that sort o' thing, so he packed up and got out. Lucky thing, too. If he hadn't of got fed up we'd all be dead now, my brothers and sisters, me, everybody. Like all my uncles and aunts and their children, and all the others. They stayed put and then the war came, and you know what happened."

I nodded my head.

"Gas chambers. Concentration camps," he said. "Oh, Christ! . . . One of my cousins got out alive. He came over here after the war. You know, sometimes I wonder how that guy can live with all the memories." He fell silent and concentrated on the smoke from his cigarette.

"Everybody has memories," I said.

"Sure," he said "Some more, some less. That friend of yours. He's got a memory or two. He was over there, you know."

"Yes," I said. "I know."

"You don't give much away, do you?"

"How do you mean?"

"You just tell me what I know already."

"What else do you want to know?"

"I want to know what kind of a *Luftmensch* that guy is."

I merely grinned at him but didn't say anything.

"You guys sure play this close to the chest," Sam went on. "I tell you something, though. He keeps bringing a pretty little number up to his room."

"Oh," I said.

"You know what I think," he said. "I think that little girl is riding for a hard fall."

"What do you mean?" I asked.

"Well, you know. That kind of a guy. Comes and goes. Like I said. A *Luftmensch*. The wind blows him here and then it blows him off somewhere else. And she isn't gonna blow with him."

"How do you know?"

"I just know," he said. "I think also she's pretty stuck on him, and she's gonna be one mighty sad little girl one of these days. Yes, sir, that's what I think."

"How do you know all that?" I asked.

"I keep my ears open," he said. "I get tired of sitting here and so I keep wandering up and down that corridor, and the walls here are not of the best, if you know what I mean. So I keep hearing a thing or two, and then I put two and two together. And speaking of two and two, there's your friend coming up the stairs. Anybody stays here longer than two days, boy, I can tell their steps a mile away." He spoke with pride. "Yes, sir, old Sam here sure keeps his eyes and his ears open."

Theodore Stappler came slowly up the stairs, stopped outside the office, looked in, and saw me.

"Forgive me," he said, in his most polite voice. "I didn't mean to let you wait. But I couldn't help it. We might as well go to my room now. . . . Hello, Sam," he said turning from me. "Thanks for keeping my friend warm."

"Aw, nuts," said Sam and smiled. "You are entirely welcome . . . . Nice meeting you," he said to me. "Come up again when you have nothing to do. I always like to pass the time of day."

Theodore Stappler and I walked down the dusty corridor. He was very serious. He said nothing but walked with long strides until he came to his room, fumbled with the lock, then opened the door and with a polite gesture beckoned me to go in first.

The room was quite dark. On the marquee of a run-down cinema across the street, neon lights flickered on and off and illuminated patches here and there, and huge shadows crawled along the walls. Theodore Stappler switched on the light and then walked across the room and pulled the blind down and motioned me to a chair.

"Have you ever," he asked abruptly, "had hallucinations?"

The question caught me unprepared. But I suspected, having come to know him a little (though it was astonishing to think that I had only met him on the afternoon of the previous day) that he was not really interested whether I had experienced hallucinations or not. Indeed, he did not wait for my answer.

Settling himself into a cracked brown leather chair, he went on, "I was sitting in the restaurant downstairs waiting for you, and I saw a man walking in. He sat down in the booth just facing me.

What I noticed first of all was that he had a thick moustache. It covered his whole upper lip. My father had a moustache somewhat like it, and the way this man sat, upright – and stern. . . . Well, I thought at first merely that there was a certain resemblance. But then something very strange happened. I was sure that the man sitting there was my father. I could have sworn it. I almost went over and said, "Hello, Papa!' But I stopped myself in time.

"The waitress came to him, and he ordered chicken. He told her he hadn't had his lunch yet. When the waitress brought him his food, he began to cut the chicken very methodically, very neatly. He cut precisely along the joints, exactly like my father. My father was a surgeon – I think I told you that. He handled the knife very well. He carved very well.

"We used to have goose often – it was his favourite fowl, and I used to have the wing."

Theodore Stappler looked at me and said softly, *"Das Flügelchen für den Theodore."* Since I looked somewhat puzzled, he translated for me. "The wing is for Theodore. That's what he always said. Funny. It sounds very odd now.

"That was the first time I ever heard of Canada. At one of those goose dinners. Two doctors from Toronto were studying surgery under my father, and he brought them home for dinner one day. One of them was called Doctor Whiteside, and the other's name I don't remember. But Doctor Whiteside I remember. He was very quiet, very reserved. They both were, and they both seemed awed by my father, the great Doctor Karl Stappler." He drew out the word "great," and smiled.

"This Doctor Whiteside I remember, I think, because he did most of the talking, in a slow, halting German. He said that the *Stappler Methode* had been widely accepted on the whole North American continent, and my father, who was a vain man, beamed and smiled, and said that if he hadn't found a new and better way of entering the thoracic cavity, somebody else would have.

"He didn't, of course, believe that. Not for a moment. He said that other men, building on what had already been achieved, would do greater things than he had been able to do. But that was all theoretical for him. A kind of humble formula.

"He told the Canadian doctors – and that he did believe – how honoured he was that they had travelled thousands of miles to study under him. 'To sit at my feet,' was the phrase he used. Oh, I remember that speech, because I was just as awed as the others.

My father always spoke of his great responsibilities and of how conscious he was of them. It was more difficult to be famous, said my father, than to be still on the way up. He had a curious habit of tossing his head a little when he made great pronouncements like that. It was a known fact, my father went on to say, that the mountain was always more difficult to climb the higher one rose. And then he turned away from these cosmic profundities and asked the two honoured guests if they wanted more goose. The sublime and the ridiculous joined together. I didn't see it then, but I see it now.

"On that occasion, too, my father gave me a little bit of the stage. He didn't do that very often. But he did then. He said to our guests that he hoped I would one day follow in his footsteps. And he asked me directly if I wanted to do that. Naturally I said yes. Because I did want to do that. And my father said, beaming, yes, indeed, that was the right thing. Ever since I was so high, he said to Doctor Whiteside, with one hand indicating my little height and with the other pointing at me, ever since I was so high, I had wanted to be a doctor, like my father. He envied me, said my father, and I knew even then that he was climbing up the rhetorical mountain again, he envied all people who were young and had the world before them. Because by the time I came to study medicine, my father said, there would be unheard-of opportunities. The advances in medical science were already stupendous. My father was a great believer in steady progress, you know. Things were getting better and better. Man was getting more and more civilized. Especially European man, you know. My father had infinite faith in European man. God's plan was now complete. He looked at European man – God, that is – and said, 'That's it. I can't do any better.'

"What would scientists not do in the future! My father went into ecstasies when he thought of it. He wanted to be a young doctor just starting out, he said, because then he could stand on the shoulders of older men and reach the very pinnacle of the mountain. He had a favourite expression. *'Die Zukunft! Die Zukunft! Wie wunderbar die sein wir!* The future! The future! Oh, how wonderful it will be!'

"Well, there you are, my dear Professor Lerner. How wonderful the world looked to my father on that day. And to me, too. You see, I was going to be a famous doctor like my father, I, too, would work out a *Stappler Methode,* and would entertain guests from remote countries like Canada. They would come to sit at the feet of the master!

"So there sat this man who was my father," he concluded with a great rush of words, "and I had to get out of the restaurant before I really went up to him and made a fool of myself. You must forgive me."

It was the first chance he gave me to ask him a question. "Why did you want me to come?" I said. "Summon me to come would be more accurate. You sounded desperate."

"Did I? I'm sorry I gave you that impression. I don't think I was desperate. Well, perhaps. Agitated, certainly. I have made up my mind," he said abruptly. "I have made up my mind to go."

"What do you mean?"

"I mean to go away, to leave, to terminate everything."

He threw me off balance. I don't know what I expected of him. I had come to see him with a sense of trepidation; I had felt something ominous in the air, but now I did not know what to feel. There was something anti-climactic about the way he announced his decision, in a pedantic, dry, matter-of-fact tone. "To go away, to leave, to terminate everything." These phrases had something rehearsed about them, something stilted. They sounded like some lines in a bad play by one of Ibsen's imitators.

"What do you think about that?" he asked me. "Are you surprised?"

"Well," I said, "in a way, yes."

"You helped me to make up my mind," he said.

"How?"

"Last night. By listening to me. By your detached view of the whole thing. By your damned Olympian view of all sides of all questions. You Canadians have it easy, so cosy, so rich, so beautifully settled in soft chairs to watch the world's drama. . . . Oh, I know," he said quickly, holding up his hand to prevent me from breaking in, "you are heroic fighters and – what do they say in the papers? – staunch and loyal allies, but you haven't had to go down into hell all together. Individual hells no doubt you have, but that – that immense hell where Held and I met, there you haven't been. Fortunate people."

"What do you want me to do?" I asked. "Go to hell?"

"There you go," he said, "turning it all into a joke. I wanted to go on and say that perhaps it is necessary that some people should be there who are the witnesses, the listeners and the observers only, to keep some sanity in the world. That is what I thank you for."

"You mean us in general or me personally?"

"Both, I suppose. But you personally now. You made me see what I have to do. Last night."

"I don't understand. I didn't tell you to run away."

"No, no," he said and stopped sharply. "What do you mean?" he continued very quietly. "Are you accusing me of – of lack of courage, of being a coward?"

I had clearly gone too far. I had not weighed the implications of my words, and I was appalled. I could only stammer that he was misinterpreting, that he was reading things into my words that I hadn't intended.

"No, no," he interrupted me, "don't explain yourself. Don't apologize. You said what you said. But how could I know that there would be this – this emotional entanglement? That here on this bed I would lie and hold his daughter in my arms, and that she would talk of our future and tear my heart, and that all the time I could say nothing without shattering and destroying her. There is now nothing I can do except to leave. There is no other way. You must understand me. You must."

He pleaded with me, looking at me silently. My heart went out to him, and I nodded my head.

"I leave you to explain to her as well as you can," he said calmly. "To tell her my story, or as much of it as you think you should tell her."

For that turn in the situation I was not prepared. He had an extraordinary gift for springing emotional surprises on one. I felt a sense of outrage rising in me. It was, I thought, an impertinence. What was he to me that I should so involve myself? My first impulse was therefore to refuse and, though I said nothing, he seemed to sense my feeling.

"You must do it for me," he said very softly. "Because I can't face her myself and watch the destruction. . . . I am willing that you should think I am a coward."

I tried desperately to think of some way that would enable me to get out of the spot in which he had placed me. "Why don't you write her and tell her, if you can't meet her on the matter face to face?" I asked him.

"Perhaps I'll do that – later. But I can't do it now."

"You think it's simple for me, don't you? But have you thought about it? What do you think I should say?"

"Oh, the truth. You must tell her the truth. You must tell her what I told you."

"Ah," I said. "*I* must destroy her, then. Is that what you want? *I* have to wield the knife."

"Oh, my God," he cried out. "I – I didn't think of it in that way.... No, no. Clearly not." He seemed confused. "Clearly not," he repeated. "You can't do it. Of course. I don't want her to know. . . well, not in exactly that way. You must tell her simply that I've gone away. If she thinks that I've betrayed her, well, then, she will think it. That is after all the best. But at least you can try not to make me out a beast. Perhaps you can find something to say."

"I have to lie, then. You want me to lie for you."

"That's not the way I want you to think of it. I want you to protect her from a knowledge of certain events."

"But can this now really be done? Once the apple has been eaten, it can't be uneaten again. If you'd never come, she would never have known, because her father wouldn't have told her. But you have come. Things can't be exactly as they were before."

"But I am going away as mysteriously as I came. From her point of view, anyway. Only I can't bear to think – to imagine what she will think of me. So I am asking you to protect her from knowledge and me from – slander, I suppose, and to protect my name – somehow to protect my name."

"You are asking a great deal," I said. I felt cold all at once and very afraid.

"I'd do it for you," he said, and at that moment I didn't doubt that he would. It seemed as if I had known him all my life, as if he and I were friends, brothers even, who had shared endless secrets. I could not believe that only the day before yesterday I had not known of his existence.

"I must think about that," I said.

"You will do it, then? You will speak for me?"

"I didn't promise. I said I would think about it. When are you leaving?"

"There is a train that goes out of here in – " he consulted his watch – "in two hours. I want to be on that train. There, you see," he gestured vaguely towards the far corner of the room, "my bags are packed. Nothing remains to be done. Only to wish I had never come. Or if I had to come, that. . . . Well, it makes no difference. Things are as they are"

He fell again to brooding, sitting in the same position I had noticed several times the night before. "That painting you have – by that fine artist – Emily Carr," he said suddenly. "That is a fine piece."

"Yes," I said, "it is a fine piece. I am glad you liked it."

"Also the river," he went on. "I like the river very much. Almost every day since I arrived I have walked to the brow of the hill by the library and looked down into the valley. That is very fine. Katherine and I walked there quite often. As a matter of fact," he concluded, speaking more briskly, "I'd like to walk there now and look at the river once more before I go. Will you come with me?"

I was glad of the opportunity to get out of his room, for I was beginning to feel trapped there. The thought of going for a walk through dark and cold and snowy streets to look at a frozen river did not, I must say, fill me with elation. It was not the kind of thing I normally went in for.

He already had his coat on and had opened the door, and so I quickly put on my own coat and overshoes and together we walked down the threadbare, creaky corridor. At the office he halted briefly, turned in his key, and told Sam that we were going out for a walk, and Sam pulled a face and shook his head and said we were nuts, but that if you were in his business you got used to nuts of all kinds, and we passed on, down the steep stairs into the street.

It was snowing. The flakes came down evenly and gently and settled softly on the pavement. Because of the cloud-cover and the snow, it was considerably warmer than it had been in the morning.

We crossed the street and he led me through a dark alley – a short-cut, he said – towards the crest of the hill. It was a short walk, and then we were there, standing against a low wooden railing which barely came up to our knees and looking down the white-gleaming hillside at the river, frozen and white below.

"I like that," said Theodore Stappler. He made a sweeping gesture with his gloved hand. He seemed to embrace the valley and the river, and for what seemed several minutes he was quite transported by the sight.

"I like the snow," he said. "It brings me happy memories. When I was a little boy, my father used to take me sleigh-riding on Sunday afternoons. Those afternoons were very wonderful. That was the only time when I felt really close to my father. Otherwise he was a rather distant man. So I was always closer to my mother. . . . Not far from where we lived there was a nice hill, like this one, only the slope was gentler. My sleigh had little bells on it, and they tinkled when I went down. I used to lie on my sleigh with my head forward, and my father used to tell me that I looked like a pointer. Sometimes my father got on the sleigh with me, and we would go down together. That's what I really liked. It wasn't often that my father unbent. He thought too much of himself, so he always stood on his dignity, and he got rather pompous. . . . Sometimes we got to the hill just after a snowfall, and the hill was so white it seemed a pity to destroy the whiteness. Just as it is now."

"Well," I said, "nobody is likely to go shooting down that hill right now."

"I wish I could be here in the spring to see the ice on the river go," he said. "It must be an exciting sight."

"Yes, so I believe."

"Have you never seen it?"

"No, never," I said. "At least not yet. Once or twice I meant to go down and see the river break up, but I've always missed the opportunity."

"It must be wonderful," he mused, "to see all that force released. A real kind of liberation."

"Yes."

"Is this a fast river?" he asked.

"Yes," I said, "it is pretty fast-flowing."

"Do people swim in it?"

"Not usually," I said. "It's too dangerous."

"There are then – what do you call them? – " He made a swirling motion with his hand – "Whirlpools?"

"Eddies?"

"Yes, eddies, whirlpools. There are some pretty treacherous eddies in the Danube. But people swim in the Danube, anyway. They also drown, some of them. Every year a number of people are caught in those whirlpools of the beautiful blue Danube, and they drown."

I was beginning to feel uncomfortable. Snow had settled around my collar, and the cold air was slowly penetrating below my overcoat. I suggested that we go back and he at once agreed, though he stood there silently for a while longer. I walked away slowly, and he joined me.

Had I anything on for the evening? he asked me and when I

said no, nothing in particular, he suggested that I have supper with him. For the last time, he said with mock-solemnity, the dragon would guard him, and me, too, he added, laughing softly, against the dangers and evils of the world.

He turned for one last look at the frozen river, and at the valley, and the lights of the cars winding their way up and down hills. I meanwhile walked on. Once again he joined me. We began to walk faster. The snow swirled about us, heavier now and denser than before. The neon signs and the street lamps seemed enveloped in snow. I was glad when we reached the restaurant, whose red and green dragon tamely beckoned, with a few of its bulbs nervously flickering, as if they were about to expire. My face felt cold. After a while, I knew, it would get hot and I would feel flustered.

"Do you like Chinese food?" Theodore Stappler asked me.

"Yes."

"Well, then, we'll have some. Sharing of dishes. It's a kind of fraternal way of eating."

When the waitress came, he said, "Joyce, my dear, this is Professor Lerner, who is a very wise man."

"Oh, come on with you," said Joyce. "Stop kidding me." She turned to me. "He's always kidding me."

"No, honestly," said Theodore Stappler, "Professor Lerner is a very learned man. A scholar and a gentleman." He took her hand. After a moment she withdrew it and took a pad and pencil from the pocket in her apron.

"Pleased to meet you," she said to me.

I nodded and smiled. My face felt hot now, and I was slightly embarrassed because I thought she might get the impression that I was blushing.

"What'll it be?" she asked.

"We're going to have some Chinese food," said Theodore Stappler. "Some chow mein, some sweet and sour spare ribs, some pineapple chicken. . . . Does that suit you?" he asked me.

I nodded. The girl was scribbling the order.

"And listen, Joyce, my dear," Theodore Stappler said, "tell the cook to make it really good because this is the last supper."

"Oh," she said, "you leaving or something?"

"Yes," he said. "Haven't I been here long enough?"

"Oh, I don't know," she said.

"And we never really got together," he said, teasing her. "I'll always be sorry about that. You've been so very good to me. You saw that I got the proper things to eat."

She laughed and gathered up the menus and went off through the swing-doors into the kitchen.

"This is a very pure city," Theodore Stappler said to me.

"In what way?" I asked him.

"They protect the morals of the people," he said. "You see, I can buy wine or liquor and get dead drunk in my room, but here in this restaurant I can't offer you even a glass of wine. So you see, the last supper won't be complete. But we can at least break bread together."

"Are you about to get yourself arrested and crucified?"

He laughed. He was very relaxed now, the way he had been when I first met him and when he told us, in so light-hearted a manner, some of the things that had happened to him in various parts of the world, before Katherine Held left us and he began to move into those dark parts of his story that had been so shattering. And now again, just after he had, in effect, forced a commitment from me that I had refused to make in so many words but that in some barely comprehensible manner both he and I assumed, he was jovial and carefree in manner.

"Crucified?" he said. "No, no. I'm not cut out for martyrdom. I'm not a saint. No, no, certainly not a saint."

He suddenly broke into loud laughter and, when I asked him what he was laughing about, he said, "Once, when I was about ten or eleven, I was watching a Corpus Christi parade – or procession, to be perhaps more precise. You know, in Catholic countries that is a big day, a big occasion. There are bands and floats, and pretty little girls all dressed in white, with little flower – what do you call them?" His hand described a circle round his head.

"Coronets?" I said.

"Yes," he said, "with little flower coronets, and there are little boys in dark suits, all marching very slowly, the boys and the girls, with candles in their hands, and then the *pièce de résistance*, the priests in their vestments, marching very solemnly under a – a baldachin, we used to call it. That baldachin was made out of a very rich brocade, and the priests looked very impressive.

"I used to watch this procession every year. I had my spot picked out. It was in front of a *Gasthaus,* a kind of inn, you know.

In front they had put up a little altar, with pictures of Christ and the Virgin, and there were a lot of flowers everywhere, and the whole procession came to a halt there.

"A small battalion of soldiers was also in the procession, with rifles, and they lined up, facing the altar. And then the priests did something, prayed, I suppose, and blessed the crowd, and afterwards the officer of the battalion gave some commands, and then he shouted, 'Fire!' and the soldiers banged away. Afterwards the little boys in the crowd ran about and picked up the empty cartridges. It was a lot of fun, and the little boys with the candles in the procession envied us because by the time they could get away, all the cartridges were picked up. . . . I never could understand why they shot off this salvo. He was after all the prince of peace. Well, one of the followers of the prince of peace – his name was Kretschmar – I'll always remember him, he was a big chap, big for his age, you understand – anyway, this Kretschmar, who was in my class, came up to me. He looked uncomfortable in his black suit, but he had marched in the procession and he was full of the glory of it, he was ecstatic. 'Stappler,' he said to me, 'have you got any of the cartridges?' I said I had. 'Give them to me,' he ordered me. But I refused. 'You are not a Catholic, are you?' He got very belligerent. I said that I was not. He knew that, of course. 'Then how come you got the cartridges?' he asked me. I held onto my loot and defied him. 'How come you stand here, so close to the altar?' he asked me. I said I stood there because I liked to watch the soldiers shoot off their rifles. Then Kretschmar asked me a question I have never forgotten. 'Do you believe in the saints,' he asked, 'and do you love them?' I said I did not. 'Do you believe in the martyrs?' he asked. I said I did not. And then Kretschmar, the lover of the saints and of the martyrs, forgot all about love and everything else the saints and martyrs might have taught him, and became the soldier of his lord, just as many years afterwards he became the loyal servant of his earthly Messiah, Adolf Hitler. Kretschmar stood up for his saints and martyrs and hit me in the teeth with his fist. I tried to kick him in the shins with my foot, but I missed and decided to run away. So you see, I was not a hero then, either. That is a flaw in me. . . . Here comes the faithful Joyce."

She came, carrying a tray with the dishes we had ordered. A soft fragrance came from them when she put them down in the centre of the table.

"I told Charlie this was your last supper," she said, "and he made it special good."

"Excellent," said Theodore Stappler. "Tell me, Joyce, do you believe in the saints and martyrs, and do you love them?"

She looked at him, plainly puzzled. "Oh, get on with you," she said at last. And to me, "He's always kidding around. Are you coming back again?" she asked him.

"I doubt it," he said. "I don't often come back to the places I leave."

"What about your girl?" she asked.

For a moment he was taken aback. "What girl?"

"Oh, come off it," she cried. "The one you used to bring in here all the time."

"Ah, well," he said, speaking very abruptly. "All good things must come to an end."

Joyce became aware of the changed tone and the changed mood, and with a toss of her head left us.

Theodore Stappler busied himself with the dishes. "Let me serve you," he said, and almost ceremoniously he divided the portions and filled my plate.

We began to eat.

"The Stapplers," he said suddenly, about halfway through the meal, "are not heroic." He put down his fork and looked at me. "In the end not even very reliable. There's a flaw somewhere. The man who looked like my father sat over there." He pointed at a booth diagonally across from us. It was empty now. "My father was a very famous surgeon, as I told you. He was *Primarius*, the chief of surgery in the most important hospital in Vienna."

He began to eat again. After a few mouthfuls, he put down his fork again and said quietly, all the while looking across at the empty booth where the man that looked like his father had been sitting. "My father died a death by water. He died by drowning in the Danube. He liked to swim in the river. It was said that he got a cramp or was caught in one of the swirls, the – what do you call it? – eddies in the river. But I think he wanted to drown. I think he committed suicide."

I stopped eating, with my heaped fork midway between my plate and my mouth.

"I'm sorry," he said. "I didn't want to spoil the last supper."

"You have a great gift for springing surprises," I said, "when one least expects them."

"Forgive me," he said. "It is all a very long time ago. The passion is all gone. I can think of it now without any really deep emotion, quite objectively. Does that shock you?"

"No," I said. "I can imagine situations like that."

"Yes," he said. "Some things, some events diminish with time. No matter how great the initial shock. Others, like the Saarbrücken events, remain forever like a festering open wound. They get even worse with time."

He picked up his fork again and ate calmly. We finished the meal in silence.

"My father had reached the end of the road," he said. "He was very high up on that mountain which he always liked to talk about. He had everything, and then suddenly nothing. He plunged from the top of his mountain into the depths of the river. Because his world also had come to an end, and he could no longer face things. . . .

"My parents' marriage was in many ways a wonderful thing. There was a deep union between them. Everybody said that. And certainly I always thought so. Until two years before the end. He became involved with a young actress then. The flames of middle-aged passion, you know. They can burn pretty fiercely. My father was nearly fifty then. A handsome, vigorous man. It was a passion in the grand manner. A real *Leidenschaft*. There was nothing secret about it. My father would never conduct a hole-and-corner affair. I will give him credit for that. The girl had great beauty and talent. She played some great roles. All the great, suffering heroines. Desdemona, Ophelia, and Gretchen in Goethe's *Faust*. I used to go and see her whenever she performed. I was in the University already, and I knew of course that she was my father's mistress. My friends knew this also, and it always created a peculiar tension whenever we went together to the theatre. In the end I went alone. I used to sit there in the theatre and feel myself torn in two. Because I identified myself with my mother. I could feel her suffering. I took her part. I felt that my father had betrayed her, that what he had done was unworthy and unfair. And at the same time I admired him for it, too. There was one terrible scene between my mother and father. Only one. And after that a kind of cold peace. And I used to sit and watch that young actress going through the agonies of betrayal and despair on the stage. Oh, but she was beautiful, her face, her skin, her arms – astonishing. I used to imagine her naked in my father's arms, and the thought was painful and also delicious. I suppose I wanted her myself. . . .

"All things come to an end. The passion cooled – on the girl's part, anyway. She married another actor. The man who used to play Hamlet and Faust to her Ophelia and Gretchen. And then it was all over. I suppose it was humiliating for my father. After all, here was the great man who had found such a wonderful way of entering the thoracic cavity! My mother forgave him, and for a while it seemed as if they were coming together again. I began to hope that the wounds would heal. The summer came, and one day he went swimming in the Danube and never came out again. My mother went into mourning for him because she loved him. She never again wore anything but black. Perhaps she mourned for lost love. Afterwards she mourned also a lost world, until she herself was lost in the chaos and in the total corruption of that time . . . . Enough. We have to go, or I'll miss the train."

"You are leaving Ophelia," I said.

"Yes," he said. "I leave her to you. Horatio will be kind to her. I know that."

He paid the bill, bade an elaborate farewell to the cashier, and then we went up to the hotel.

"I haven't even told Sam that I'm leaving," said Theodore Stappler as we climbed the stairs. "I still have to settle my bill with him. It doesn't leave us much time."

Sam's splendid ear detected us, for he came bounding out of his office before we had reached the top of the stairs and said, "Well, well, I thought you guys was never going to come back. . . . You got a visitor."

"Oh?" said Theodore Stappler. "Who could that be? I wasn't expecting anybody."

"Who, he asks me," Sam said. "Who do you think?"

"Katherine?"

"Who else?" said Sam.

"Where is she?"

"In your room. You wouldn't want me to toss her out in the snow, would you? Not everybody is nuts and walks in the snow."

Theodore Stappler was no longer listening to him. He pushed past him with a movement of great impatience, hurried along the corridor, and without first knocking entered his room.

❦ XII

I HESITATED A MOMENT AND STAYED BEHIND. SAM WENT BACK into his office and I followed him.

"How long has she been here?" I asked.

"Oh, 'bout twenty minutes or thereabouts," he said. "She looked pretty wrought up, so I let her in the room. Say, you know something. When I opened the door, I just looked in like, and I saw a couple of suitcases standing there, by the window. How come? He isn't leaving or something, is he?"

"Yes," I said, "as a matter of fact, he was going to go to the station right now. I was going to drive him there."

"So," said Sam. "What do you know. How come he didn't tell me nothing about it? He wasn't going to run out and not pay, was he?"

"Do you think he would do that?"

"I seen all kinds," said Sam. "In this business you see all kinds. Why didn't he say nothing, then?"

"I think he just made up his mind to go. I mean this morning, or this afternoon."

"Does she know he's leaving?" he asked.

"I – I don't know," I said at first, evasively, but added more firmly, "No, I don't think she knows."

"That's what I think," said Sam. "Like hell she knows. She doesn't know a damn thing. He was just going to leave her. Just like that. Like a little thief. Like I told you. I know those guys. Here today, gone tomorrow. I came, I screwed, I buggered off."

"I wouldn't be too harsh on him," I said. "In some ways he can't help it. He has to leave. In some ways he's doing her a favour by leaving." I caught myself. It was astonishing how I was already playing the role of apologist for Theodore Stappler.

"Oh, come off it," said Sam. "She won't be thinking that, any-way. He wasn't gonna tell her. But by now she's gonna know for sure because them bags was just standing there by the window, and she was in that room for twenty minutes. If she opens up a drawer, I bet it's empty. So empty drawers and bags. Two and two makes four. She's gonna figure that out. There's gonna be fireworks. If I know dames, there's gonna be fireworks."

I was afraid of that, too, and for a moment I considered leaving, but this would have meant deserting him. Besides, to put the matter in less dramatic, less heroic terms, I was also very curious to know what was happening. I was also relieved, for Stappler's stratagem was clearly not working out. It was now impossible for him simply to steal away and leave me to do the explaining. That was, for me at least, a merciful turn of events.

"I'll see what's happening," I said to Sam and walked slowly down to his room.

He had left the door open and, when I came into the room, I saw Theodore Stappler and Katherine Held standing together. He held her gently in his arms. He was talking to her in a soft voice.

They became aware of me and separated.

Still holding her hand, Theodore Stappler said, "Katherine had an awful row with her father. It was about me."

She turned, as if surprised. When she saw me, she nodded to me and the mere suggestion of a smile passed across her face. But she didn't say anything, didn't greet me.

"I'm very sorry," I stammered. "I don't want to interfere."

"No, no," said Theodore Stappler quickly, "please stay. Please stay," he said again, more urgently than before, as if he were afraid that I might indeed leave. "I – we may need your help."

"Well, if I can help. . . ."

I still hesitated because I still felt very uncomfortable.

"Please close the door," he said.

I did as he asked. The girl didn't say anything. She looked very pale, very beautiful, too, I thought, though she had never before struck me as particularly beautiful. The weak overhead light highlighted the dusky-gold of her hair. She had on a black dress that fitted tightly, and defined with soft precision the con-tours of her young body, her throat, her breasts, her hips.

I noticed that she had thrown her overcoat across Theodore Stappler's bed, and now she disengaged her hand from his and walked over to the bed and sat down and folded her hands in her lap.

"I really don't want to intrude," I said, speaking directly to her now. "I think I'll only be in the way."

"It's all right, Dr. Lerner," she said. "If Theo wants you to stay, please stay. I – I really don't know what to do, anyway. I'm all confused."

"I've taken Dr. Lerner into my confidence," Theodore Stappler said to her. "I've told him a great many things – things that I didn't tell you. Things that I couldn't tell you." He stopped talking, but went on gesturing with his hands, in a choppy, desperate kind of way, as if he couldn't find the customary words. "After I left you yesterday, I went back to his apartment and stayed the night there."

"Well, as long as it wasn't with another girl," she said, with the merest trace of irony.

"No, no," he said quickly, as if this had been a real possibility, "I wouldn't do that." He crossed over and sat down beside her on the bed.

I felt useless and superfluous. If there had been a little door so that I could have disappeared quietly, I would have slipped out of the room. There was a chair on the side and I sat down.

Had she not noticed, I wondered, that his bags were packed? How could she fail to have noticed? Had she asked about it before I came into the room, and if so, had he told her that he was leaving? But that seemed hardly possible.

"We had a long talk last night, Dr. Lerner and I," he said to her.

"When I came home last night," she said, "I had another of those long and awful talks with my father."

"About me?" he asked.

"Of course," she said. "It's always about you these days." She got up and walked over to the chair where I was sitting. I had thought they had altogether forgotten I was still there.

"Theo probably told you," she said to me, "that my father has been very unhappy about me."

"Yes," I said. "And as a matter of fact you told me yourself."

"Oh?"

"Yes."

"When?"

"When you talked to me in my office yesterday afternoon."

"Oh," she said and seemed surprised. "I'd forgotten.

"My father," she went on, "thinks that Theo is a most unscrupulous, even a—I won't say it. They had some dealings years and years ago. And my father now says that. . . ." She stopped, then went on quietly, "I – I – perhaps I should say it. It'll be better so. He says – my father – he says that Theo has come here to blackmail him."

Everything seemed suddenly to be frozen as the terrible words came from her lips. Theodore Stappler spun round where he sat on the bed and stared over towards us, but he said nothing.

When I am caught in such moments, I suddenly become awfully conscious of my whole anatomy, of my ears, and of my nose particularly, and of my hands, even – absurd though it may be – of the blood coursing through my body. But I can't move. Only my nose twitches. Now the sudden thought struck me that we had all three of us become figures in a waxworks, a tableau entitled, "The Blackmailer at Bay."

"And do you believe him?" The dry voice of Theodore Stappler at last mercifully broke the silence. The figures in the waxworks moved. I shifted position, feeling again that I should not be there at all. Katherine turned from me to face Theodore Stappler, and he rose from the bed and came over to her.

"And do you believe him?" he asked again. He asked the question very matter-of-factly, as if the whole affair were of no great significance.

"No," she cried out. "No, no, I don't. I don't want to believe him. And that's why I came. Because I trust you. Because I want to be with you. You know that, Theo. But why don't you stop hinting? He won't tell me straight out what really happened, and you don't, either. You both treat me like a little child. Whatever there is between you, surely it can't be as terrible as all that. And it happened so long ago, anyway. Why can't we be done with it? Why can't you end the quarrel?"

"When I came here to see your father," Theodore Stappler said, "I never expected that I would find you, and when I found you I never expected that I would come to feel so – so close to you. That was not in the calculation."

"I don't know what you're talking about," she said after a moment's silence. "Calculation? What is this? I thought you just happened to pass through this city and that someone had told you we were living here, and. . . ."

"I didn't tell you the whole truth," he said. "Not because I wanted to deceive you. But because you had nothing to do with it all. There was no need for me to involve you, and so I told you that I was just passing through here. But I didn't come here by accident. I came on purpose. To find your father and settle accounts."

By degrees his voice had become cold, bereft of all sentiment. He had evidently decided not to spare her anything. And indeed his words made her recoil. She gasped a little and took a step or two backwards, away from him.

"Settle accounts?" she cried out. "What do you mean? Then when my father said you came to blackmail him, was that true?"

He didn't answer her at once, and she asked the question again, almost desperately, imploring him almost to say that it was not true.

"I don't know what to say," he answered, after he had thought for a while, and his words were measured and carefully weighed. "It is not true in the way he meant you to understand it. I'm sure of that. Because he has made me out to be a – a swine. He has made me out to be a run-of-the-mill little swindler, a petty little blackmailer. And that's not true. That's not true at all. I'm grateful to you because you never believed that."

She seemed relieved, perhaps because of what he said, but mainly, I thought, because his tone changed. He spoke softly and very sadly.

"But if it's not true in the way he meant it," she said, pursuing the point, "is it true in some other way? I don't understand it."

Again he hesitated, as if he were turning the whole matter over in his mind, trying to find some way of making clear to her the dilemma in which he so obviously found himself.

"It depends," he said softly. "It depends what you understand by blackmail. If he means by this that I want some money from him – the ordinary, sordid kind of blackmail – then that's completely false. I never would take any money from him. Not a cent. Not even if I were starving and needed money to buy bread. No, no, not that kind of blackmail. But there are other kinds of blackmail. There is emotional blackmail, and in many ways this is much worse than the other kind. One person holds another in his power. He can play with him and he can hurt him. And if he said to you that I wanted to hurt him in this way, then that is true."

"But why?" she cried out in torment and confusion, and I felt suddenly infinitely sorry for her and almost got up to intervene, to call a halt to this slow and painful revelation. But it was now inevitable that she should know. It couldn't be stopped now. In a sense I was grateful, too, and selfishly so, that it had not fallen to me to bear the news and to have to twist and squirm when she pressed me, as undoubedly she would have done, to tell her what I knew.

"But why did you want to do that?" she cried again. "Why did you want to hurt him? He's such a kind man, my father, so gentle. What did he do to you that you went out of your way – so far out of your way – to find him?"

"Don't ask me," he pleaded with her. "Please don't ask me. I don't want you to know. There's no point to it. You don't need to know. I don't want you to know."

"You think I'm a little child," she said. "You treat me like one, anyway. What do you mean, there's no point to it? That's just an insult."

"That's the last thing I want to do," Theodore Stappler said, "to insult you. I only want to save you from pain. And that's why I am going to leave tonight. I want to go so that everything can be as it was before I came."

She turned pale. Her whole body became rigid.

"Look," Theodore Stappler said and pointed to his suitcases standing in a far corner of the room.

Her eyes followed his finger and came to rest on the suitcases.

"They're packed," Theodore Stappler said, his eyes following hers. "Surely you knew that."

"I?" she said. "How should I?"

It suddenly dawned on me that she had not, in fact, been aware that all his things were packed. She had probably been too preoccupied with other matters when she came into his room to notice the suitcases, or if she had noticed them, she obviously had not paid any attention to the fact. Suitcases, after all, are fairly common in hotel rooms.

"Everything is packed," he said. "The drawers are empty. . . . You didn't notice that?"

"Theo," she said, "I don't usually look into other people's drawers."

"Well, they are empty," he said, almost belligerently, as if daring her to go and test the truth of what he was saying. "And I intended to leave on this evening's train without seeing you again. I wanted to vanish."

She shook her head. A look of total incomprehension came over her. She passed her fingers through her hair, as if cobwebs had got caught there and she wanted to brush them away.

"If you don't believe me," he said, "ask our friend here. Ask Professor Lerner."

She turned towards me, her face drawn and that look of incomprehension still there, and her eyes asked the question.

I cleared my throat. "It's true," I said. "What he says is true. Theodore is going to leave. And I was supposed to tell you after he had gone."

"But you see," Theodore Stappler interjected, "nothing is going right for me. All my plans go wrong."

"But why?" she asked me, her voice almost a whisper. "Why would he do that? After all he said to me about what — about what I meant to him. Why would he betray me now?"

I got up and moved closer to where they stood. "I don't think he wants to betray you." I spoke almost as if Theodore Stappler were not there, as if he had already gone, and I felt for a moment that I was carrying out the task he had given me earlier. "When he said that he was leaving for your sake, I believe that he was telling you the truth. When he said that he wanted to spare you unhappiness, he was telling you the truth."

"To leave someone you say you like — even love — very much," she said, "and to leave suddenly and without any explanation — that's a funny way of sparing someone unhappiness."

"I suppose there are degrees of unhappiness and degrees of evil," I said, in my most pedagogic manner. "We have often discussed that in our classes."

"But this is different," she said.

"Why?"

"Because it is happening to me and I don't understand it." She turned sharply and, her voice rising in anger, she said to Theodore Stappler, "Then all you told me, here — " she gestured towards the bed, which suddenly seemed to me to bear the imprint of their embracing bodies — "it was all a lie, then. An awful lie."

"No," Theodore Stappler said. He reached out his hand as if to touch her, but she drew away from him. "It was true," he said. "At first it was perhaps not true, but it became true. If you had only been someone else. If your father had been someone else! If there was not between him and me this – shadow. But that can't be changed. And so there is only one thing for me to do."

"To run away," she said contemptuously.

He winced when she said that and looked over to me as if he were seeking some support from me.

"To run away like a coward," she went on. "Why couldn't you tell me?"

He only shook his head, silently, hopelessly.

"What did you want to do – to us? To my father and to me?"

"To you – nothing. Only to protect you. I've liked you more than perhaps any other woman I ever knew – except my mother. And to your father – nothing now. Nothing any more. Nothing at all. Neither good nor bad."

"But you hate my father?" she said. "You do, don't you?"

"No," he said. "Not now. Not any more. At first, yes, I did. When I first came, I did. But not now."

"But you wanted to hurt him?"

"At first, yes. But not now."

"What did you want to do to him?" she asked.

"I don't know," he said. "You won't belive that. But it is true. I wanted to hurt him, but I never really knew how I would do it, how I would hurt him."

"But why did you want to hurt him? Why? What did he do to you? Was it so awful that you would come all the way from God knows where? How can I believe anything you say?"

He did not answer her.

"Why?" she pressed him. "You can't be silent now. You must tell me. You must."

Theodore Stappler turned to me. "Help me now," he said. "I can't tell her. You must speak for me."

I had not expected this, and his request startled me. For now he wanted me to tell the precise reason why he had come. Clearly, he could not want me to dissemble or to invent. But why could he not say it himself?

"I – I really don't know what you want me to say," I stammered. "I – I am hardly competent. . ."

"You can tell her better than I," he said. "I – I don't trust myself. . . . You are not involved. You are outside it all. Tell her what I told you last night."

"But you told me so much that. . . ."

"Tell her what you think is important. The issue. The issue. The central issue."

How was I to sum everything up? How to compress it, how to say it? I tried to order my thoughts, so that I could say precisely what the issue was, and I said to myself that I would try to speak as drily, as dispassionately, as nearly without any intonation even, as possible – almost, I thought, as if I were a judge summing up a case. But when I actually began to speak, my voice trembled and my heart was beating so strongly that I had trouble keeping myself under control.

"Many years ago," I found myself saying, and though I had not intended to achieve this effect at all, I realized that I had begun as if I were telling a fable. "Many years ago a man undertook to lead some people into safety because they were persecuted in the country where they lived. This man – who is your father – undertook to lead them across the German frontier into France. They paid him money, and he in turn dealt with corrupt officials. But then – under pressure – this man – your father – led these people into a trap. He betrayed them and they were arrested. Theodore – Mr. Stappler and his mother were among the people who had trusted their lives to your father. By some accident – by some chance – Theodore Stappler escaped, but watched helplessly when your father led the others to be arrested. Eventually they all perished. Except for your father and Theodore Stappler. . . . Mr. Stappler says that your father sold himself to the devil – he made a deal with the forces of evil. And saved himself at the expense of others."

I stopped. For an eternity, it seemed, there was silence in the room. The full impact of the words appeared curiously muted. We did not look at each other. We were each of us in our private world, it seemed, isolated one from the other. I fixed my eyes before my feet and noticed that my shoes looked very dusty and was suddenly seized by an urge, which I resisted, to bend down and wipe the dust off my shoes.

All at once I heard, as if it came from a far distance, Katherine Held's voice, barely a whisper, saying, "No, no. That must be a lie. How could he? We had to escape ourselves. . . ."

"That was afterwards," I said. "After what happened."

"And do you believe it?" she asked. "Do you believe what – " she motioned mutely towards Theodore Stappler who was standing behind her – "what he said?"

I hesitated for some time, but then I said, "I think I do."

"You take his word alone for it?" she asked. "One man's word? Is that sufficient? One man's word? Answer me," she demanded when I remained silent. She spoke louder now, and more belligerently. "You teach history!" She seemed to be taunting me. And in a sense she had a right to do that. "One source only," she continued. "There is only one source. . . . Did you ask the other man?" she pursued me. "Did you ask my father?"

"I could hardly do that," I said. My collar seemed suddenly very tight. I felt the blood rushing into my face. "Even if there had been time. But I am not a judge. I had no right to ask him."

"But you have a right to judge him?" she asked.

"I am not judging him," I said.

"But you believe a slander against him," she cried out. "How then are you not judging him?"

Theodore Stappler, who had seemed almost abstracted, standing slightly apart from us, as if the whole thing hardly concerned him, now spoke.

"The facts are not in dispute," he said. "The motives – well, that is another matter. And the question of full responsibility. That is another matter, too. But the facts are not in dispute."

She turned sharply. Her whole body quivered. "It's a lie," she cried out. Her voice was out of control. It was a piercing sound that issued from her lips. "It's a lie. A lie. A lie. A lie."

She rushed towards Theodore Stappler, and for a moment I thought she was going to attack him. He stepped back until his back touched the wall.

"You're everything he says you are," she almost hissed at him. "He could never do what you accuse him of. And behind his back, too, to a stranger, and without giving him a chance to defend himself."

"The facts are not in dispute," Theodore Stappler reiterated.

She stepped furiously towards the bed and grabbed her coat and began struggling to put it on. When I stepped forward to help her on with it, she rounded on me. "Leave me alone," she cried. "Leave me alone."

Still wrestling with her coat, and without bothering to put on her overshoes, which were standing beside the door, she rushed out of Theodore Stappler's room, and we could hear her running along the corridor and down the stairs.

"Why did she have to come?" Theodore Stappler mumbled.

"Why did she have to come?"

"Where did she go?" I asked, of no one in particular. "She left her overshoes here."

"It doesn't matter now," he said.

"Someone – you or I – should go after her," I said. "The snow will be very deep now. She won't get far without overshoes."

"Yes," he said, "someone should go after her."

I looked at my watch. "You've missed your train," I said. "It left about five minutes ago."

"There will be other trains," he said.

"I'll go down," I said. "Perhaps I can still find her. She can't have got very far."

"All right."

I got my coat and threw it over my shoulders.

Sam was standing outside his office, looking down the stairs. "What happened?" he asked me. "That kid was awful upset when she went running down those stairs. He give her the gate or something? Like I told you it was going to be?"

"No, no," I said. "Nothing like that. Do you know where she went?"

"Out," he said. "What other way is there to go?"

I pushed past him and ran down the stairs into the street. It was snowing very heavily now. I could hardly see anything except the dense, heavy flakes coming down like a vast, eternal army. Headlights of cars lit up the falling flakes for a moment and then disappeared into the darkness, and the snow swallowed them up. I trudged to the next corner through the snow, but I could see nothing beyond a few yards and realized that my search was hopeless. There was no chance that I could find her.

So I turned back, and just as I passed the restaurant and was about to open the door to go up again to Theodore Stappler's room, Katherine came out of the restaurant.

"I ran down to look for you," I said.

"Why?"

The question seemed ludicrous but an answer more ludicrous still.

"I phoned my father," she said. "He'll be here soon."

"Why did you do that?" I asked.

"So he can speak for himself," she said.

"Does he know that's why you called him to come?"

"I told him he had to come," she said. "Before *he* leaves."

"Theodore?"

"Yes."

"He won't leave tonight," I said. "His train has already gone. There's no other one tonight."

"I see."

"We can't stand out here in the snow. Let's go wait for your father in Theodore's room."

She hesitated a moment, as if reluctant to go back, but when I took her arm, she turned and came with me, and together we walked up the stairs and returned to Theodore Stappler's room.

🌿 XIII

THEODORE STAPPLER WAS SITTING MOTIONLESS ON A CHAIR, facing the window. He had raised the blind so that the flickering lights of the marquee on the little run-down cinema across the road were visible through the falling snow. The door was still as I had left it, half open.

He heard me come in and. without turning around, he asked, "Did you find her?"

"Yes," I said. "She is here."

Katherine had come into the room, but she had taken her wet shoes off in the corridor and was holding them in her hand, and so he had not heard her.

He turned round in the chair and looked solemnly at us. "What now?" he asked. He put his hands together, palm to palm, as if he were about to say a prayer. "If you want to know all the details of – of my case," he said, speaking now specifically to her, "you must ask our friend here. Professor Lerner will tell you – if he feels that he can. I have told him all. He is my representative. He has promised to act for me."

"I didn't promise," I said.

"No, you didn't," he said. "And yet you have consented. I won't say anything because I can't bear it. It is intolerable. I can't bring myself to speak about it. Not any more. Last night I spoke – to our learned friend here. It is all over. I will not speak of it again. It is finished."

He let his head fall forward onto his chest, and so sat brooding for some time. Then he turned again to Katherine and demanded, "Why did you have to come? I didn't want you to know. Why couldn't you let me go?" He broke off, as if he realized himself the unreasonableness of the demands that were clearly implied in his questions.

"I didn't prevent you from going," she said. "You could have gone any time – yesterday or the day before."

He shrugged his shoulders, as if to say that nothing really could be gained by further discussion.

The next half-hour or so seemed interminable. We sat, each of us a little island, and waited. I was tense at first, but after a few minutes I became curiously calm and abstracted, as if I were in limbo. The silence in the room was broken only twice, quite inconsequentially, by Theodore Stappler – the first time when a heavy footstep marched slowly up the stairs and came bearing down the corridor, and I tensed up because I thought that Joseph Held was coming, but Theodore Stappler said calmly, "That's my neighbour in room six. Sam calls him Number Six. He walks, says Sam, like a regiment of soldiers. Sam says that Number Six talks with his feet, but rarely with his mouth," and the second time when a man and a women came up the stairs together, talking in suppressed anger, a kind of prologue to a bitter quarrel, and Theodore Stappler said, "They are my neighbours on the other side. An innocent little couple who've come here from somewhere in the country on their honeymoon. They've been married a week, and already, you see, they're quarrelling. But they'll soon make love and all will be well."

Neither Katherine nor I pursued the subject, and silence settled again. I concentrated, more than I had before, on what was going on outside the room. The walls were thin, and I could hear the young honeymoon couple pursuing their quarrel, for their voices were now raised in anger, but I could not make out precisely what they were saying.

Theodore Stappler said all at once, "What are we waiting for? There will be no resurrection. What has happened has happened. Nothing can be undone. I am waiting for another train. Tomorrow. But what are we waiting for together?"

"My father," said Katherine Held. "We're waiting for my father. He should be here soon."

"Your father!" he exclaimed. "Your father is coming here?"

"Yes," she said. "I phoned him and told him to come."

"But why?" he asked. "What's to be gained? I have nothing more to say to your father."

"But my father may have something to say," she countered. "And I want him to speak before – before a witness. If Dr. Lerner has heard your story, he should hear my father's too."

"Must I be here?" he asked. "And must I face him again?"

"Do you have any choice?" she asked, almost mocking him.

"No," he said. "No choice. Not any more. Let it be done."

Again we waited in silence. I concentrated my whole mind on the direction of the stairs, to hear at last someone slowly, laboriously climbing them. The man's footsteps came to a halt at the top of the stairs, and I heard muffled voices. The man had obviously stopped by the office and was asking where Theodore Stappler's room was.

"That's my father," said Katherine very softly.

None of us stirred.

The footsteps continued their way, came closer, and halted outside Theodore Stappler's room. Then there came a light knock on the door.

We rose, almost all at once. Theodore Stappler went to the door and opened it.

Face to face, I thought. Once more, face to face.

But Joseph Held, looking smaller even, more insignificant, framed there against the dim corridor in a dim light, than I had expected, hardly looked at Theodore Stappler. He pushed past him into the centre of the room, his eyes sweeping quickly across the whole room, stopping briefly to glance at me and then coming to rest on his daughter.

"You are all right?" he said, his voice wavering between a question and a straight assertion. "Nothing has happened to you?"

"No," she said, "nothing has happened to me."

"Thank God," he said, "thank God." He seemed immensely relieved. "I didn't know what to make of it. Over the telephone you sounded absolutely desperate. Frantic. Incoherent almost. I didn't know what to think. I didn't know what to make of it. I was half scared to death. I came as fast as I could. But there is much snow. It is hard to drive."

"Nothing has happened to me," she repeated. "I'm perfectly safe. If that's what you were worrying about. Nothing at all has happened to me. As you see." She motioned over to me, almost as if I were acting as her chaperon. "This is Professor Lerner," she said then, introducing me. "You've heard me speak of him."

"I am honoured to meet you, sir," said Joseph Held. He came towards me with outstretched hand, and he bowed formally when I shook hands with him. It was almost as if we were meeting at some tea party and were getting ready for some pleasant chit-chat.

I asked him to take his coat off, and he did so. Then he turned again to his daughter and asked, "Why did you call me here?"

I wanted you to come," she said, "because . . . . because. . . ." Her voice broke, and the sentence trailed off. She looked at me, as if she were asking me to speak for her, just as earlier Theodore Stappler had asked me to speak for him. But I couldn't bring myself to do it. Joseph Held was after all a total stranger to me, and I couldn't suddenly confront him with an accusation.

"Because what?" he asked, very quietly, and without any seeming emotion.

I remembered what Theodore Stappler had told me about his first meeting with Held, and how he was able to keep himself under control. So it seemed now. But his eyelids suddenly began to twitch and betrayed his inner tension. He must surely know what had happened, I thought. He must surely have an inkling of why he had been summoned in such haste. But it was also clear that he was waiting to hear it from someone else, in order to be sure exactly what the limits of knowledge and revelation were.

"Because what?" he asked again, more insistently.

She saw that no one in the room would speak for her, not I, and not Theodore Stappler. So she took a deep breath, like someone about to dive into depths where no air is, and said, "Because Theodore – Mr. Stappler said something about you that I don't believe. And I wanted you to come here and tell him that it isn't true."

"What did he say?"

"That you betrayed him," she said, her face pale and her voice now barely audible. "And his mother. And others."

"Ahhhh." A cry that was half a moan and half an expression of suppressed anger broke from him. After a few moments, when he had sufficiently recovered himself, he rounded on Theodore Stappler.

"You promised me," he cried out. "You promised me that it would be between us – between you and me – between us only."

"No, no," Theodore Stappler said quickly. "I promised you nothing I promised you absolutely nothing. . . . But I didn't go out

of my way to tell her. I didn't want to tell her. I wanted to leave. . . .
Look. My bags are packed. I would never have come back. I
wanted to leave you alone with – with whatever knowledge you
have. . . . But she came here this afternoon, and. . . . Ask Professor
Lerner here. He is my witness. He will tell you that what I said
is true."

Held disregarded the request. "Why do you make the innocent
suffer?" he asked. "Why? What is gained?"

"I did all I could to prevent it," Theodore Stappler asserted.
"All."

"You talk about me as if I were six years old," Katherine broke
in. "I don't understand. . . . What I want to know is if it's true. Is
Theodore telling the truth, and were you telling me things about
him that weren't true? That's what I have to know. Why can't you
tell me? Is it true? Is it, Father?"

"I must sit down," Joseph Held said. "First I must sit down."

He walked over to the chair by the window where Theodore
Stappler had been sitting when Katherine and I had returned to
his room. Joseph Held's forehead was sweaty, and he drew a
handkerchief out of his pocket and mopped his brow, and then,
speaking very deliberately, he said, "It is true and it is not true. . .
It is true that some – certain things happened. I wish to God that
what happened did not happen. And I wish also that I should
have had the power to make them not happen. But I did not." He
turned away from her and spoke to Theodore Stappler. "You
promised me that it would be between you and me," he said, as if
he had completely forgotten that only moments before he had
said the very same thing and that Theodore Stappler had denied
that he had ever made such a promise. "Between you and me
only," he repeated. "That you would not. . . ."

"I made you no promises," said Theodore Stappler. "None.
But even so, I didn't want to involve Katherine. I told you that
already. But let's not talk about promises."

"Why should there be promises anyway?" Katherine asked.
"Theodore – Mr. Stappler – says that there were some people who
were – arrested because of you. And I can't believe that. You
are not that kind of man. You. . . ."

"No man knows who he is," Joseph Held said. "Until the
moment comes. No man knows what he will do and what he will
not do until the finger points to him. . . These were extraordinary
times."

"But did you?" she pressed him. "Did you – betray these people? And were they arrested because of you?"

Joseph Held closed his eyes and leaned his head forward against his chest. For a long, long time he seemed thus to take counsel with himself.

"Certainly – some people were arrested," he said at last. "That is true. But I am not so black. Not so very black. And yet God knows black enough. . . . Mr. Stappler says I did it for money. I saved people for money. But I did not betray for money. I sacrificed some people to save others."

"Yourself," said Theodore Stappler.

The word fell like a stone.

"Not myself," said Joseph Held. "Not myself only. I was afraid. Of course I was afraid. But I didn't think of myself first of all. I thought of my wife and – and of my daughter." He turned to Katherine. "I was threatened," he said, "and there were hints also about you and your mother – of what would happen if I didn't do what they wanted. And that was my choice."

He suddenly turned and addressed me. I thought he had forgotten all about me, and I had in fact tried to make myself as inconspicuous as possible. But now he drew me into the circle.

"What would you have done?" he asked. "Doesn't everyone act to save his loved ones first?"

It was a question I found impossible to answer. For I had already asked myself precisely that question. Faced with a similar situation, would I have done what he had done? Would I have acted on pure principle? Challenged directly by Joseph Held, I pondered the question again, and in absolute honesty I could not answer it. So I took refuge in evasion, all the while aware of my cowardice.

"That all depends," I said.

"Aha!" Like acid, Theodore Stappler's voice cut through my careful and deliberate words. "The *Herr Professor* is taking up his position on the fence again."

"I'm not a judge," I mumbled.

"A man is still free to choose his own way in any given situation," Theodore Stappler said.

"But you yourself," Joseph Held broke in, "were not everything you wanted to be in that situation."

"No," Theodore Stappler said. "I am the first to admit it. But you have no right to throw that in my face."

It was curious how we seemed to have reached a stalemate, how all roads led us into a labyrinth, where one not only lost one's way but was in constant danger of sinking into a morass and suffocating. There was no light there and no air.

"You," Theodore Stappler pursued Held, pointing his right index finger at him, "you were supposed to lead us to safety. But you led us into a trap instead."

"I was in a trap myself," Joseph Held defended himself. "From the moment that I made that first deal with them. That was my sin. And I am the first to confess it. If it could be undone I would undo it. God is my witness."

Katherine had been standing there without saying a word. But she was tense and nervous, and her eyes moved restlessly around the room, from Theodore Stappler to her father and back again. Now she asked her father, "What did you do? What exactly did you do?"

Joseph Held looked at his daughter in a kind of astonishment, as if the question had shocked him. It occured to me that he probably thought she knew more than she actually did.

"Has he not told you?" he asked. "Has he not given you his side of the events?"

"No," she said. "I only know in the most general way, and only what I have heard here this evening."

"I see," he said. And then, after a moment's silence, "So I must tell you, after all. I thought I would never have to tell you. That it could be spared you. You remember that after Austria was taken over – you were a little girl – after the *Anschluss*, I used to be away from home every few weeks. You have asked me about that. Not for a long time but you used to ask me about that."

"Yes," she said. "I remember."

"I was a lawyer," he said, turning to me. "I had connections with some people high in the police. Two or three months after the takeover, one of these men – I knew him well – I had played cards with him and drunk coffee and wine with him – came to me with a proposition. I couldn't practise law any more, you see. I was making arrangements to leave the country with my family. In the meantime I did a little work, whatever I could do – I helped people to get their papers in order and I arranged their documents. And one day this man – his name was Wirt – approached me and made me a proposition. 'You can help your people,' he told me. 'You can help yourself – and of course there will be something for me, too. So everybody,' he said, 'will be satisfied. Everybody will be happy.' And for a while it worked. There were people who had to leave the country, and who were willing to pay for it. They had no visas for other countries, and I arranged things. I helped them. I saved them. And after all, Mr. Stappler came to me. I didn't come to him. . . .

"But then, that last time, it didn't work any more. Suddenly there were no supports any more. I don't know why. I could never find out. I went to see Wirt, as always. I gave him part of the money, as always. He took it, as always. And then he said, '*Das Spiel ist aus*. The game is over.' I asked him what he meant. He told me what I had to do. I asked him why, but he was cold, like a stone. He wouldn't say anything. . . I – I – oh, God, I don't know, I don't know. I cried out to him, 'No, no!' I begged him, but he only threatened me. I had to do what he said. I am not a hero. . ." His voice trailed off, and he was silent.

"Then you knew," Theodore Stappler's voice, calm and quiet, cut through the dark silence. "When you met us at the station, when you came into the compartment and spoke to us, to me and to my mother, you knew all the time. You knew that we were doomed. And you said nothing. Not even the slightest of hints."

"*Man ist doch nur ein Mensch*," Held whispered.

"But you managed, anyway, to save yourself."

This accusation Held did not answer directly. "I thought still," he said, "that perhaps I could do something. At the last minute. When I met that other man – in Saarbrücken. I thought that perhaps there. . . but it didn't work. All the doors were shut. But I tried there. I tried. I tried. . . . I did save some people. Some. Only in the end there was a price. And that I didn't know. That there would be a price. And how high it would be."

"You walked with them. Down the platform you walked with them. You did their work for them. That was the price."

"In the end," said Joseph Held, "that was the price. But I saved some people before that. But never mind – in the end that was the price. I will not deny that."

"You saved yourself," said Theodore Stappler. "You delivered us up. Without a struggle. And you told me that you were a man of honour. That you would be with us and stay with us. You told me that we were all in the same boat and that you would not jump out."

Joseph Held nodded his head slowly. He made no effort to

justify himself further. Indeed, he seemed to be a totally beaten man. I wanted him to go on pleading for himself, to put forward some further explanations, however commonplace, however platitudinous, but he seemed now to have decided against that course.

"In the end," he said at last, very softly, "I thought only of myself, and of my wife and of my daughter, and of no one else." He tried to say more, he gestured with his hands, but words would not come.

No one said anything. In the silence we heard a young couple, talking and laughing, coming up the stairs. For a moment I thought they were going to stop outside Theodore Stappler's room, but they passed on and knocked on the next door, and the door opened, and I recognized the voices of the young honeymoon couple. Their quarrel seemed now to be over, for they all sounded very happy, and it seemed as if they were about to have a party.

Suddenly Theodore Stappler spoke, and what he said surprised me.

"Why don't you ask me why and how I saved myself?"

"We both live with our questions," Held said. "Each alone. I alone. You alone. I bore it, all alone. For all these years. I shared it with nobody. Not my wife, not my daughter. I took it on myself. I alone." He spoke now entirely to Theodore Stappler. He whispered to him, *"Mein Leben ist schärzer als die Nacht und tiefer als die Hölle."*

The phrase made me shudder. It shook me to the very depths. Darker than night. Deeper than hell. That, he said, had been his life. I saw suddenly the tragedy of Europe in the lives of these two men. For really, nothing that either of them, acting alone, could have done would have much changed the awful pattern of events. Clearly, Held should have refused to act, to have become embroiled in the pattern of corruption. But his sin was moral weakness rather than criminal villainy.

"We both live with our questions," Theodore Stappler echoed Joseph Held. "You are right. Each alone. You alone and I alone. And I ask myself over and over. 'Why was I saved? And what for? To do what? To come here and find you out?' But that was not worth it."

He seemed unutterably weary.

I glanced over to the bed where Katherine Held was sitting. I had almost forgotten about her, and I saw now that tears were streaming down her cheeks, silently, and she made no effort to wipe them away but sat with her arms folded in her lap. I had often asked my students how we are to judge extreme situations and the reactions of fallible human beings to them. And now, asking myself the same question, my mind simply refused to come to grips with it. That was in a sense cowardly, an evasion of responsibility. Faced with the question now, here in this room, I could only think of platitudes: how thin the veneer of civilization is even in the most civilized nations and how fortunate most of us are to be spared the most extreme tests of courage and virtue, for how many of us could pass them?

In the room next door the party got livelier. Someone had put a radio on, and loud and frantic music came bursting through the walls, and then I heard the shuffling of feet. There was obviously dancing.

In our room all passion seemed to have been spent, but there was no relief. A dull ache remained. Nothing had been settled, nothing resolved. I longed for something tremendously dramatic to happen. Absurdly, I suddenly thought of Charlotte Corday stabbing poor Marat in his bathtub. A confusing and absurd thought. No one in this room would stab anyone. The two antagonists seemed to have disarmed each other. But yet I longed for some climactic moment to occur, for some cathartic relief.

"Let's have another drink," a man's voice shouted in the other room, so that the words could be heard plainly, and then I heard the sound of glasses clinking and laughter and confused talk and snatches of song and the radio blaring louder than before.

But we in this room were frozen. Then suddenly I heard a heavy fist banging on the door of the next room, and a thunderous voice shouted, "Sharrap!" There was a sudden hush of silence. Then someone opened the door, and there was some loud and animated conversation, and whoever it was that had protested so loudly agreed to join the party, and things seemed gayer then they had before. The shouting and the laughter now rose with greater abandon.

"There is nothing more that can be done," Joseph Held said. "If you will allow me, I will now go."

He rose, as if with a great effort. Old and wizened he seemed, a pitiable figure. I had got up also, to try to help him into his overcoat, when there came a knock, timid and hesitant, on the door. I was closest to the door and opened it.

A tousle-haired young man was standing there, a bit unsteady, holding a large glass of whisky in his hand.

"My name's Art," he said. "We're having a party in the next room."

"I had an idea there was a party going on," I said.

Art raised his glass. "Here's to you," he said. He took a long gulp from the glass. "We're having a little party," he said again, wiping his mouth with the back of his hand. His tie was loose and his shirt collar was open. He wore a navy-blue suit, obviously new, but already badly creased. "A celebration kind of," he explained, focusing a pair of tame, watery eyes on me. "On account Mary and me just got married, about a week ago."

"Congratulations," I said. "I wish you a great deal of happiness and a long life."

"Thanks," he said. "Thanks a lot." He seemed suddenly shy and modest. "Well, that's what I really came for," he said quickly. "We thought if all the people in the hotel'd come and have a drink with us we wouldn't have to worry on account of the racket."

"That would make a large crowd," I said.

"Naw," he said. "There's only four rooms taken, and one party's out. So there's only you and Number Six and us."

Glum looks met him and he shrank back in some confusion.

"Thank you very much," I said, "but I don't think anyone here wants to have a party just now."

"Don't worry about us," Theodore Stappler called out to him. "Just go ahead and have a good time."

"Well, I'm sorry," said the young man. "In that case I guess I'll just go along. But any of you come and join the party any time you feel like it. Here's to you," he said, now speaking directly to me. He raised his glass to me in salutation and invitation all at once, and then turned and went back into his own room.

Joseph Held stood dressed and ready to go, and suddenly Katherine, who had seemed hesitant, joined him, and said, "I'm going with you."

"I am glad," he said.

Theodore Stappler made no move. He looked on, waiting for something to happen, perhaps for some manifestation.

Joseph Held opened the door and stepped out into the corridor. She let him go and for a moment turned, and she and Theodore Stappler stood looking at each other like two lost souls, I thought, who had momentarily met, had found something that drew them together and now were driven apart again, to go separate ways. So at least it seemed to me.

"I didn't want you to know," said Theodore Stappler, sadly shaking his head. "I didn't want you to get hurt."

"I'm sorry," she said. "About everything." Her voice was hardly audible above the din of the music coming from the other room. "What can be done?" she asked. "What can be done?"

His body seemed to stiffen. His face became pale, almost a mask. But he did not answer her. No word, no gesture came from him. I longed for him to speak, to let the fountain of frozen emotion flow, but evidently he could not.

She raised her hand to him in a gesture of greeting and farewell, and then turned and joined her father outside in the corridor.

Then suddenly Theodore Stappler got up and almost ran to the door, as if he meant to follow her and call her back, but stopped short and merely looked after them, as they slowly descended the stairs and disappeared from our view.

So it ended, with a whisper. The cathartic, cleansing emotion was not released. Perhaps it could not have been. Held's dark night and deep hell were there still. He carried them with him. And Theodore Stappler's tragic burden was there still. It had in no way been lightened. For me, the witness, who had inexorably been drawn into the circle, what was left for me to do? It was at this very moment, in fact, that I suddenly decided that I would set all this down, so that the act of writing would in itself be a kind of relief.

"You've missed your train," I said to Theodore Stappler when we had sat down again.

"There will be another train," he answered.

"You're still determined to leave."

"Of course. More than ever now. What else is there for me to do? Nothing." He looked at me and said in his most acid voice, "*Die Zukunft ist wunderbar.*" After that he became silent.

Someone turned up the volume on the radio next door, and then I heard the shuffling of footsteps in the corridor. The dancing had begun again.

There seemed nothing for me to do any more. "I think I'll go now," I said.

He nodded but didn't answer me, and so I took my coat and left.

In the corridor the young man confronted me. "Come and have a drink," he said.

A drink was exactly what I needed, and I allowed myself to be gently pushed into the room. A great shout of welcome greeted me. The couple who had been dancing stopped and came over to me.

"That's Bill and Mary," said Art, introducing them. "And that's another Mary over there. My Mary, that is."

"Hi," said his Mary demurely.

"And that's Number Six over there. His name's Bob." Number Six sat silently in a corner, drinking his whisky with slow and deliberate determination.

"And he was just in Number Eight," said Art, pointing at me.

"I'm not staying here," I said quickly. "I was just visiting some-one."

"That's all the same," said Art. "We don't mind. What's your name?"

"Mark," I said.

"Where you from?" he asked.

"I live in town," I said.

"Well, that's all right," he said. "Here," he continued, pointing to the dresser, "get yourself a drink."

Three bottles of rye whisky, one full and the other two half empty, stood on the dresser, and also a pitcher of water and two tumblers.

I poured myself a drink, raised my glass to the company, when Bill cried, "Hey, wait a minute, wait a minute! This is a celebration. It's their honeymoon. He's gotta kiss the bride before he drinks. The bride! The bride!"

He got hold of the girl, the other Mary, and pulled her gently over, so that she stood between him and me. I kissed her on the cheek. She giggled.

"You can do better than that!" he cried. "On the lips. You gotta kiss her on the lips."

I felt compelled to kiss her on the lips.

"Atta boy!" Bill seemed delighted. "Dja see Art, Mary? Look at him. He's jealous."

"Naw," said Art. "I got trust in Mary. And Mary's got trust in me. Haven't you, honey?"

"Well, I'm not so sure any more," she said pouting. And turning to me, she said, "He was making eyes at a waitress just before, when we were having dinner. That's why we were having a fight when we came up."

"Aw, nuts," cried Art. He fairly leaped at her, caught her up in his arms and began to smother her with kisses.

"Atta boy!" cried Bill.

"Now are you sure?" Art demanded, but got no immediate answer. "Open your mouth," he commanded. He put his glass to her lips but tilted it up too far, and most of the whisky spilled on her dress. She only laughed and took the glass from him and drank.

"Are you sure?" he insisted.

"Sure, darling," she said. "Sure I'm sure."

"That's right," said Bill. "You gotta make sure all the time." He suddenly began to sing in a loud, croaking baritone, "Shenandoah, I hear you caaaaalling. Hoyohoy, you mighty river. Shenandoah. . . ."

"Aw, cut it out, Bill," cried Art. "Don't sing that song. We don't want to hear that song."

Bill's wife sprang to his defence. "Why can't he sing that song? He used to be a sailor. Only I stopped him 'cause he was never home. What's the use of being married if your man is never home? So I badgered him till he gave it up and we moved here from the coast. But he can sing shanties if he wants to. You sing, Bill," she ended defiantly.

"But not that song," said Art truculently. "He can sing if he wants to, but something with a little pep to it, something cheerful, not that moaning stuff. We're supposed to celebrate."

"Okay, okay," said Bill. "How's this?" He cleared his throat. "On the road to Mandalayhay, where the flyin' fishes play," he sang.

"That's better," cried Art and joined in. Together they roared out the song, substituting a confused bellowing for the words they only knew in part. They ended amid general laughter, and Art tottered over to the dresser, got hold of a bottle and went around the room filling up everyone's glass.

"Now you, Mark," he said when he came to me. "You sing us a song. C'mon! Sing us a song!"

I had had two large drinks and was beginning to feel warm and cheerful. I raised my glass and began to sing the first song that came into my mind. "Roll out the barrel," I sang, "let's have a barrel of fun."

They all joined in and sang lustily when suddenly, out of the corner where everyone had forgotten that he was, Number Six roared, "Sharrap!"

We stopped singing and looked at him.

He drew himself laboriously up from his chair and stood there, swaying slowly backwards and forwards, like a fragile little tree in the wind.

"Sharrap!" he roared again, though we were all silent and stood looking at him. He peered about with glazed eyes, his tongue trying to formulate words.

"Le's sing," he cried. "Sure, le's sing. . . . Le's sing, patriotic. . . . O Canada," he roared out, "our native home and land." He stopped. "Tha's not right." He tried to steady himself on the back of his chair. "What country needs," he said, swaying dangerously now, his hand missing the back of the chair and groping vainly about for it. "What country needs is. . . . is flag. Tha's what th' country needs. Nash'nal flag. We don't want no. . . . Nothing. Flag. So we know – so we goddam well know who we're supposed – what is supposed – what – who we. . . . Can't be nobody . . . . Gotta be somebody." His hand clawed desperately at the empty air. Then quietly he slumped down on the floor and lay there, like a sack of potatoes.

"He's out," said Art.

"Cold," said Bill.

"Take him to his room," cried one of the girls.

"Give us a hand," said Bill to me.

He was heavy, and he stirred uneasily when we began to lift him up. Art came over to give us a hand. Together we carried him to his room and carefully deposited him on his bed. He snored contentedly, and we went back again to the other room.

Art filled all the glasses.

"Let's have some music," cried his bride, the other Mary. She reached behind her and turned on a little portable radio which stood on the night-table beside the bed. Music blared out.

"Let's dance," she cried excitedly. "C'mon, Art. Let's dance."

He got up, not very steady on his legs any more, and at once sat down again.

"Oh, come on. Dance with me."

"Okay, honey," he said.

They whirled about, out of the room, dancing along the corridor, and then back into the room again. Art was barely able to keep up with her.

"Not so fast," he cried. "Not so fast." He was winded.

The music stopped, and he sank down exhausted on a chair. There was a commercial, and then the music started again, a slow and languorous tune.

"C'mon, Art," she said, attempting to pull him up from his chair. "Dance with me."

"I can't," he said. "I can't dance any more."

"Aw, come on."

"Naw, I've had it."

She turned to me. "You dance with me, then," she said.

"I'd be delighted," I said.

We moved slowly to the music, out of the room, and danced along the corridor until we came to the head of the stairs. There, in the office, I saw an elderly man who had evidently taken over from Sam. He stared morosely at us. He too, had been drinking. We turned and danced towards the room again. A scent of cologne and whisky rose to me as she nestled closer into my arms.

"Gee," she said. "You dance real swell." She laid her head against my cheek.

Suddenly I became aware of Art standing in the door, glowering at us. When we came level with him, he stretched out his hand and grabbed me by the shoulder.

"Hey," he said. "What's going on? You trying to make a pass at my wife?"

"Of course not," I protested.

"You were whispering to her," he said.

"I didn't," I said. "I didn't say anything. I was just thinking."

"Yeah. I heard you. I know that kind of thinking. And you," he said, turning to his wife, the other Mary. "You danced pretty close."

"I never," she said. "Besides, he didn't mean nothing."

"Oh, yeah." His tone was belligerent. He balled his hands into fists.

I said hurriedly, "I was thinking about someone else. Another girl." But my arm was still round Mary's waist.

"Oh, yeah," he said and pulled her away. "I can't trust you neither," he said to her. "So now we're even."

"You've got to trust her," I said, feeling like an idiot.

"Not with guys like you around," he said.

Bill was suddenly between us. "Let's have no fights," he said. "They was only dancing."

"He made a pass at her," said Art.

"He never," said his wife, the other Mary.

"Did you?" Bill asked me.

"No," I said. I no longer really cared about anything. "What's all the fuss about anyway?"

"There," said Bill, the peacemaker. "He never. Shake hands, you two. We don't want any fights. We don't want the p'lice around here."

Art seemed reluctant. But at last he growled, "Okay," and thrust out his right hand, drawing his wife closer to him with his left. "Let's have another drink."

He filled all the glasses again. "That's it," he said, emptying the last bottle. "All gone."

He drank his drink down quickly and then went over to the bed and lay down. "Come here, Mary," he said. She lay down beside him, and he pulled her close to him and kissed her.

"Well, we might's well go home," said Bill to his wife. "The party's over."

I helped them into their coats and then watched as they staggered carefully down the stairs, out into the street.

I was left all alone. On the bed the honeymoon couple had dropped off to sleep, fully clothed, in each other's arms. I looked about the room, surveying the debris – the empty bottles, the glasses on the floor, the cigarette stubs everywhere. I stared for a few moments at the figures on the bed. How peacefully they slept, all conflicts for the moment resolved. I felt that I must make them more comfortable. So I tiptoed over to the bed, somewhat unsteadily, and pulled off their shoes. Then I put on my coat and hat and my overshoes, turned out the light in the room, and left.

Outside Theodore Stappler's room I stopped. What was he doing? Curious how I had almost forgotten that he was there. I knocked on his door. There was no answer from within. I turned the knob and entered his room. Darkness met me. But the light from the corridor was sufficient to make the outlines of his room perceptible to me. He sat where I had left him, as if he had never moved at all.

The shapes in the room, the bed, the chairs, the chest of

drawers, the still form of Theodore Stappler himself, sitting frozen and immobile in his chair, began to see-saw and swim before my eyes. I steadied myself and held onto the door.

"Theodore!" I called to him.

He seemed startled. "Mark?"

"Yes."

"Have you come back?"

"I haven't left yet."

"What were you doing?"

"I danced."

"You danced!"

"I drank."

"Oh!"

"I helped to celebrate."

"What?"

"God knows. A marriage. I suppose it was a marriage."

"A new life."

"I suppose."

"Good. The world has to move on."

"Why are you sitting in darkness?"

"I don't want to see anything."

"Why don't you go to bed?"

"I don't think I could sleep."

"What are you thinking about?"

"Nothing. Nothing."

"About Katherine?"

"I try not to."

"Joseph Held?"

"Nothing."

"Do you need anything?"

"No. Nothing."

"I'm going now."

"Yes."

"Will you be leaving tomorrow?"

"Yes. Yes, of course."

"Let me drive you to the station."

"If you wish."

"Good night, then."

"Good night."

I closed the door of his room and walked down the silent corridor. In the office, the old man, the watchman and night clerk, his head leaning against the desk, was sleeping and snoring. Gloom overcame me. I felt a desperate need to dispel it. I began to sing. "Shenandoah, you rolling river," I sang, and "Roll out the barrel," I sang, passing the snoring watchman, groping my way down the steep stairs and wondering vaguely how, as clouds seemed to envelop my head, I would be able to steer my car home through the thick snow.

❦ XIV

I STUMBLED OUT OF THE HOTEL VICTORIA INTO THE STREET.
Whiteness in darkness. It had very nearly stopped snowing. Only
a few perfunctory flakes were still drifting down from the black,
invisible sky. But a great deal of snow had fallen, and though cars
and buses had cut deep furrows into the road, the snow on the
pavement was almost undefiled.

For a moment I felt as if I had stepped out onto a strange and
unknown street. The landscape seemed curiously unfamiliar, like
a landscape in a dream. The buildings were sombre, forbidding
shapes, rising from the white pavement into the darkness above.
There was very little traffic on the road. I did not know what time
it was. It seemed the dead end of the night.

Slowly I became aware of the cold, and I buttoned my overcoat, something that I had evidently neglected to do while I was
still in the hotel. Slowly, like a sleeper returning to consciousness, I began to place things. Over there, somewhere – I could not
really recall where – there was my car, where I had left it in the
afternoon – or perhaps it was now yesterday afternoon. Now the
sequence of events began to move through my mind: how I had
spoken to Sam, how I had sat with Theodore Stappler, how I had
walked with him, how I had eaten with him – his father's suicide
– how Katherine had come, how she had summoned her father,
how the two victims had confronted each other once again, how I
had danced, how I had drunk. But though things moved, in a curiously slow and stately procession, through my mind, they did not
seem to matter. Nothing mattered. I could attach no real significance to any single event that day, which now probably already was
yesterday.

Still, my head now seemed clearer. And if I kept standing there on the pavement, in the snow, long enough, I would freeze. At any rate, my ears would freeze. So march, I said to myself, and find the car. Take one step and then another step, and move. Where was the car? Why, sure, I suddenly remembered, I had parked the car very nearly outside the hotel – the victory hotel, as Theodore Stappler had called it. I stumbled on through the snow and ploughed my way through the virgin blanket of snow to the end of the block, only to realize when I got there that I had gone the wrong way. I was now fully aware of myself, moved with more assurance, less automatically, turned with more delibera- tion, and suddenly realized that I had been standing very nearly be- side my car when I had first come into the street.

It hardly seemed like a car, but rather like some sort of humped animal completely covered in snow. Gingerly I began to remove some of the snow, so that I could open the door and get the long-handled brush, which lay ready on the back seat, and then I started to remove thick layers of snow from the rear win- dow and from the windshield and from the hood, until at last the body of the car emerged from under the blanket of snow.

I got into the car and turned the ignition on. The battery was cold. It coughed and wheezed, at last caught. The engine shud- dered, growled. I waited for it to warm up a bit, then slowly let the clutch in. The car groaned, pulled slowly away from the curb. I steered with care, concentrating wholly on the task. Every de- cision seemed to demand my most deliberate concentration, be- cause I still had the sensation that I was driving through unfamil- iar streets in a faintly familiar city.

But somehow I got home. At last familiar objects surrounded me. Emily Carr's trees were there, towering on my wall, the tangled roots almost coming out of the canvas and spreading into my brain. There was my desk, a half-read essay lying on top where I had left it before I went out. There was my bed. I took off my shoes, my jacket, my trousers. But could not move any fur- ther, could not bring myself to change into my pyjamas.

I began to sing to myself, absurdly. Shenandoah haunted me, the rolling river. Clouds enveloped me, thickened about my head; the room swayed, see-sawed, but I managed, barely, with the greatest difficulty and in the slowest of slow motions, to pull back the blankets and crawl between the sheets.

By a stagnant lake I lay entangled in roots. I struggled to free myself. On my left and on my right there were two men whose faces never came into clear focus, although I kept looking at them, staring and staring. I thought I knew them, but just as I was about to fix them firmly, the outlines of their faces wavered until I could see only a nose, an ear, a mouth, but never a complete face. They stretched their arms out towards me, as if beseeching me to help them, to get them out of the bog, to free them from creeping roots that were threatening to strangle them. But how could I help them? I was myself entangled.

Around us there danced, arms linked together, three or four couples, I could not be sure exactly how many. Perpetually they moved round us. They did not seem to notice us at all. The entangling roots which held us captive did not bother them. Nor did the soft earth. They danced and danced, a joyless dance. No birds sang. No music played.

Only from far, far away came the sound of bells ringing, not sonorously, but jangling and discordant. The sound came closer and closer until it seemed to be within my ears, within my head, and I threshed about trying to stop it. I came up, as from a great depth. My hands groped about. Was I asleep? Was I awake? Was I dreaming?

My hand, instinctively, lifted something. The bells were silent. The ringing inside my head stopped.

A voice cried out to me.

"Dr. Lerner! Dr. Lerner! Dr. Lerner!"

"Yes," I answered. "Yes."

It was a girl's voice. It seemed vaguely familiar but, like the faces of the two men, the voice would not stay still.

"My father!" the girl's voice cried. "My father! My father!"

"Who are you?" I asked.

"Please come. Please help me."

"Who are you?" I asked again.

But there was silence.

"Hallo!" I called. "Hallo! Hallo!"

The line had gone dead.

I was conscious of being awake now, propped up on one elbow on my bed, my other hand holding the receiver. Darkness enveloped me. To my right the first faint glimmers of the dawn were beginning to show through the window. What time was it? I replaced the receiver, groped about for the lamp on my night-table. Yellow light bathed the area around my bed. And now I could not be sure what had happened. Had somebody actually called me or had I been only dreaming?

My alarm clock was ticking away. I checked the time. It was just ten minutes past seven. The alarm was set for eight and I turned it off. Clearly I was not going to fall asleep again.

Slowly, slowly I gathered my thoughts about me, tried to get things into focus, above all to place the voice that had called to me for help.

If indeed there had been such a call, it must have been from Katherine Held. No one else could have called me. I sat up in bed and fumbled for the telephone book, which I kept in the drawer of the night-table. But when I dialled the number, it was busy.

She had called to me for help. She had asked me to come. I was weary. My head was throbbing. My mouth felt as if I had been chewing rusty nails. Automatically I pulled on my trousers and noticed that I still had my socks on. I went into the bathroom and splashed cold water on my face. My shirt was crumpled, but I did not bother to change it. I just put my tie on. Before I left, I rang the number again, but it was still busy. I copied down the address, and then I left.

Everything seemed jumbled; event melted into event. I no longer knew where dream ended and reality began. Once again I drove through streets heavy with snow, streets still dark, though the winter dawn was now breaking, the sky was lightening. It seemed to me suddenly as if I had been driving all through the night, that I had not been to bed at all. I welcomed the dawn, as if it meant that I could stop moving now.

But why had she called to me? Why had she cried for help? Why must I be further involved in events that had nothing to do with me? I felt resentful all at once and stepped on the gas, but the car began to skid, and I came to with a start.

But why did they feel, Katherine Held and Theodore Stappler, that they could summon me so peremptorily? I felt victimized. And now her father, too! "My father!" she had called to me. "My father!" And I had obeyed the call, at once, and without any question.

I drove across the steel-girdered bridge, sensing below me the frozen river. Across the river and up the hill I had stood that afternoon with Theodore Stappler. How long ago that seemed now. I could no longer differentiate the past from the immediate present. Everything was now, and yet everything seemed to have happened somewhere in the distant past. And I could no longer be sure of my own part in the events. The more I tried to detach myself, the more involved, the more entangled, I became. Yet some necessity drove me on. They had all now, in one way or another, called on me for help – Theodore Stappler, Joseph Held, and now Katherine, too. And yet how could I help them? What could I do? It seemed that I must listen and yet was powerless to act. For I could not ultimately pass judgement. If Theodore Stappler and Joseph Held had paralysed each other, they had paralysed me, too. We seemed now to circle endlessly around the problem which Held's action posed. And was I now to be called on again – this time by Held's daughter – to help her resolve a dilemma that had so suddenly opened up before her?

I reached at last the street where they lived. A grey light was over everything, and all was silent. Only my car moved through the snow. I shut off the engine and sat for a few moments, looking at the house. The house was dark. No one seemed to be up yet. Suddenly I doubted whether I had, in fact, been summoned. Perhaps it was all part of the dream. But I had heard the voice. And the voice had called to me for help. It had called me to come.

So I walked cautiously up to the door and rang the bell. No one stirred. Nothing happened. I rang the bell again, this time keeping my finger on it and wondering vaguely if I was making a fool of myself. What if I were rousing people who had no desire to see me? Should I then say, "I thought you called to me for help?" And what if she were indignant and denied it, saying that my help was not wanted?

The bell was still ringing, when the door was suddenly opened and she stood before me. She was barefoot. Her hair was dishevelled. She wore a blue, woollen dressing-gown, and I thought she must have just got out of bed and that she had not called me at all.

"Oh, Dr. Lerner," she said, "oh, Dr. Lerner. You came." Her voice was barely a whisper. "I thought you would never come." She reached out her hand and drew me into the house. "Dr. Lerner. . . . my father. . . . I think my father is dead."

She closed her eyes, and her body swayed as if she were going to faint. I reached out my arms to her and drew her to me and saw how pale she was. I led her into the living-room, to the chesterfield where Theodore Stappler had sat on that first day, talking to her and waiting for her father.

I was afraid. What was I to do? Was he really dead? And if so, how had he died? Where was he? I shuddered to think of the body lying somewhere in this house.

Katherine seemed barely to breathe. Her body felt stiff against me, and I hardly dared to speak to her. At last I asked her if she had called someone else, a doctor or an ambulance.

She shook her head. "No," she said. "No. Only you. I spoke only to you." Suddenly she burst into tears. Her body was shaken by sobs. "I – I went to – to wake him," she said, the words coming between sobs, haltingly. "He – didn't answer me, and I – I went in – and – and – saw. . . ."

"He died in his sleep, then?" I felt totally inadequate to deal with this situation. My mind was clear, nothing of the hangover remained, but I was suddenly conscious of the beating of my heart, and when I got up my legs felt weak, as if they were about to buckle under me. But I had to go upstairs. I had to see, and then, if he were indeed dead, I would have somehow to take charge of things, for she was clearly incapable of doing anything at the moment.

"I'll go upstairs to see."

She nodded her head and, shivering, drew her dressing-gown closer about her.

I mounted the stairs in this strange house, which yet I seemed to know. The stairs seemed steep, and my ascent was slow, almost as if I were climbing a high mountain and were moving into altitudes where it was hard to breathe. I steeled myself against what was to come. At the top of the landing I paused and looked about me. There were three doors. Two were closed and one was open. I heard a tap dripping. Otherwise everything was silent. I looked first into the room with the open door. That was Katherine's bedroom. I then opened the bathroom door and shut off the dripping tap. Now only the third door remained. I could not bring myself to turn the knob and open the door. I knocked on the door. Three times I knocked. There was, of course, no answer. And so I opened the door and entered the room.

The curtains on the window were half drawn. The room was in twilight. And by the grey light of the winter morning I saw the body lying on the bed. I walked softly to the foot of the bed and there, without thought, but simply obeying some impulse, I began to call his name.

"Joseph Held!" I called. "Joseph Held! Joseph Held!"

The body of the dead man seemed curiously heavy as it lay there, the rigid head sunk into the soft pillows. The eyes were open and stared up at the ceiling. The lower part of the body was covered by blankets. His heart must have stopped suddenly, I thought. There were no signs of heavy convulsions. The clothes of the dead man were carefully folded, and he had put them on a chair beside his bed.

I moved closer to him. I was no longer afraid. I reached out my right hand and pressed his eyelids down and closed his eyes. When the eyes were closed, the face took on the relaxed and yet brooding expression of a man in deep slumber. The dark night and the deep hell – had they come to an end now?

For some time yet I remained there, looking down at the still face. Then I pulled the sheet and the blankets over the whole body, and covered also his face.

Only then did I notice the empty pill bottle lying on the night-table beside his softly ticking wristwatch. I picked the bottle up and examined it. What kind of pills had there been in it? The label on the bottle didn't tell. It simply said, "Take one or two before bedtime."

How many had he taken? There would have to be an inquest, I thought. What would be said there? Death by accident? Suicide? What end would be served? I thought of the girl and of her agony, which could only be prolonged. To what end? But if no bottle were found? There could then be no questions. His heart had stopped. Did it matter how?

I turned the bottle round and round in my hand until I almost hypnotized myself. It was a curious sensation. But it made it easier for me to slip the little bottle into my pocket, with my conscience somehow neutralized. And so with one more look at the shape of his body, stiff and inert under the sheets and under the blankets, I left the room, closed the door behind me, and began the slow descent.

I found her huddled on the chesterfield, her knees drawn up against her body, her face turned into the cushions, as if she had crawled into a deep cave to seek some comfort. I touched her gently on the shoulder, and she turned with a startled cry. Her face was almost white. All the blood seemed drained from it. Her eyes were dry, two large, dark orbs staring at me.

"Is it – finished?" she asked, in a barely audible whisper.

"Yes," I said. "It is finished."

Her head drooped forward, buried itself again in the cushions. But no sound came from her, no cry, no whimper. She seemed oblivious to everything.

"Who was your father's doctor?" I asked her after a while. For the machinery of burial had to be set in motion.

She did not answer me, and I had to repeat the question. At last she gave me the name of the doctor and, when I went to the telephone, I saw that the receiver was off the hook. She had neglected to put it back after she had called to me for help. I looked up the doctor's number and, when I dialled it, a female voice informed me that the doctor was out of town and that another doctor, whose name she gave me, was taking his calls. I decided to call my own doctor, who was also a friend of mine, and managed to catch him just as he was leaving his house. When I explained to him what had happened, he said he would come at once. Everything seemed very matter-of-fact now, an ordinary death on an ordinary day in an ordinary house.

I went back into the living-room to wait for my friend to come. I sat down beside Katherine but did not talk to her, only occasionally stroked her hair, and that seemed to soothe her. Then I suddenly began to wonder what she would do now. I could not think of her staying on alone in this house. Who would look after her, especially during these first few days when the shock was most severe? I asked her if she had someone she could call on, but she said she didn't want to bother anyone. I asked her if she would mind if I arranged something with friends of mine, and she said she would leave it all to me. I thought at once of Brian Maxwell and his wife. They would help.

I went at once into the hall to phone the Maxwells, and Mary answered. As soon as I had explained what had happened, she agreed at once to help, and I said that I would bring Katherine over.

My friend arrived, obviously in a hurry. Just after I had phoned him, he said, there was a call from the hospital. He had to be there as soon as possible. I led him upstairs. On the way up he asked me if I had known the dead man for a long time. I told him I hadn't. Had he been ill for some time? I said I thought he had not been well, but that his daughter would be able to give him more precise information.

Once more I entered the room where the dead man lay. My friend pulled back the blankets and the sheet and began to examine the body. I asked if Joseph Held had had a heart attack. My friend said that that appeared to have been the cause of death. I made no mention of dark nights or of the depths of hell. Nor of the little bottle, empty of its pills.

I asked him what I should do next, since there was no one else to make the necessary arrangements. He gave me the name of an undertaker. Then he wrote out a death certificate.

We went downstairs again. He spoke briefly to Katherine, in a professionally kindly way, prescribed some sedatives for her, and left. I phoned the undertaker and was told that they would come for the body as soon as possible, within an hour.

We sat in a deep, brooding silence, waiting. The presence of death permeated the house, coming down from the room upstairs where the dead man lay. I tried to think of something to say, but all that I could think of seemed inane. The name of the one person who linked us together I didn't want to mention. And neither, evidently, did she. For we did not speak of Theodore Stappler.

"You should get dressed," I said.

"I can't go upstairs now," she said.

"No. I understand."

"Can you wait – till afterwards? Till they have. . .?"

"Of course."

There was a long pause. I felt suspended in a curious kind of no man's land, waiting.

Then suddenly she asked, "Dr. Lerner – those others he mentioned – my father – yesterday. The ones who – who -- forced him to do – what he did. What about them?"

"I – I don't know," I said.

"Do you think that they are – haunted, too? In the night?"

"Perhaps," I said. "But perhaps not." And added, "That's the horror. The real horror."

"Someone should pursue them, too."

"Yes," I said. "Yes."

"But will they?"

I could not answer her.

"I think I can go upstairs now," she said. "I'm not afraid any more. I'll go and get dressed now."

Her voice was suddenly choked. Tears began to course down her cheeks. I drew her close to me and wiped away her tears with my hand.

"I'll be all right," she said. "I can manage."

The men came while she was upstairs getting dressed. I went upstairs with them, and together we stood, Katherine and I, and watched them carry down the body.

And then we ourselves left.

I took her to the Maxwells and afterwards drove home. I could not think about very much, perhaps because I was too exhausted, perhaps because my emotions were frozen and in a state of shock, perhaps because I was simply unwilling to think about what had happened.

It was now nearly noon. I had a lecture at two o'clock, and I decided to give it. It was a lecture in an introductory course, one of those courses which, in one grand tour, guides first year students from the fall of the Roman Empire to the beginning of the First World War. I had reached the Reformation, and I decided to go and talk about Martin Luther.

But first I took a shower and changed into fresh clothes, and suddenly I thought about Theodore Stappler — curious how I had shut him out of my mind — and I decided that he should know what had happened. I don't know what I expected him to do. Perhaps it was merely some hankering after sensationalism on my part, a kind of morbid desire to know how he would take the news, that drove me to phone the Hotel Victoria.

"Victoria Hotel!" The voice on the other end was blunt.

"Is that Sam?"

"Yeah. Who're you?"

"Mark Lerner. . . . We met yesterday."

"Oh, yeah. I remember. Want to talk to your friend?"

"I do."

"He just went out. About ten minutes ago. Any message?"

I hesitated for a moment. If I let Sam give Stappler the news, then I would not be the first to see his reaction. But as soon as I thought that, I felt ashamed. And so I said quickly, "Yes, yes. Tell him — tell him Joseph Held died last night."

"Who?"

"Joseph Held. H - E - L - D. Joseph Held."

"He died?"

"That's right."

"Was he a friend of his?"

"Well — no. I don't think so. He was the father of the — the girl. . . . You know."

"That's too bad. What he die of?"

"I don't know. A neart attack, I think."

"Well, that's the way she goes. Here today, gone tomorrow. Anything you want him to do? Your friend, I mean?"

"No. Tell him I'll be at the hotel about three-thirty."

"I'll tell him."

I talked about Martin Luther in a dry, perfunctory manner. I could not breathe life into a subject which I usually found fascinating. But today I could not involve myself. My words remained lifeless. It was hot in the classroom. The air was stale. Together we went through the motions – I talking in a slow monotone, the students scribbling notes. Some facts, I suppose, were thus transmitted. The dry bones of history. But no meaningful contact was established between me and the students. No current flowed. Dry bones don't hurt anybody.

The bell rescued me from the sound of my own voice. I hurried out of the classroom, without waiting, as I usually did, for students to come up and talk to me, and drove downtown.

Sam seemed to have been waiting for me, for when I began to climb the stairs, he suddenly came out of the office and called to me, "Your friend's gone."

I stopped and looked up at him. "You mean for good?"

"That's what he said. He said to tell you."

"Did he really mean it?"

"Well, whatever he meant, he checked out of here."

"But the train doesn't leave until the evening."

"I know that. But he left, anyway. Bags and all. And he's not coming back."

I walked slowly up the rest of the stairs until I stood level with Sam, and together we went into the office and sat down. I don't know why, but I found it more difficult to believe that Theodore Stappler had left than that Joseph Held had died.

"Did you give him my message?" I asked Sam. "Did you tell him that. . . .?"

"I told him. I told him exactly what you said. And when I told him that this man Held was dead, he cried out, 'Oh, my God, that's not what I wanted. That's not what I wanted.' For a moment I even thought that he'd had something to do with it. With the guy dying, I mean. So I told him, 'He had a heart attack. In the middle of the night.' He didn't say any more. He just stood there for a while and then went to his room. About ten, fifteen minutes afterwards he walked out, with his bags all ready. He paid his bill and told me to get him a taxi. I said, 'Aren't you going to wait for your friend? He said he was going to come for you.' But he said to tell you he was sorry. He couldn't see you. He said there was nothing he could say to you."

"And he left nothing for me? A note? Or. . . ."

"No. Nothing like that. It was just like I told you. He told me what I told you. Then the taxi got here and the cab-driver came up and helped him carry his bags down, and he said good-bye to me and left. I thought it was kinda strange, but that's the way he wanted it, I guess, and that's the way it was. He always played things close to the chest, so it didn't surprise me in a way. I always figured he'd leave that little girl standing. But in this business you keep your eyes and ears open, and your mouth – well, you can keep that open, too, but there comes a time when it's better to keep it shut. And there wasn't any more that I could say because I could see that it wasn't going to do any good. No damn good at all. So I just said, 'So long,' and that was that."

And that is how it ended. Theodore Stappler left as silently, as mysteriously even, as he had arrived. Obviously he felt that he could not face me again – or Katherine Held. In a way I could understand him. And yet I felt that he should have stayed, that he should have tried in some way, though I admit I couldn't say exactly how, to help her. At the crucial moment he had abandoned her, had left to others the task of consolation. Perhaps that is what I resented most of all.

Where he went to, how he left the city I didn't know. He was not at the station, for I drove there immediately after I left the hotel, and again later in the evening, some twenty minutes before the transcontinental pulled in. He did not get on. So he disappeared in the dead of winter, without a trace.

I drove away from the station through the snow, through the familiar streets, with the intention of going to the Maxwells, to be with Katharine Held, to do what I could to comfort her and help her, though God knows there was little enough that I could do.

But after I had crossed the bridge and was again on the south side of the river, I parked my car and walked back onto the bridge. There I stood for some time, looking down at the frozen river. And then I quickly pulled out the little bottle which I had found beside Joseph Held's bed and tossed it over the railing of the bridge and watched it disappear.

Then I walked away, quickly.

🕸 Postscript

1960

EIGHT YEARS HAVE PASSED; EIGHT SUMMERS WITH THE LENGTH OF eight long winters. It was the end of May, a glorious, warm May, the days long and sunny, the nights cool, and so after our brief spring we were moving into our paradisial summer.

I was getting ready for the press the book I had been working on for these past six or seven years – *Intellectual Cross Currents in Post-Revolutionary France*. Parts of it I had already published in scholarly journals and read before learned societies, and my friends and colleagues in the profession were always telling me how eagerly they were awaiting the appearance of the book. Well, we all say that to one another, of course – and partly mean it, too. I have great hopes for the book. I have something of importance to say, I think, about the impact of extreme situations on the main personalities involved in those extraordinary events, and something to say, too, about the influence of ideas on action, and about the impact of action on ideas.

Work on the book, though slow and laborious, has been exhilarating, like climbing a high mountain. And now that the task is nearly finished, I feel suddenly tired, drained of energy, sorry in a way that the labour is done, afraid of a kind of emptiness, of a void that one must travel through between the ending of one phase and the beginning of another.

I am not complaining. My life has been rewarding enough. It is not, I realize, the kind of life that would suit everybody, but it has suited me, it has been what I wanted it to be.

I have watched with interest and satisfaction the growth of this city and of this university, have felt involved in it and derived some pleasure from playing a small part in it. I live now in one of

the new high-rise apartment buildings that have gone up everywhere and changed the skyline of the city. My living-room window overlooks the river valley, and I look down on the magnificent
river winding its way through the city, and watch the changes of
the seasons as they reflect themselves in the mirror of the river,
until I think that I could not live without the river.

I have gone on collecting paintings and the walls of the apartment are glowing and alive with the works of Canadian painters,
some famous, some hardly known, but all of them acquired because I responded to them immediately, spontaneously. Last year,
when I was in Toronto, I bought a Lawren Harris – one of those
silent peaks, all white, rising out of a blue sea, all still, serene and
yet curiously tense, as if at any time the white mass would shatter
and break itself. In a way which I find hard to express, this painting seems to go together with my Emily Carr, and I have hung
them together, side by side, in my bedroom, on the wall facing
my bed, so that I look at them when I wake in the morning and
just before I turn out my light to go to sleep.

I took my mother with me to the gallery where I bought the
painting. She thought it was a forbidding piece, too stark, too cold
at the heart. Dear Mother! She does at any rate know now where
I am. This is no longer *terra incognita*, and she no longer tells me
to come back to the East. She has also very nearly given up urging
me to get married. There are now only occasional hints in her letters that it would be nice if. . . And when I am with her, she tells
me sometimes that, even if not now, I might in later life be lonely.

Seven years ago – it is painful for me to recall it, more painful
still to write it down – I almost married Katherine Held. I loved
her, and for a while she seemed to return that love, though never
perhaps totally, never with complete abandonment. I suppose we
were engaged, though there was never a formal, public declaration. Yet there was an understanding.

Katherine was always honest, incapable of dissembling, and in
the end she could not go through with it. It is hard to say why. She
said she did not know. I have felt that the events in which we were
involved that winter had something to do with it. We could never
wholly free ourselves from the ghost of her father and from the
curious, ghostly presence of Theodore Stappler, though we rarely
spoke of them.

After the death of her father she stayed on at the Maxwells',
who took care of her and became very close friends. I thought at

first that she would find it impossible to go on with her studies, but quite the contrary happened. She threw herself into her work with a sort of fierceness that was almost awesome. If I had thought at first that she would want or need my sympathy, that turned out to be wrong, too. She was too proud to be dependent.

I contrived to see her more often than was perhaps strictly necessary – after lectures, and in the evenings from time to time at the Maxwells' house. She was reserved at first, though she must have been clearly aware of my growing interest in her. Of the affair that had first brought us together we spoke only once. She did not try to defend her father's part in it but talked about the betrayal with a curious kind of detachment, as if it were the action of a stranger we were discussing. She had of course to build some sort of dam around her emotions, so that they would not rise up and drown her. And Theodore Stappler she seemed to have banished altogether.

As soon as she had finished writing her examinations in the spring, she left the city without waiting for convocation. She had decided to go to Toronto and look for a job. But there was a kind of urgency, bordering at times on desperation, in her preparations to leave the city that made it clear to me that she could not bear to stay in the city a moment longer than she absolutely had to. The ghosts were too real here.

I drove her to the station and saw her on to the train. And when I drove back to my apartment, alone, through the sunny streets, I felt suddenly lonely, felt suddenly a need for her. I told myself that I was merely sentimental, overcome by the spring, by the green grass of the neat lawns, by the trees in bloom. But it was no use. I was surprised myself by the persistence of my emotion, by its intensity, and when I did not hear from her for over a week, I phoned the Maxwells every day to find out if they had heard, until they must have been astonished by my concern and by the thinly disguised ardour of my questioning.

I was going to go east that summer, in any case, to work in some of the great libraries, but I had first planned to do some writing. I now decided to go at once, and as soon as I got to Toronto I went to see her.

She had taken a room on Bedford Road, just off Bloor Street. I didn't know her telephone number, and so I called on her without warning. But when she saw me, she received me with a great cry of joy, and I took her in my arms and kissed her, and she cried out how glad she was, how glad to see me.

So my serious courtship of her began. It was a glorious summer. Ages and ages seemed to have gone by since those bitter days in January. And yet, and yet. . . . Sometimes — and in the most unexpected places, too – those presences rose to haunt us. Once I took her to a night club and there, in the dim light, I saw her suddenly start and stare at a couple who were just stepping out onto the dance floor and, putting her hand up to her mouth as if to stifle a cry, she said, "That's Theodore!"

It was not Theodore, but we could not banish him that evening. At last, to lessen my irritation, I asked her, "Were you in love with Theodore Stappler?"

She plainly did not like the question. It took a long time before she answered me. "You wanted to know that once before," she said.

"You never told me," I said.

"Why do you want to know now?"

"Because I love you."

"And I love you, too," she said. "What difference does it make how I felt about another man? That's all in the past."

"But did you love him?" I insisted.

She turned the question into a game. "I won't tell you," she said. "I'll let you guess, but I won't tell you if you guessed right."

But I was not in the mood for games and kept on pressing her, until she herself became exasperated and said, "I think you're jealous." And after a few moments of silence she asked, "Are you a jealous man?"

"I never thought so," I said.

"I think you are," she said. "I think you are."

Perhaps she was right. For I really felt jealous. I wanted to cry out to her to stop, and I resented the sudden thought that the figure of Theodore Stappler might always be there, looming in the background. But the cloud passed, and the next time we met all was calm.

There were one or two awkward moments when my mother, with the kindest of intentions, began to probe into Katherine's background and asked about her mother and father, though I had explained everything that I thought my parents needed to know.

Yet, taken all in all, it really was a glorious summer – to feel the excitement of a new life beginning, to feel the glow of a young girl next to me.

I went to Boston for three weeks to work in the Harvard library and could hardly wait to get back to Toronto, and there one hot and humid July evening, when we had gone to the Island to find a faint fresh breeze, I asked her if she would marry me, and yes, she said, yes, yes, and I said that we should do it at once, within the next two or three weeks, and at first she said yes, but the next day when I called for her she was upset and clearly unhappy.

She had not been able to sleep all night, she said. She didn't know what she should do, but she could not return to the West, she said, not at once. The thought was unendurable. She said she wanted to wait until the spring. It would give her time to set her emotions in order. I was stunned. But nothing that I could say, nothing that I could do, would change her mind. She protested that she loved me, but she could not commit herself totally now. So I had to leave without her.

At Christmas I returned, impatient and full of hope. Her letters had been warm, though from time to time I felt a certain reticence, a withholding of emotion that was hard to pin down precisely, but was yet there between the lines. And within a week of our reunion those vague misgivings were confirmed. Between us there was a shadowy wall. Somehow she had moved away from me, and though I tried desperately to draw her closer again, to bring her again to that point where she had said yes, it was impossible.

Did she no longer love me, then? I cried, and she closed her eyes, as if in pain, and said, yes, she did, she did, and would always love me. But there were things. . . She begged me to understand her. But how could I understand her, how could I know what she meant? For if she loved me, if she would always love me, why could she not marry me? But she only shook her head and said no, no, it could not work out.

I pleaded with her to change her mind. I told her that if she found it impossible to return with me and live again in the city where she had witnessed that final encounter between Theodore Stappler and her father, then I would move from there. I could always get a position at another university. But no, she said wearily, no, it would not work, and broke into tears, and I drew her close to me, and she clung to me, crying all the while, and when I kissed her she seemed to abandon herself to me with a passion that was hardly comprehensible to me after what she had said, and for a moment, as I held her in my arms and felt her heart beating against mine, I thought that perhaps she would say yes after all.

But it was a forlorn hope, and when we parted just before New Year's, we both knew that it was the end of the affair, even though, for my sake mainly, I suspect, we left the door ever so slightly ajar. Perhaps, I said, perhaps when it was spring again and when I came again. . . . She whispered yes, perhaps, perhaps yes, but at the same time shook her head, as if to say no, no, it could not be.

When the spring came I heard from the Maxwells that she was going to marry a young student of architecture, and then she wrote to me herself. After they were married, she said, they would go to live in Vancouver. There they now live, happily. So the Maxwells tell me. They have three children, a lovely house, a lovely garden. Her husband has become a quite famous architect.

Wounds heal. Below inveterate scars forgotten griefs are reconciled. I gave myself up to my work, to my writing, to my students. Katherine Held and Theodore Stappler now were somewhere on the outer periphery of my mind and sometimes would invade it briefly, only to float out again. Sometimes, wrestling with some intractable moral problem that history raised for me, I thought of Joseph Held and tried once more to come to terms with his action, but I could never settle the matter in my own mind, and it remained one of those loose ends which dangle somewhere in the attic of one's mind, untidy and uncomfortable, but fortunately out of the way, safely hidden amid the other bric-à-brac that gathers dust there.

So it was with enormous consternation that I listened to the voice of the operator who called me early one Tuesday morning in May, while I was working in my office, and said there was a telegram for me. And then she read it to me.

"If you are still there, meet my plane tomorrow at midnight. Theodore Stappler."

Silence.

"Are you still there?" she asked. "Sir? Sir? Are you still there?"

"Yes," I managed to say. "Yes."

"Did you get the message, sir?"

"I think I did. Did you say it was signed 'Theodore Stappler'?"

"Yes, sir," she said. "That is correct."

"You are sure?"

The question surprised her. "Of course," she said, and was about to spell the name for me, but I interrupted her, thanked her, and hung up.

I suddenly began to tremble and feel cold. For it was as if someone had come back from the dead. Not that I had ever imagined that Theodore Stappler was dead. It was simply that he had in a real sense ceased to exist for me apart from that affair in which he had involved me. And now, mysteriously it seemed, he appeared again, summoning me peremptorily to come and meet him. And what if I refused to heed his summons? What if I pretended that I was not "still there" and let him arrive without meeting him?

But of course I had no intention of doing that. As it was, I could hardly wait for the two days to pass. I was so excited, so shaken, so consumed by sheer curiosity that work was completely impossible for me. I could not concentrate on anything, and was waiting for him at the municipal airport fully an hour before the plane at last touched down.

He was the last person off the plane. I had already begun to think that he was not coming after all or that he had so changed that I had failed to recognize him. But when I saw him come striding in, there was no mistaking him.

He saw me, too, raised his hand in greeting and cried out, "Mark! Mark!" He pushed his way quickly through the crowd, dropped the little case he was carrying and suddenly embraced me, European-fashion, and kissed me on both cheeks.

"I hoped that you would be here. But I didn't dare to hope," he said. I was astonished to see how moved he was.

He had hardly changed at all, though he seemed taller and thinner than I remembered him. I recalled that first glimpse I had had of him, eight years ago, on a cold winter's day. He had looked sleeker then, more elegant, with his homburg set at an angle that made him look rakish and yet distinguished. Now he wore a European raincoat with wide lapels and a soft felt hat.

"I meant to get in touch with you many times," he said as we made our way through the crowd to get his luggage. "But somehow I could never bring myself to write to you."

"What brings you back here?" I asked him. "After all these years?"

"I'm only passing through," he said lightly, almost playfully.

"I'm on my way to the far North." He said it as if it were the most commonplace thing in the world to go to the far North.

"Well!" I said, and found myself trying to be as casual as he was. "That's interesting. To do what?"

"To practise medicine," he answered, quite matter-of-factly, as if it were obvious that that was what he was going to do, and he plainly enjoyed seeing me stop and gape at him in astonishment.

He moved on ahead of me. The luggage was now coming off the plane, and he picked out his suitcases. I took one, and then we made our way out of the airport to my car.

It was not until we were edging our way slowly out of the parking lot that I turned to him and asked, "Are you a doctor, then?"

"Of course," he said, "of course. That took you by surprise, didn't it?"

"Certainly," I said. "And you knew perfectly well that it would."

He laughed. "I suppose so," he said. "But it's not really so extraordinary. I'd studied medicine before the war. I come from a medical family. So I went back and picked up where I had left off and finished my studies." He paused for a moment and then said in that dry ironic tone of voice which was his special trademark, "My father had always predicted a wonderful future for me. And you? Are you married? Have you a family?"

"No," I said. "No."

"So," he said. "You are alone. Like me."

"At least I'm anchored to a place."

"Yes," he said, with a dry laugh. "Unlike me." He looked out of the car for a while without saying anything. Then said, "It's magnificent to fly into this city at night. Suddenly, you know, out of an immense darkness there comes a great circle of light. God, how marvellous! But frightening, too. Because the darkness is so vast and the circle of light so small – by comparison. . . I've made a reservation at the Macdonald."

"No, no," I said. "You will stay with me."

"Thank you," he said. "You are very kind."

When we got to my apartment, he looked about with some astonishment and said. "Well, you have joined the affluent society." He seemed to be looking for something, but couldn't find it. "Where is that painting I admired so much?"

"The Emily Carr? It's in my bedroom."

"I must see it," he said. "I have often thought of it. And of the river."

"You can see the river, too," I said. "From the big window there. But it is too dark now. You'll see it in the morning."

He stepped over to the window, drew the curtain aside and stared down. "The dark and silent river," he said, and then drew the curtain again.

"Are you hungry?" I asked him.

"Well," he said, "I could eat something."

"An omelette?"

He gave me a quick glance. "You have a restricted repertoire," he said.

"How do you mean?"

"You cooked an omelette once before for me."

"So I did," I said, "so I did."

"You also supplied some Benedictine," he said.

"I think I can duplicate the Benedictine, too."

"But not the girl," he said, sitting down on the chesterfield and stretching his long legs. "But not the girl."

"No, not the girl. Not Katherine. I cannot supply her."

"A pity," he murmured, "a pity."

"Come into the kitchen," I said, "and I'll cook the omelette."

He slowly got up and followed me. "What happened to her?" he asked me with a studied casualness that only barely disguised his intense interest.

"She is married. She has three lovely children. Her husband is an architect. They live on the coast."

"So."

When the omelette was ready, I cut some bread and we sat down at a little table in the kitchen and ate.

"I nearly married her," I said. "At least I wanted to."

"I expected that," he said. "I thought you would. She admired you. She thought you had a great deal of integrity."

"Are you mocking me?"

"Oh, no," he said, "no, no." He seemed genuinely surprised by my reaction. "I'm sorry if I offended you," he added softly.

"It's all right."

Yet there was a tension between us.

"Why didn't you?" he asked.

"What?"

"Marry her."

"She broke it off."

"So. Why did she?"

"I think because there were too many spectres about."

He thought for a while. "Was I one of the spectres?" he asked then.

"You were never identified," I said. "But I always thought that you were there."

"I must plead innocent," he said. "I tried hard enough to disappear." He had finished eating and pushed his plate aside.

"Where did you disappear to?" I asked him. "You didn't leave that night."

"No," he said, "I didn't leave that night. I merely moved to another hotel. Close by the station. Because I couldn't bear to face you again. I stayed in the city for three days. Until I was sure that he was buried. For some reason I felt I had to stay until he was buried. It was absolutely necessary. And then I left."

"You left me to do what was necessary," I said.

He sensed the reproach. "I know that. But what could I do? What would you have wanted me to do? How could I have faced her? What could I have said to her?"

I could only shrug my shoulders. I poured us out some coffee and some Benedictine and we went into the living-room.

"I remember coming back to that hotel where I stayed – Victoria – and Sam told me that Joseph Held was dead. The news shattered me. I couldn't believe it. His death was my death also. Do you understand that?"

"I don't know," I said. "In a way, I suppose, yes."

"Well, it was, it was," he insisted. "I felt that. Deep, deep within me." He sipped his Benedictine.

"But you are alive after all," I said.

"Yes, but in a different way, in a different way," he mused, but did not elaborate. "What a futile journey it was, really," he went on. "To come all this way – for a death. To find that we were after all in the same boat. And so much corruption. . . . And so many, so many who were more to blame than he or I, walking about in sunshine. Ah, well, after three days I left. But part of me was buried with him. In Montreal I got news of my uncle's death – my father's brother. My aunt begged me to come to her. The estate had to be set in order. She needed me. So I left for Vienna at the beginning of March.

"When I got there, it seemed like a city of the dead to me. Like a sepulchre. The great Hapsburg palaces looked like tombs, monuments for a dead capital. The city was still occupied, still divided into zones. There were a lot of uniforms about – British, American, Russian, French. They were always rumbling through the city in their jeeps. I took things in hand, haggled about with lawyers, conferred with officials. I had to do it all, my aunt was quite helpless. So I set the estate in order. My uncle had left me some money, but I couldn't take it out of the country. So I vegetated there. I did nothing, absolutely nothing. I didn't even read. I just sat about in cafés. My life was totally useless, totally without purpose.

"One day I was walking in a street full of rubble – the bomb damage there hadn't been cleared away yet – when suddenly an old man called to me. He had passed me, had looked at me, and then turned round and called to me. He called me by name. 'Stappler!' he called me. 'Stappler!' And then I looked at him and recognized him. He had taught me mathematics years and years ago. And he recognized me, after all these years! Zeitelberger was his name. He had a walrus moustache and a red, red nose. He was a man of great compassion and deep humanity. 'Stappler!' he cried. '*Du lebst noch! Du lebst noch!*' He could not get over the fact that I was still alive. He embraced me there, right there in the street, as if I were his son, you know, and he had just found me.

"He, too, he said to me, he, too, had survived. He lived. He seemed proud of that fact, as if the mere fact of survival, of just living, was already an achievement. He lived, he said, 'here,' and pointed vaguely somewhere in the direction beyond the bombed-out houses.

"But Zeitelberger saved me. He took me to his room. He lived alone – his wife had died during the war – and there we talked. He rambled on and on, in an amiable way, but somehow I found it comforting to come to him, and so I went again and again to see him. He didn't badger me, but quietly kept on saying that I should do something with my life. 'Teach people,' he said, 'heal people,' he said. Teaching and healing – that was all he talked about in his rambling way. 'Study,' he said, 'study.' Well, that seemed the best thing to do. I lifted myself out of my despair. I was fortunate because I could do it. My uncle had left me some money. Not a great deal, but enough to scrape by. So I went back and started again."

"I admire you," I said. "I don't think I could do that. The thought of cramming for examinations again would be too horrible."

"Oh, yes," he said. "It was a kind of purgatory. Four years in purgatory." He laughed. "The second and the third were not so bad. I found a little girl, a lost girl who'd drifted into the city from somewhere in Bohemia, had been in camps, and on the streets. I took up with her, and we lived together for two years. I nearly married her. But then we began to drift apart, and perhaps it was best that we ended it.

"I couldn't stay in Europe. I had to come back to this country. So I did. And had to do many things over again – to intern, to write examinations again. A second spell in purgatory, only this time briefer. And here I am, you see, a new man."

"But why are you going where you are going?" I asked him.

"I don't know, really," he said. "Impulse perhaps. I saw a post advertised. They need a doctor for one of the ships that sail along the Arctic coast. I thought it would be interesting. So I thought I would do it and signed up with the Northern Transport Company. I'll stay with them for a while. And then I'll see what happens. There should be something to do for me there. There are not many doctors up there. Perhaps I can be useful. . . . Besides," he continued after a pause, "I've had enough of cities. I don't know what I want. I don't know what I'm looking for. Not exactly. But I have an impulse to go."

He got up from the chesterfield. "I'm tired now," he said. "I'm very tired."

It was nearly four o'clock. The dawn was already breaking.

"You can look out now and see the river," I said.

We went to the window and drew the curtain aside. The river flowed below us, calm and peaceful in the soft, grey morning light. We stood watching for a few minutes and then went to bed and slept late into the morning.

He left again the following day, on Thursday. I took him down to the airport. He embraced me and kissed me on both cheeks, as he had done on his arrival.

"Whatever it is that you are looking for," I said, "I hope you find it."

"A new life," he said, smiling.

"Write to me," I said.

He nodded, shook hands with me and went out through the gate to the waiting plane. Once more, on the ramp, he turned and waved to me, and then disappeared into the belly of the plane.

1964

BETWEEN THE TIME OF HIS DEPARTURE AND THE TIME OF HIS death Theodore Stappler wrote me eleven letters. The first of these letters is dated June 29, 1960, from Tuktoyaktuk, a little Eskimo settlement some ninety miles from Aklavik, and the last, a brief note, is written from Mayo, in the Yukon Territory, on January 12, 1964, a short while before he left his hospital to set out on a mission from which he did not return.

Here they are, these letters, before me on my desk, written in a bold and even hand. I have been reading and re-reading them ever since I was informed, by a polite young RCMP officer, that Dr. Theodore Stappler, who had on all documents given my name as his next of kin, had disappeared somewhere up a nameless high mountain, some eighty miles out of Mayo. Together with another man, an orderly in the hospital, he was trying to reach a badly injured prospector who was lying helpless on the mountain and bring him down. So far as could be ascertained, said the young officer, speaking in that curiously neutral and passive voice of officialdom, a crack had developed in the massive snow field which they were traversing, and a huge wall of snow had thundered down the slope and buried them. Their bodies, said the officer, had not been found and were not likely to be found.

I don't know what Theodore Stappler was seeking, but his letters make clear that he found there, in the Arctic wilderness, a kind of peace, and a sense of unity with elemental forces. And he also followed the advice of his old teacher and healed people. Perhaps he taught them, too.

"I must run," he writes in one letter. "I have to look after a fourteen-months old Eskimo baby." Two days later he continues the letter. "I stayed for ten hours to help the child, and now I am fairly sure that the child will live. I do what is possible."

Or he tells me of a small, fat man, whose father was a Portuguese whaler and whose mother was an Eskimo woman. "The traits of both peoples go beautifully together, and here produced a man of great vitality. And great good humour, too. He came to me because his stomach gave him trouble. The only thing wrong, he said, was that he had grown fat and his stomach hadn't kept pace with him. What an expressive language Eskimo is when you see and hear it spoken!"

When he first went to the North to serve on one of the ships of the Company – so far as I can determine, he stayed with the Company for only about eight months – he was struck by the immensity of the landscape, by its great silence, by its timelessness.

"Here," he writes, "you are really close to the absolute elemental quality of nature. It takes some time before you become aware of any variation in the landscape at all. After a while you see that the surface of the ice is constantly changing. So all is movement and yet all is still. So it has been for billions of years. Time and silence acting together have produced a no-time."

He returns again and again to this subject. "Very curious," he writes, "seems to me the concept of time here. Perhaps I should say that time does not exist. Particularly here, in the great silence, in the great stillness. There is no movement by which you can measure time. Time has been abolished, has been swallowed up in space."

"It is only now, when there is no night at all, that I have suddenly become aware of how we take the rhythm of night and day for granted. I miss the darkness which invites one to sleep and to rest. Imagine it. Nothing but day. Light all the time without break. The Arctic summer night is not simply a variation of night, it is an endless, timeless, eternal day. And the polar night is an endless, timeless, eternal night. Not only the people who come here from outside, but even the natives, get curiously restless and nervous and come to me for help. I can only tell them to have patience. But for me there is a great peace here."

His very first letter spoke of spring, just beginning at the end of June. "The birds have arrived to build their nests just when I have. I take that as a good omen. They must built their nests on the ground. I discovered two nests yesterday. There were tiny little blue-green eggs in them. I stole one of the eggs – they looked so lovely. The birds lay their eggs, hatch them, and bring up their young. Then, after three months, when winter starts and the long, harsh polar night begins, they fly south again with all their little young who were born here. I shan't fly with them. I shall stay here."

In one of my own letters to him I accused him of having sought an escape from the problems of the world, of gratifying some romantic impulses. He indignantly denied this in his next letter to me. He demanded to know with some vehemence what I meant by "escape" and by the gratification of "romantic impulses." These were just words, he said. They meant nothing to him. He was not interested in gratifying any impulses. On the contrary, he said, he wanted to free himself from the burden of self. What was important, he said, was that he could live and be useful.

I did not pursue the argument. For long stretches of time there were no letters, and then there would be two or three within two weeks.

I don't know when he moved into the Yukon Territory. For the first communication I had from him there was also the last. It was very brief.

"Dear Mark," it read. "I must go to help someone who is badly injured and in terrible danger. It's not going to be easy. It is very cold outside and the snow is deep. But this time I shall not be late. It is not a romantic impulse that drives me! When I return I'll write you a long letter to make up for my long silence. I shall tell you all. Theodore."

He had declared that I was his next of kin, and though he can no longer tell me all, I at least have set down all I know about him. For now that he is dead, he seems to me most alive. It is strange.

The Author

Henry Kreisel was born in Vienna in 1922, and received his elementary and secondary schooling there. Following the Nazi occupation of 1938 he escaped, with the help of relatives, and fled to England. He got work in a textile factory in Leeds. Because of his Austrian nationality he was interned in 1941 and sent to Canada. He was released after a year and entered the University of Toronto, where as an undergraduate he led his class in the field of English Language and Literature. He took his Master's degree in 1947, and in 1954 got his Ph.D. from the University of London. He is now Academic Vice President of the University of Alberta.

Since the publication of his first, highly-esteemed novel, *The Rich Man*, in 1948, he has published short stories in *Prism*, *Queen's Quarterly*, and in the collection *Klanak Islands*. Some of his stories have appeared in anthologies and have been translated into German and Italian. His stories have also been read on the C.B.C. programme *Anthology* and in 1960 he was awarded the President's Medal of the University of Western Ontario for his story "The Travelling Nude." He has written radio plays for C.B.C. *Wednesday Night* and C.B.C. *Stage*. His critical articles have appeared in *Tamarack Review*, *Queen's Quarterly*, *Canadian Forum* and *Dalhousie Review*. In 1960 he was elected a Fellow of the International Institute of Arts and Letters. *The Betrayal* was first published in 1964. Dr. Kreisel is married and has one son.

SELECTED NEW CANADIAN LIBRARY TITLES

Asterisks (*) denote titles of New Canadian Library Classics

McCLELLAND AND STEWART LIMITED
publishers of The New Canadian Library
would like to keep you informed about
new additions to this unique series.

For a complete listing of titles and
current prices – or if you wish to be added
to our mailing list to receive future catalogues
and other new book information – write:

BOOKNEWS
McClelland and Stewart Limited
25 Hollinger Road
Toronto, Canada M4B 3G2

McClelland and Stewart books are
available at all good bookstores.

Booksellers should be happy to order from our catalogues
any titles which they do not regularly stock.